Halloween Hollow

Aisling Storm

Contents

To the things that are unseen,

but never unfelt by the heart.

Topics & Trigger Warnings:

LGBTQIA+, polyamory/CNM, paranormal, grief, impact play, consensual bondage with protagonist, physical violence, kidnapping and non-consent with antagonist, DID, reference to childhood sexual abuse.

Prologue

1970 ~ Liverpool, United Kingdom

Mulligan

He knew that they knew, his brothers in the mystical arts. *They had to know.* Old Sir Kragon's power grew daily, and they *must* be able to sense it.

Mulligan's friends had been like brothers to him. But some loyalties weren't worth keeping. Not when you stood on the edge of greatness, a power promised unlike any witch or warlock had ever heard of. The power bestowed from the great Goddess Atë, directly to old Kragon. And Kragon had been grooming Mulligan to be his second in command.

Mulligan knew he should feel guilty for going behind the backs of those who were loyal to him. But he knew they wouldn't understand. The light in their souls spoke too loudly—they were too pure and assumed others to be innocent as well. They all believed in shared power...but Mulligan wanted *more*.

Especially after Selene had chosen William rather than himself. Wil had everything—money, the right family, the girl everyone wanted—and Selene hadn't been the first girl to prefer Wil over Mulligan. For some reason, the ladies preferred the good chaps. Sometimes that miffed Mulligan's attitude, but he tended to prefer the less pristine ladies anyways. And a handsome chap now and then.

William was the left prop position on their rugby team, Castian the right. But they couldn't win without *him*, the lead hooker for the team. They had been playing as the 3 lead players since he had joined the team. It was what had connected them at first, really. But he liked to play dirty, and they usually didn't. They were rule followers, the two of them. They frequently told him that he didn't need to push his dirty little tricks in the game and that if he just followed the planned plays, the team would take victory cleanly. But what kind of win was that? *Not fun at all, I say.*

But all of this was so old school, anyhow. Attending The Mystical Arts Academy at Liverpool had been his dream as a young boy. But now, he'd graduated from a general university in London with his business degree and was preparing to graduate from the Advanced Program at The Academy and leave all of this behind. There was so much more out there than the others could see. More power, more ownership, more for *him*. As a boy, he had had nothing—had been nothing. His mother had cleaned the antiquated, rich businesses on the east side of London just to help them scrape by. The miserly old business owners would scoff at him as he tagged along, too young to be in school just yet. Mulligan would never forget their sneering faces. He'd promised himself before he was even old enough to remember otherwise that he would one day be richer than them all. Those plain-faced, weak-livered mundanes were *just* like his father.

Father had abandoned them when he learned of Mulligan's developing powers in his primary school years. Mother had run away from her coven when she was barely past legal age, running away with his father, who was clearly just a weak mundane. Mundanes, or non-magickal humans, were boring. *Why did others even bother with them anyways? They were weak.*

His father hadn't been able to stomach his mother's powers. She had dampened them more and more over his primary years, trying to keep her husband with them. But he had left anyways. By then, his mother had weakened most of her gifts. The depression she bore made it difficult to re-engage them. After his father had left, his mother's guilt at his not having things as easy as other children drove her to find a way to send him to summer camps at The Mystical Arts Academy for Children.

She couldn't afford the full school year, but she worked her fingers to the bone to afford to send him for the summer programming.

There he had cultivated his talents alongside other students, some whose rich families afforded to send them year-round as William and Castian's families had. A few, like him, attended only when they could. By his secondary years, his developing skills in the dark arts had afforded him a full scholarship, and he had delved in, seeking to find himself in his own magical powers.

But his mother grew sickly his junior year, and without the money to travel back and forth, his mother had died before he had been able to travel. Not willing to focus on his heavy grief, he dove ever deeper into his study of the dark arts, growing under the tutelage of Sir Kragon Night. Sir Kragon had been the one to observe Mulligan's growing powers and submit his name to the coven for a full scholarship. He knew he owed Sir Kragon a great deal for his opportunity to grow and enhance his powers, otherwise he could not have afforded to be there.

So, when Sir Kragon began to ask him to do small favors—ones he mustn't tell others about as they defied the coven's order—he'd felt he had no choice, really. But secretly, he began to enjoy completing each favor as though he were winning some dark contest against not only his peers, who had always had so much more than he had, but against the even more powerful leaders of the international coven. Each dark deed accomplished felt as though he were gaining power over the impenetrable, as no one got past them.

His raw, hungry, and needy taste for power grew steadily each year post-initial secondary graduation. He was willing to be second only to Sir Kragon. After all, the old man was teaching him everything he knew. And Old Kragon had the favor of the Goddess. But one day, he would control the rest of this miserable flock of magickal sheep. The coven would know *him* as their leader.

Maybe even the world.

Chapter One

Maggie

Holy fuck.

Thunder rumbled, growing louder. The dark clouds had begun to move in over the two-lane highway through the mountains almost an hour ago. *This was going to be an ugly ass storm*, Maggie guessed, as she tried to navigate the narrow two-lane back road that usually saved her time on her long drive home.

GOOD. She absolutely loved a fantastic storm.

Maggie had never really been afraid of storms. Not even when, as a little girl, her Nan would check on her when the thunder rolled. Expecting tear-filled eyes, her grandmother would always find her young eyes filled with delight and wonder instead, or at least that's what she told Maggie every time she insisted that Maggie should be more careful with things. That she was rarely scared of things she should be. Her grandmother worried too much.

Her grandparents would tell her stories through the years of her love of storms, explaining it as being a young person born not of her own time but with "a hippie soul," like her mother had been. Maggie had always felt in tune with the earth, even as she had grown up loving computers. Electronics of all kinds, really. In her backseat was not only her laptop in her backpack but an old Atari game system she had picked up at a rummage sale last weekend. She was going to fix it, like Pop had shown her before. She just hadn't had the time.

Not after she got the call from her Nan last Sunday night. Her Pop had taken a fall down their old rickety basement stairs and had broken his hip. Maggie had immediately said she would come home, despite mid-terms this week at her final year at Boston U. But Nan had assured her she should finish her exams before heading home to check on them. Plus, Auntie Esme was there, she said, and according to Nan, that was "enough wild girl in this house," anyways.

She knew her grandparents were proud of her for completing the educational goals she had set for herself. Neither of her grandparents had attended university. Education hadn't been as important to their families growing up, they told her. Her grandfather preferred working with his hands, able to fix almost anything. Running his little shop in their small town of Essex, NY, while Maggie grew up had been enough to keep them content. Well, that and Nan had mixed lotions and balms for many of their friends, helping with the aches and soreness of aging, and sold it at a steady little profit. It afforded them just enough income to live debt-free, happy, and even save a little to help Maggie with her undergraduate degree.

Graduate school had both pushed her growth and kicked her ass over the last two years. Winning the STEM scholarship to complete her advanced master's program in technology had been amazing but difficult. Most of her classes were virtual now, thanks to changes afforded by the pandemic. Students had been allowed to attend in person or via virtual options when lectures were scheduled, and Maggie, being more of an introvert and quiet, definitely preferred virtual. Much of her thesis work on nanotechnology was research-based and independent, and she knew that once she got past mid-semester exams, she could work from home for a few weeks or maybe even until end-of-semester exams.

So after her last exam this afternoon, she had packed the things she had needed in her little red '77 VW Cabriolet Bug, whom she lovingly referred to as Margot since she'd found her when she was 17. She and Pop had worked on Margot, getting her up and running, and even redid some of the upholstery and the tan convertible top to get it into tip-top shape. She had a little rust around her lights, but Maggie felt that was part of her story. *Margot must have seen a lot since '77*, she often thought. Of course, autumn in the northeast meant she had the top up, especially with the storm coming on. *Margot would protect them all though.*

She felt—er—heard Morpheus from his crate. *Boy, he wasn't happy.* If hisses could kill...well, she would have died a thousand deaths through the years by now.

Morpheus had been her cat for as long as she could remember. Agile but cranky, he was rather particular about life. And he was very particular about not liking being closed in that crate. But Maggie knew he wouldn't have liked being left behind either, and with this storm looking so wild, she hadn't wanted to let him out of the crate in the car, afraid he might startle at the storm and then startle her—and then they'd be wrecked on the side of this old, dark road.

Maggie nervously tucked a long, auburn lock behind her ear and pushed up her black, thick-rimmed glasses with her knuckle, turning on her high beams. Her little moonstone ear studs from her Auntie Esme glistened in the moonlight in her rearview mirror. That was until the moon slipped behind billowing thick clouds, and the rain broke through like a monsoon.

She groaned at the sudden, wild stream of water that her wipers suddenly couldn't keep up with.

Through the dark, her lights glinted off an old, gated entrance to a drive ahead. The road curved left near its entrance, and an old streetlight near the gate was flickering in the darkness. She could have sworn one of the iron ravens at the top of the gate post winked at her in the wavering light. The wind had really picked up, and the now autumn-toned leaves of the many nearby trees that lined the old two-lane road this high on the mountainside, flooded her windshield along with the pounding rain.

Every time Maggie had driven past this old place on her trips home, she had always wondered at the imposing iron gate where she could see the very tip of the turrets of what seemed to be a mansion through the trees in the distance. Not many houses were seen from the road in the western heart of the Green Mountains. People liked their privacy. But that dark and foreboding gate had always held curiosity for Maggie. *It was like it was a portal to a cavernous world cut in the side of the mountain for an old wizard*, or so Maggie fantasized.

She hadn't gone much further when she heard her little car's engine begin to chug strangely. Maggie kept the vehicle in good care, so she couldn't imagine what might be wrong, well, other than the many decades old parts found in junkyards that keep her going. And old parts died eventually, she knew. The sputtering only got louder, and Maggie had just enough time to pull off into the wet, grassy slope alongside the two-lane road on the curving mountainside. Maggie grabbed the hoodie she had shoved into the backseat earlier and pulling it on, she got out of the car.

The rain had at least lightened a little for the moment, but the lightning and thunder still crackled and lit the sky. Maggie felt the vibrations echoing through the earth—through her, really. She wondered how she could feel so much sometimes, but she always had. She didn't think others noticed things as much as she did—sounds, energies, feelings, nature even. She opened the hood of the car and checked various connections and fluid levels with her phone flashlight. But in the dark, with the rain threatening to get worse again, she really wasn't going to be able to tell much.

She got back in the car again, uncertain what she should do. Her hoodie hadn't done a lot to keep her dry, and her jeans and tank top underneath her hoodie had gotten pretty damp. She grabbed an extra ponytail holder off the stick shift, pulling her hair up on top of her head. That at least helped with the dripping on her face part. She *HATED* it when her glasses were wet. *But it was better to be able to see wet than not to see at all,* she shrugged. She was as blind as a bat without her glasses.

Checking her phone, she knew what she'd see. Zero bars of service. *Zero!* It was always that way from the moment she entered the mountains. She was shit outta luck.

"Sir Morpheus, what are we gonna do, huh?" She heard him get quiet. He really was a good listener, even if he seemed persnickety most of the time. Not that her cat had answers for her. He didn't know this place any better than she did. But she had passed that old mansion a short way back. The one with the old iron gates. She knew the temperature was going to drop tonight. It always did in the New England areas on a crisp fall night. *And holy hell, was she wet*—she couldn't sleep in her car like this.

Knowing she didn't have a lot of choices, she grabbed her phone and charger and put them in her backpack. Her laptop was in there, along with a few other necessities.

"Ready for this, Morph?" Maggie said uncertainly. The cat chirped at her, but Maggie wasn't so sure it was in agreement.

Opening her big umbrella, she slung her backpack on her back and grabbed her cat's crate. Promising Margot she would be back soon, she locked the door and headed out. She walked back down the small highway, where she hadn't seen a car since it had grown dark an hour or so ago. The flashlight on her phone did her little good in the rain. She heard Morpheus' hisses and disgruntled sounds and knew some of the rain must be getting inside the front of the crate. Trying to keep the umbrella in place to shield them both, she had just gotten close enough for the iron gates to come into view when a strong gust of wind blew her umbrella out of her hands. Flying up and spinning madly, it flew across the road, sliding down the slope of the mountain on the other side of the road to catch in a thicket of bushes. *Yeah, she wasn't going to try to get that tonight.*

"It's a good thing I don't scare so easily," mumbled Maggie to herself as she glanced around. Minimal streetlights and a dark two-lane road that hadn't seen a vehicle in a while, other than hers. Dark trees on a pitch-dark mountainside with a wicked storm where even the wolves feared to tread. Or at least she hadn't noticed any living things, although she was sure they must be out there. She shivered. "I might be crazy for doing this. For all I know, this could be the end," she laughed to herself. *Ah well, if it was, so be it.*

"As above, so below," she said, thinking of her Auntie Esme's favorite saying. Somehow, saying it out loud made her feel better. She never was sure why, maybe because it brought her beloved aunt's joyful face to mind.

She approached the gate and noticed it was locked. She pulled on it, jangling the bars. *It was so tall!* Taller than she had ever noticed while driving. Bushes that hadn't been taken care of in some time were trying to overgrow it. Out of the corner of her eye, she swore the raven was laughing at her, but when she looked at it—right in the eyes—it was as still as the hard iron it was made from. She heard a crackle come from near one of the bushes, and she noticed a box that was making sounds at her.

Once upon a time, it had probably been a good little intercom for whoever lived up in that house. But someone definitely needed to look at those wires. Clearly, there was a short in the audio.

"Wh—" she heard a crackly voice trying to come through. It sounded youngish, not like the old wizard she had imagined living there. Maybe.

"What t—he—" She heard again, the voice sounding cranky and irritated. Reminding her for a moment of Morpheus. If Morpheus had a voice to speak human words.

She tried to yell back into the intercom, noticing the button on the box and unsure if it was a call button or a talk button, the words once printed on the box having rubbed off long ago, many decades after it was likely installed. But she wasn't sure the box was working any better from her end, and the sound of the wind and thunder sure wasn't helping.

"What th—ev—liv—fuck—" She heard from the intercom again. "Just come—" she heard, the rest garbled.

She jumped as suddenly the gates pinged and began to creak open slowly. She wondered if she should hear any type of spooky music as the long drive called to her, beckoning her to enter its hallowed and ominous, bare, tree-lined hall. Every now and then, old iron streetlights on either side of the lengthy drive partially lit the way up the winding drive. As she drew closer, the trees opened to the view of the majestic old mansion. Three stories, with two turrets, and a massive front wrap-around porch with a small balcony over it. The mansion was old and dark, with black shutters against smokey gray exterior stone and brick. Iron and glass windows in some upper-level sections were broken and old torn curtains flapped ominously in the storm. The front light was on, but it was flickering an uncanny welcome.

While it was all eerie, Maggie was strangely not afraid. It really was an old massive home that seemed built for classic horror movies. She wondered if it had ever been used for any. If not, it sure should be. She smiled and wondered if Dracula might find her here.

She jogged the last few feet of the drive and up the five wide stairs of the porch, eager to be out of the driving rain and chilling wind. Every moment that passed, the temperature seemed to drop by another degree. Sir Morpheus even seemed to let out a chirp of relief when she got out of the rain and under the covering of the massive porch entrance.

Reaching up and grasping the heavy metal door knocker, she heard it echo as she glanced around, waiting for someone to answer. The porch really would be lovely after a fresh coat of paint and a few plants. The old porch swing was nice, in a peeling sort of way. *And maybe an accurately working light,* she thought. She wondered if the wires might be old and need replacing. She could hear a dog scampering and then a loud bark on the other side of the door—which startled her at first with how large it sounded.

The door groaned as it was pulled open. The entry was vast and intimidating, especially with that flickering light into the dim interior. A quite handsome guy, looking to maybe be in his 30's or so, held back a rather large pitch-black German Shepherd by the collar.

"Down, Xander!" he commanded firmly. But instead, Morpheus screeched in his crate and started the large dog on a round of excited barking all over again.

Morgan

Morgan couldn't believe this old, damned house. *Why was everything so difficult??*

"Come on in here, hurry! It's got to be freezing out there. And you're wet..." He looked startled at her, looking around, unsure what to offer her. *She looked like a half-waif,* her hair plastered to her head like that underneath her oversized college hoodie. She looked all of 17, if that, with her backpack on and, of all things—a cat carrier under her arm, *with a screeching, hissing cat.*

He grabbed a blanket off the back of the couch from the nearby sitting room and tossed it at her. *He wouldn't touch a minor if someone paid him.* Even if her eyes underneath those geeky glasses shone like a Cheshire cat, the color of dark merlot—*he would not be drinking tonight.*

"Why don't you take off a layer there on the entryway carpet, you are absolutely dripping everywhere!" he yelled quickly over the sound of his barking dog and the shrieking cat. "Let me put Xander in the laundry room, I'll be back!"

He headed towards the back of the house through the kitchen with his big barking pup.

'What the hell was that boss? That fur bag with an attitude just told me to get the fuck out, and this is my house!' Xander irritably yelled. Well, to others, it would only sound like barking, but Morgan and Xander could understand each other. Xander had been his familiar since Morgan was a gangly young teen.

'I just need you to stay back here for just a few minutes,' Morgan impressed to Xander. Morgan didn't have to speak aloud. There was a telepathy of sorts that occurred between witches and their familiars. He put Xander in the back laundry room, grabbing his just-dried robe from the clean laundry in the dryer before shutting the door firmly on the protesting dog.

'But boss, this is my house! I have to protect it! That demon cat may try something, and you won't even know! Clearly, you can't hear him!' Xander barked at him through the heavy wooden door.

'You'll be fine, and I'll let you out in a few minutes, but you are going to have to be good. You like cats, remember. They aren't all demons,' Morgan reminded him. Wondering at the fact that Xander could understand the cat. That likely meant that the cat was a familiar as well. *To a witch, or a demon, or anything in between.* Morgan breathed a quick breath, reinforcing the wards of the home. He didn't do witchcraft very often anymore, but he remembered enough.

Quickly he walked back out to the front hall through the kitchen.

His breath caught in his throat.

She had taken off her soaked hoodie and was wringing out her hair, which had been hidden underneath that sweatshirt hood. Underneath, she had a thin tank top on, and not even the thin bra she wore underneath could hide the way the cold wind and rain had only heightened her beauty. She literally glistened, standing there. Her long, auburn hair tangled in wet strands down one side as she rang it out over the entryway carpet.

Morgan shook his head to clear the cobwebs. He'd think about the light he'd naturally sensed in her later.

"Sorry, it was already soaked anyways," she said, referencing the carpet. "I figure you'll want to wash it eventually."

"No worries," he got out. Almost forgetting wards and familiars, as his groin tightened at her hardened nipples poking out through her white tank and thin violet bra.

She has to be college-aged, he assured himself. But he still scolded himself for being a creep. Maybe just starting college, those big round eyes under those thick glasses just seemed so young. When he was younger, he would have given anything to run into a girl like her at school. Smart-ass English major meets wet and hot geeky girl on a dark, lonely doorstep? But he'd turned 34 this year, college was ages ago. Now he just thought about how many steps and people he would have to interact with to get that entryway rug properly cleaned. *Damn him and his need to honor his uncle's things the right way.*

He handed her the robe, still warm from the dryer. Barely holding himself back from wrapping it around her protectively to cover all the exposed flesh.

"Lucky for you, this just finished drying," he said. He gestured to the half bath just off the entryway. "Why don't you take a few moments and change or dry off, or whatever. There are some towels on the rack in there. I'll make something warm to drink. Do you prefer coffee or tea?" Expecting her to prefer the typical college cappuccino.

"Tea would be lovely, actually, if you have it?" she asked, heading into the nearby small bathroom. Surprise to him. *It seemed like no one enjoyed tea anymore.* But his uncle had left him hoards of it, which worked for him.

He had actually just arrived at The Hollow, his great uncle Castian's estate, last week. His great uncle had died about a month ago, unexpectedly, in a car accident. Morgan had intended to get out here more during college—and then after. His uncle had meant a great deal to him. *He still wasn't even sure what to do with all this.*

When his own mystical energies began to grow stronger in his early teens, his parents had sent him off to live with his great uncle. His mother was a witch, just like her uncle Castian, but rarely practiced the arts. She had married a mundane, or a non-magickal human, despite her parent's hopes that she would keep the magick in their line going strong. Though she had continued to use some of her magick over the years, she had forgotten much of it out of laziness. While she had no qualms about magick or witchery, as she continued to celebrate some of the Wiccan traditions she had been raised in, it just wasn't her focus in life. She had become quite used to traveling with her husband on his business trips, and not keeping up with a teenager had actually been something she had taken to.

Not that he had been that busy of a teenager. He had never been very sporty, preferring novels and video games to the great outdoors. Although herbs and flowers did grow and respond well to his energies. His father had been an avid rugby player in his youth, and finding something in common to talk with his father about had only grown more difficult as he got older. As a kid, Morgan had often felt like he didn't belong in his own home—like he didn't fit in with either one of them.

So being sent to live with his great uncle hadn't brought him much hope either, as he had heard Castian had been an enthusiastic rugby player in his youth as his father had. But Castian had been different from his father. He had many other things that they found in common—enjoying a good game of chess, or discussing old literature, and especially studying the magickal arts together. Morgan had learned so much from him over the four years he had spent there during high school.

Morgan had known growing up that not everyone was magickal. He had learned to mask once he went to elementary school, with early signs of light shooting from his fingertips, learning that his life was far rarer than he had known. His mother and he connected during those early years over small moments of magick, but she hadn't been a good teacher, delighting more in what she could do for herself than what she could share with her son. He eventually became quietly frustrated, knowing there was more he could learn. He was tired of talking rugby, a sport he had gradually begun to nearly hate, as it was all his father would ever talk about.

So being sent to his great uncle Castian's grand old estate was actually the best thing that could have ever happened to him. Not only had he developed his skills with his uncle's training, but he had also gained confidence in his strengths. Here he had had far more normal teenage years than he might have ever had living with his parents.

But Castian had been from old-school England, where tea was the drink of choice. Not sugar-laden coffee. Coffee had its place for sure, especially in American busyness. But tea reminded you to slow down and breathe, to take in a good book, maybe. And that was Morgan's livelihood. To deliver good books to the masses. Or at least his publisher would like him to.

Lately, he had just been stuck. He needed a new idea or two. Something to inspire him.

Chapter Two

Maggie

Gods and goddesses, he was handsome, thought Maggie. She knew she was pulling a line from her aunt again, but it *so* fit. *Gah!* When he had looked at her like that, she had felt the heat shoot straight to her core. Even if he clearly had a decade on her. The smattering of grey at his temples whispered his years.

Speaking of her aunt, her phone pinged.

```
Where are you? I hope this weather hasn't affected your drive. (Auntie Esme)
```

```
Sorry, I meant to text sooner. But my car broke down somewhere after
Rochester, but before Middlebury. I'm okay, there was this nice house that
let me in. I'm going to call for a tow truck. (Maggie)
```

Yeah, that wasn't going to go over well. Almost immediately, she felt the buzz of her phone, her Nan calling instead of more texts.

"What in the world has happened, my Margaret? Esme said your car broke down?" her Nan asked, instantly fretting.

"I don't even know, Nan. My car has had no problems at all before today! Just out of the blue, it seemed to sputter and die," she said, exasperated.

"Thankfully, I got it to the side of the road. Hopefully, I can get it towed and find a nice hotel nearby once I do."

They talked for a few moments about her plans, but Maggie told her she had to go.

"The sooner I get the tow truck out here, the sooner I can get into town and find a place. *I promise you*, I will let you know what is happening," she assured her worrying grandmother.

Her grandmother had always been a little more high-strung than the rest of them. Pop had promised her it wasn't as bad before Maggie's mother and father died.

But they didn't talk much about those days.

Maggie tried not to pry too much. She knew it must be hard to talk about what things were like before tragedy occurred. When she was younger, she'd asked more questions. A kid wanted to know about her parents, ya know? But gradually, her Nan had become more and more irritable at her questions, to the point that Pop had said she should probably stop.

Pop had promised to answer any question she had, as had Esme actually, but by then, Maggie had just felt too much heaviness in her young heart to bring it up again. She hadn't wanted to be the reason everyone was so sad.

She had a hair pick in her backpack, thankfully, so after she used the red hand towel from the rack to wipe any remaining trace of streaked mascara off, she began to pick through her tangled dark red waves. Her Auntie had once said that if there were a dark rose with burnt tips, that would be the color of the Fredrickson women's locks. Esme had assured her that her mother had had similar hair, as did Auntie Esme, and supposedly so did her grandmother before it had grayed. Nan had boxed up much of the family photographs after her parents died. She had snuck to look at them in the boxes in the attic a few times, but her guilt was worse than being able to hold the images of them.

Sometimes she wondered if her mother might look similar to how Esme did now had she survived the crash. Auntie Esme was beautiful, body and soul, even in her late forties. Everyone loved to be around her, she radiated life. But she had never settled with anyone, just flitting from one relationship to another. Maggie thought the loss of her sister might have influenced that somehow.

Maggie's parents had been killed in a horrible car accident when she was just a toddler. Her grandparents had said they had left her with them while on vacation. But when they didn't return, and no one could reach them, it took two weeks before it was reported that their vehicle was found at the bottom of a ravine in Russia. *Maggie had always wondered what took someone to Russia for a vacation, especially when you had no known family or even friends there.* But no one would ever answer her questions, often just hushing her and moving the conversation along. Eventually, Maggie gave up on that one too.

Maggie held her necklace between her fingers. The necklace had been her mother's, given to her by Nan when she started school, almost earlier than she could remember. The tiny dark obsidian star was encased inside a tiny clear glass circle, interwoven with dark silver metal roots that somehow shot through the glass, encasing the star. It was hers, and it made her feel closer to her mother somehow, this beautiful woman she would never know. Sometimes Maggie thought she could hear her mother singing sweetly to her, as she was just waking in the early mornings. She figured it was leftover memories from a childhood long ago.

She held the pendant for a moment more, sending her love to the skies.

She had rung out her hoodie as best as she could and her jeans—hanging them over the rack. Interestingly it was a warming rack, so it might actually help them dry a bit before she needed to leave. She didn't feel comfortable in this stranger's house completely naked in his robe, so she left on her tank top, panties, and bra, albeit damp, under the warm robe for now. She tightened the belt, trying to figure out how to walk without tripping over the long hem. He was taller than her, but not extremely. *Yeah, she really was kinda short.*

She left her bag in the bathroom, pocketing her phone in the soft terry cloth robe. She could hear the hissing of her despondent cat long before she left the bathroom.

"I'm sorry, I'm sorry!" she insisted as she took him out of his crate. Scratching his black forehead. "I couldn't let you out into a house I don't know without me."

She swore she heard the black cat say, *'Yes, you could,'* quite snarkily, his tuxedo chest huffing out in disdain. *But no, surely not.*

He allowed her to carry him with her, making her way toward the kitchen. Maybe it was in the hope of some food or being unsure of that big, burly dog. Cats truly only seemed to allow being held when it worked in their favor. She shook her head. *Especially Morpheus.*

"Now be good," she hushed, entering the kitchen. Despite the old and in need of repair aspects of most of the house, the kitchen was surprisingly up to date.

"WOW," she blurted, looking around with wide eyes. The subway tiles and the sparkling metal of the industrial appliances shone in their modern newness, especially in comparison with the heavy tattered drapes she had just passed in the hallway. *If he was an ax murderer, he was a master chef version or something.*

"I know," he said, coming back into the room with a can of tuna in hand. Morpheus' eyes lit up. "So, long story short, I recently inherited this old house from my great-uncle. He didn't like change much, but he did like good food and had an on-staff chef who refused to cook in the previous kitchen the way it was." He shrugged. "So, he let him update it."

"But clearly not the rest of the house," Morgan said, looking around. "Thankfully, things like the furnace and plumbing are good. He 'refused to live in squalor,' he would say, so the amenities are all pretty much up to date. Well, except the damn electric," he said as it flickered around them. "I had a cleaning company come in before I got here. They did a decent job preparing it for me...as best as they could anyways."

Morgan had forked the tuna out onto a small plate, Morpheus beginning to purr, having jumped down from her arms haughtily, now wrapping himself around the man's ankles like a tuna whore. *Cause what a cat wouldn't do for some good tuna...* Have you met cats?

I mean, the man's smokey blue eyes, shy smile, and rough chin scruff made her wonder what he would do if she wrapped herself around his ankles too. *And up his thighs...*

She felt heat pool between her own thighs. *Dear GODS, she didn't even know his name.*

"So, I'm Maggie. Margaret Fredrickson actually," she said, pushing her sliding glasses up and shoving her hand out awkwardly in front of her. Her hand seemed even smaller than normal, hanging out from his rather large robe sleeve. "Just finishing my final year in the grad program at Boston, but traveling through on my way home to Essex, when my car broke down out there in this horrible storm."

He took her offered hand and firmly shook it while also attempting to multi-task the teapot on the stove.

"I was really hoping you wouldn't mind if I could call a tow truck, my reception was horrible out there, but I seem to get some service in here," she mentioned, gesturing with her other hand that was filled with a cell phone. His absentminded attention to her hand distracted her, his thumb grazing down her wrist, distracting her as she felt the zing from his touch.

He let go and turned back to the stove, turning the burner on.

"I'm Morgan...Smithe," he said after a moment. "Writer and clearly not an experienced rehabber, but the new owner of a dark and spooky mansion. Really, it's not so bad once you get used to it. I lived here with my uncle as a teen." He smiled to himself, clearly at some memory.

"Sure, I don't mind—" he started again, but the electricity suddenly clicked and shut down completely, leaving them in the shadows created by the flame on the gas stove.

"Fuck—" Morgan stopped himself, glancing quickly at her in the dim light they'd been thrown into.

"Sorry, my mouth gets the better of me some days." He began to rummage in a nearby drawer, eventually pulling out some candles. Just enough light to see each other and the hungry cat, licking his paw as he paused in his unexpected meal and glanced at them in what surely seemed like annoyance for being there.

"No worries, this seems to be my kinda night," she said, rolling her eyes at the sky. *Seriously, it couldn't get worse, but at least the company was enjoyable to look at.*

Morgan had a dark gray t-shirt on, which pulled a little across his shoulders. His waist tapered down to narrow hips in dark black jeans, and he had bare feet peeking out from below the hem. He wore a silver necklace, but she couldn't quite see what the pendant was, hidden underneath the v of his neckline. A few thin, dark tendrils of hair peaked above the shirt at her invitingly.

His hair was a little messy on top, a wavy dark piece falling over his forehead, looking like he barely finger-combed it out of the shower. A bit of a devil-may-care glint in his quiet eyes. But that shy smile he gave every so often through what seemed like a somewhat cranky demeanor, was a bit of a surprise. Or maybe a trick to gain her trust, who knows? But it so often felt like men today thought they knew everything and wore their suave attitudes on their sleeve. Morgan had a dark restlessness to him, and his eyes seemed to glint with knowledge, but he didn't give the 'know-it-all' vibe. It was a strange mix of openness within a closed and cautious exterior.

Surely, he wasn't an ax murderer, right?

He had lit the candles and he now moved toward the laundry door, saying, "Sorry, I've gotta..." And before she knew it, his German Shepherd came bounding out with a bark, and Morpheus screeched and ran to hide underneath the small table and chairs nearby.

"He just—with the power going out, I know him," Morgan started to explain.

"No, no, don't worry about it," Maggie said. She got it. Had Morpheus been the one in the other room, she would have worried too. "Morpheus just takes a minute...or five, to warm up to other animals."

Thankfully, the big Shepherd didn't try to chase Morpheus out from under the table but came to inspect Maggie. She'd always had an uncanny way with animals, rarely having one not like her. This one seemed no different. The large dog sniffed her bare toes, then curiously looked at Morgan after sniffing the robe edges. He nudged his head under Maggie's hand, quickly ready to be petted.

"Well, clearly, Xander likes you," he said. The teapot started to whistle. Thankfully the power being out didn't affect the gas stove. Pouring her water and setting out a few tea bag options on the counter, he told her to pick as she'd like, and he was headed to stoke the fire in the sitting room.

Picking the Earl Grey, she began to let her water steep. Wondering if he would have tea as well, she noticed the other empty cup he had brought down and added a few tea bag choices to his saucer. She grabbed both cups and followed him, too curious to wait very patiently. He had walked through a door off the side of the kitchen to what Maggie found to be a den of sorts.

The room was cozy, even if not yet updated. Old and faded dark green patterned wallpaper lined the walls. An imposing fireplace was on one wall, with a decent size flat screen over it, which was off with no electricity. Morgan had set one of the candles on the large trunk that seemed to be used as a coffee table in front of an overstuffed leather couch. A pair of high wing-backed chairs graced both sides of the couch, angled towards the fire, their green, gray, and gold lines glinting in the fire he was stoking as he added a fresh log.

High, arching windows lined the front wall with heavy, gray draperies pulled-back and showcasing the wind and storm outside as it whipped by furiously. He shifted at her entrance but didn't look up. "I'm not so sure you'll have much luck with a tow truck tonight." He glanced out the windows for a moment, "It's pretty wicked out there."

She felt her nerves rise a little, and she set the teacups on the trunk in front of the couch. "I'll just try really quick if you don't mind?" she asked anxiously.

He told her to check the magnet on the fridge, as he'd just recently used a local repair shop to tow his uncle's old 1965 Ford F-100 in for some work. Her penchant for old classics made her eyes light up, but she decided to ask more about that later. She needed to call, and the sooner the better. She typed in the number, and while it rang, she headed back into the den.

It rang for a while without an answer, and she eventually hung up, sure she had called the wrong number. But when she double-checked, it was right. She tried again. This time it was picked up on the 3rd ring.

"Mikes. This is Mike," the gruff older voice said.

"Hi there," she began, aimlessly walking around the room, past a floor-to-ceiling bookshelf filled with books. That would need to be looked at more closely, too. "I am traveling through the area, and my car broke down. Just off Route 125. Maybe 20 minutes out? I noticed you are in Rochester. Any chance you can tow me and my vehicle in tonight?" she asked a tad pleadingly.

"Where you at now, missy, you say off 125?" the gruff voice asked. "Bout 20 minutes, is that out there by the old Smithe Mansion? You got his writer nephew helping ya? Morgan. Yeah," he said, and she could just imagine him nodding his head while he talked.

"I, yes sir—that's where I am," she said. Oh yeah, he had said he was a writer, so at least that was confirmed.

"Well, it's Friday, so towing ain't gonna happen before Monday, proba-bly," he broke through her thoughts. "Tree went down across the bridge leading out of town over here. I hear Hancock ain't much better, what with their water main break having everyone up in a tizzy in this mess."

"Oh..." she sighed. That sucked. What the hell was she going to do? She couldn't just stay here.

"You might as well just stay right there," his gruff voice came across the line, crackling a little bit. She glanced at her phone. Great, the battery was low. And they still had no power.

"That Morgan Smithe is a good boy. Knew him when he was younger, when ole Castian was takin' care of 'em. Couldn't find a safer place to be in this storm," he assured. "I'll get out there when I can get through, early next week, probably." And the call abruptly clicked off.

She lowered her phone silently. How does one ask a stranger if you can stay at their house for a few days? *And who the hell does that??*

"Soooooo..." she started in. But Morgan interrupted.

"I heard. I know Mike, he's good people. Took care of my uncle's cars like they were his own," he said. "It sounds like you may need to bunk down here for a few days. At least until you can get into town. Your car too." She wasn't so sure he looked happy about it, though, as he got up. "I don't mind running to your car to make sure it's good for the night and get any of your other things. Would you like me to?"

Holy crap, would she. I mean, Mike said he was a good guy, right?

"Holy shit, that would be the best. I have a duffel bag in the backseat with some clothes and stuff. And there is a bag by it with some stuff for Morpheus, my cat," she said, running to the bathroom quickly to grab her keys.

"It's a '77 VW Bug, red. You can't miss her. She's my baby, *please* take care of her," she pleaded with him.

Chapter Three

Morgan

A body would do a lot of things for those soulful, pleading eyes when she looked at them like that. He tried to stop thinking about what all he would do.

Grabbing the keys from her outstretched hand before he did anything impulsive, he warned her to be careful with the house. "It's kinda an electrical mess, so if the electricity comes back on, prob a good idea to leave it be." He threw on a rain slicker from the coat closet near the door, sending Xander a silent message to watch out for things. "I'll be back."

It would probably be best if he stayed busy anyways rather than follow his earlier train of thought. He broke into a light jog, thankful the rain had lightened up for now. She was older than he first thought if she was in her final year of graduate school at Boston U. But those big round eyes still made her look pretty young. *College girls were flighty.* Or that had been his experience. He had made a few decent female friends in his lit classes, though.

His love for old English literature had won out in the end when he decided to go to college. His Uncle had mentioned he should consider going to the old Academy after college, like past generations of witches in his family. But honestly, Morgan had little interest in the witchcraft community. He had minimal interest in any community, really. The few friends he'd made in college hadn't really stuck afterward. He had always stayed mostly to himself, enjoying some brief relationships in high school and college, but tended towards one-nighters with mundanes. Girls seemed unusually drawn to what he knew was the dark mystic arts in him, but they didn't know that. He knew with his dark hair, penchant for not shaving, sullen and quiet nature, and you add in that mystical draw—let's just say he hadn't had a hard time finding sex when he got old enough to figure it out. Had even attended some rather kinky parties in college. Dominance in sex especially drew an often smokey darkness from him. But real relationships had been few and far between. He just didn't open up easily.

But he was more than his mystic side. He had little interest in engaging with others in the mystical community. And he sure as hell didn't want mundanes to look at him like he had two dragon heads when they realized he was a witch.

Witch, wizard, whatever. He thought some of the Coven made too big of a deal about gender references and roles. He tended to lean into witchcraft when he engaged his magic, and every wizard he had met seemed to crave power. And he didn't. He really just liked to be left the hell alone.

So, writing had worked well for him.

He arrived at her little car, nodding in appreciation of the work done to take care of the classic. *Uncle would have appreciated that.* A tinge of sadness slid into his gut.

He unlocked the car, grabbed her bags, and double-checked the windows were sealed against the rain. She had pulled it off to the side far enough to avoid any unsuspecting drivers, although he figured there wouldn't be many with the bridge being cut off the way he had overheard on her call. Mike was loud, and his gruffness carried. But he was honest with his numbers and did good work on classics. Her car would be in good hands.

After locking the car, he broke into a jog again, heading back to his uncle's home. The Hollow was his home now, actually. *Why was it so hard to think of it that way?* He'd lived there for nearly four years before college.

Maybe it required him to accept that his uncle was actually gone.

Morgan hadn't been able to write since Castian died. He couldn't quite figure out what was holding him back from his typical process. The ideas just wouldn't flow. Writer's block didn't usually last too long for him. He had been picked up early on, even before graduating, by his agent Max. Max worked for one of the publishing industries that catered to both the mystical world and the mundanes. Morgan wasn't always so sure how Max had found him, but always suspected Castian might have had some sort of influence. He had started writing his first fictional series "Mystic Mysteries" early on in college, but it wasn't until the final year that Max had reached out to him and mentioned he'd found some of his work online and wanted to represent him. His writing had taken off after that, selling quickly in both the mystical and mundane worlds.

He jogged his way up and around the side of the large home to the back door, pausing, curious.

The front light was on as he passed, and it was steady.

His wards felt secure. But his eyes squinted a bit as he felt through the drenching rain. Nothing was off in the space. He sensed each of their essences—Xander, quietly guarding from his spot by the fire in the sitting room. Her cat, an unusual presence all his own, but the feline somehow felt like he was guarding as well. He could now sense that the cat was much older than he had first thought, much, much older. And her. She had a light to her that radiated in purples and blues. Honest, true. There was an uncharted but powerful energy to her. He wondered if she knew about her own light. And there was the ghostly essence, but he knew that presence, it had been here since long before he first arrived at his uncles as an awkward, 14-year-old boy. Uncle had assured him right away that Althea wouldn't cause problems. They had a deal of some sort. While he had always sensed her, she had never presented herself over the years.

No other forces were here or drew near.

Morgan went ahead into the home. *His home,* he reminded himself. Whispering under his breath, he again reinforced the wards on the home. Noting he had utilized more magick tonight than he had in a long while. He wasn't sure how he felt about that.

He stripped off the rain slicker, taking his wet t-shirt with it, and dropped them in the laundry basket on his way through. He grabbed a towel from the clean stack he'd folded earlier but hadn't yet managed to put away, and towel-dried his hair and face.

"O.M.Gee..." she was saying as she bound into the room, suddenly halting—words caught in her throat as she ogled him.

He saw that. That fire that sparked in her eyes as she looked him up and down. But he wasn't sure what, if anything, he wanted to do with that awareness. He felt the pop, the spark of electricity—literally—running between them. She definitely had magick of some sort in her. Attraction was always intensified when it occurred between two mystical beings. He wondered if she was playing some kind of game with him, had some ulterior motive for this innocent schoolgirl thing she seemed to have going. He'd give her credit—she must have worked the spell all the way down to her inner core—he couldn't sense a dark layer of mirth beneath the presenting, innocent facade. She must be good at this. Or he had been out of the game for a while.

He slowed his movements. He had intended to quickly grab the t-shirt he knew was also in the dryer from earlier. *Maybe he'd play this out for the moment.* His eyes met hers, his light tangling with hers. The electric current snapped hotter in the room between them.

He glanced down at the bags he had dropped when he entered and looked back at her through closely guarded eyes.

"Your things," he snapped out. He wasn't sure why he felt so angry. Maybe because he had thought her guilelessness was so refreshing earlier. But standing there in his robe, with the knot slipping, he wanted to drag her close to him, and taste her berry-tinged lips—see just how hot those eyes could burn.

Maggie

"I—I—I..." For the life of her, she couldn't remember what she was going to say. Drops of rain still rested on the tips of his hair and dark lashes, his eyes glittering a midnight blue. Scattered dark hairs smattered across his chest and thickened as they narrowed down his belly to his... *YEAH.* Gulp. *What was she in here for?* His eyes looked like they could eat her alive.

"Oh yeah," she squeaked. "I fixed the front light."

His eyes snapped towards the front hallway. "You what?" he asked incredulously.

She was pretty used to this. Men struggled when she fixed things they couldn't. She rolled her eyes. "I fixed the front light. It was just a loose wire," she said. She had kinda hoped for more from him than putting her in that 'girls can't fix anything box.' Ah well, what else was new? She set down the screwdriver she had found in the kitchen drawer and picked up her bags. She turned away, walking back towards the front of the house.

So much for helping him.

He followed, having grabbed a shirt from the dryer on the way in. *GOOD.* That helped her think a little more clearly. She shouldn't be thinking about jumping the bones of someone she had only recently learned the name of. Not that she hadn't done that before. Her Auntie had helped raise a forward-thinking girl, and Maggie was very sex positive. In all kinds of ways and with all kinds of folks. Consent and happiness were her only rules. Otherwise the lines were blurred and meant to be played with.

Not that she was playing with his lines. Not tonight, at least. She was tired.

"I really appreciate your letting me camp here tonight," she said, taking a breath. She really needed to be grateful for his kindness. Not so heated—not so turned on or pissed.

"Yes," he stated, like he had snapped something back into place. Xander jumped up when they entered the room, immediately walking alongside Morgan. "Let me show you a room you can stay in. I'm really only currently using the main floor. There is so much more to this place, but I have the 2nd and 3rd floors mostly closed off for now due to electricity issues and windows that still need to be replaced. My uncle hadn't used those floors in years, other than the office."

He ushered them down the hall, Morpheus following them reluctantly. There were two small wings of rooms at the end of this hall. He mentioned he had been using one, and the other had been cleaned and prepared for guests as well. Both rooms had their own bathrooms. He gestured to his room across the hall but turned to the other door and opened it.

The moonlight was especially bright as it poured in over the tall four-poster bed before he turned on the small bedside lamp. She noted the fresh welcome it portrayed, unlike the mood he had just showered her with. A twinge of guilt edged his voice as he assured her she would have complete privacy in here and that the door locked if she wished. He opened the adjoining bathroom, pointing out the fresh stack of towels that he said a cleaning person had left when he had asked that the rooms on the main floor be readied before his arrival.

He bowed out, eying Morpheus as he left, who had settled himself on the small loveseat in the room. Morpheus, his eyes squinting as he studied Morgan's back, sizing him up. Morgan bowed his head in respect of the senior cat's and exited stage left. Er—across the hall to his own rooms.

She was glad to finally have the space to herself, but she noted that hint of disappointment in her gut that had wished he had grabbed her and kissed her the way it had felt like he might. But she was finally glad to get out of her wet clothes. Thankfully, the clothes in her bag had stayed pretty dry. She pulled out a tank and some sleep shorts. Her bra was wet, so she hung it over the shower door for now.

"It's a good thing there is a lock, Morph, or there could be trouble," she said to her cat as she clicked the lock closed. She just wasn't sure if Morgan was the trouble, or if she was.

Chapter Four

Morgan

Xander was laughing at him.

She had fixed the light somehow. He had spent hours trying to figure out what was wrong with that light yesterday. I mean, he hadn't taken it apart, but he changed the light bulb, checked the fuse, and YouTube'd the hell out of it.

'Maybe you should keep her around,' Xander pointed out.

'Yeah, maybe I'll replace you with her,' Morgan snarked back. And his pup rolled his eyes at him and put his head on his paws. Morgan would feel bad, but they had that kind of rapport. Xander had been with him since he had come to visit his great uncle's home for the first time as a young boy. His Mom had brought him when he was about 8 years old, when his uncle had told her he had a present for him. Thankfully, his mother let him keep Xander after she saw the immediate connection between them. For the first time, it had felt like someone really understood him. His dog had truly been his best friend through the years.

Xander filled him in on the details he'd learned so far from the cat. Morpheus was definitely older, although Xander wasn't sure how old. He'd learned that Morpheus had been the girl's mom's familiar. But something about the girl not knowing she had magick. Not even knowing her mother had been a witch. But Xander said it had been hard even getting that much information out of the cat. Something about having eaten and needing a nap.

Guilt twinged within him. He should have trusted his first intuitive response. Her innocence rang clear. There had to be more to her story, witches rarely awakened this late in life.

Morgan sat down at the desk in his room. His laptop had been open for days, a blank new document opened, awaiting his ideas to become an outline. He'd never experienced a drought this long. He wished he knew a spell of some sort that cleared the cobwebs of his thoughts, but that required motivation to dig into his uncle's stuff. His thoughts drifted for a moment to the girl in the rooms next door. He wasn't so sure that was going to help. He didn't write erotic novels. He wrote paranormal intrigue.

But he hadn't written a word in weeks. Not since he had heard of his uncle's death. He still remembered the call from his mother, his head buried in contracts from wrapping up his latest book deal. He was supposed to be adding another book to the Mystic Mysteries line. Three more, eventually. His agent, Max, had tried calling him three times yesterday. Max knew he was avoiding him. But he had no new antagonist for his hero to uncover yet. He should be writing.

But he had come here. Taking care of the details his mother hadn't had time to do for her own uncle. He had arranged for the body to be transferred for the funeral and to the family plot in Newcastle. Uncle Castian had been all that had been left of his mystical generation of the Smithe's. And now there was Morgan. Who didn't want to be a witch at all. He just wanted to live in peace and write.

When ideas actually came to him.

He slept. Somewhat fitfully. His dreams were filled with a young girl, just about 19 or 20 or so, naked and dancing in the wind, long blond hair whipping around her voluptuous form. And along the edges of his dream, watching him watch the young girl was his young, intriguing raven blood haired houseguest.

Maggie

She'd actually slept decently last night on the old feather mattress, despite unusually erotic dreams of the new mansion owner and a young blond girl, around Maggie's age. But definitely not Maggie. Still, she had woken tingling with sensation that she had decided to do nothing about, for now.

The water pressure left a little to be desired, but Maggie was just glad for a clean shower. She wondered at the old showerhead, though. It looked like it had seen better days. She'd look at that later. Thankfully, the bathroom had some little travel toiletries in a small wooden basket. She hadn't packed those at all, knowing she had all that at home. Even a toothbrush. The soap was lovely, fresh lavender, and she noticed small bits of amethyst.

The bathroom was intriguing. Its dark stone tiles—with scattered clear quartz, and she thought amethyst again—had an ancient feel. But what really heightened the old-world factor was the gigantic iron and glass arched windows that went from wall to wall, with heavy dark green velvet curtains that hung floor to ceiling on both ends of the wide wall. The antique clawfoot tub was the center of the show, and one could pull the heavy curtains closed behind the tub if they wished...but then they couldn't use those lovely large candles displayed along the ledge of the windows overlooking the tub.

If it were up to her, she would never pull those curtains, especially with how dim the overhead light was in here. She remembered the moonlight last night, and this morning the sun shone through the trees along the back edge of the property so beautifully. She was fairly comfortable with her body, with a penchant for exhibition anyways, but there was no one out there other than the wildlife. There seemed to be no one for miles, and thank gods, Morgan wasn't an ax murderer. Maybe she'd try that tub tonight.

She had woken early to a text from her aunt, checking on her to make sure she was alive. She would rather be sleeping, dead to the world—but she needed to get moving anyways. Normally she would be working already. Hopefully, she could get on his wifi and check her work. *Maybe the grades from this week's exams were up already.*

She dried off after her shower with a thick towel from the small closet she had found next to the shower. A slight chill—not in a bad way—ran through her at being naked in front of such a large window. It was like eyes viewed her, approvingly almost...but she knew no one was out there.

She dressed in another clean tank, this one with a built-in bra. Her bra wasn't actually all the way dry yet. She wasn't very heavily built, running small with her barely B-cups, but she had good natural lift that allowed her to get away with going without a bra now and then. She pulled some cut-offs up her short legs, wishing, as she often did, that she were taller. Throwing an open flannel shirt on to ward off the chill of an autumn morning, she got her comb out of her bag and combed her still-wet hair up into a high ponytail, a few shorter tendrils falling out loose around her face.

She grabbed her glasses and laptop, thankful she had plugged it in last night thanks to Morpheus, or it would have been dead. She had been so tired, but he had sat by her cord, ominously looking at her like she would lose her head until she finally plugged it in. Otherwise, she barely got to the bathroom and brushed her teeth before crashing last night. Pocketing her phone, she went to the kitchen and started some hot water for tea, which was still left out on the counter from last night.

After the teapot whistled, she took her stuff and settled on the porch, on the old wooden swing, testing it gingerly to make sure it didn't break. She connected her laptop for now through her hotspot, but with only one bar of service, the connection took forever to load. Thankfully the scene in front of her was gorgeous with the turning autumn leaves and the first rays of sunrise.

"I should totally get you the wifi password," he said, yawning from the doorway, scratching the scruff on his chin. She hadn't heard him come out, and almost jumped a mile, but he didn't notice, his eyes half closed. His pup looked ready to wake the world, he was so excited to be up. Maggie saw Morgan carrying his running shoes and figured the two must run together. Xander was extra-large, even for a German Shepherd, and she wondered that he was so quiet and well-behaved. She rarely even heard his paw steps, despite his massive size and energy. Morgan must have to exercise him regularly to get him to be so calm and focused. She should exercise Morpheus. She snickered at the thought. Morpheus would more likely *exorcize* her.

She saw Morgan look at her out of the corner of his eye, catching her laughter. His gaze traveled up her bare legs, pausing momentarily on what was likely her chilly nipples before meeting her eyes. A brief zing ran through her, straight to her clit.

"I, er—started the coffee," he said, yawning again. "And can get that password. Sorry, I don't have it memorized." He finished tying his other shoe and moved quickly back into the house.

Her nips gave her away all too easily at all the wrong (*or right*, she often thought) times. She pulled the purple flannel a little closer against the chill and tucked a strand of hair behind her ear. Pushing her glasses up, she tried refreshing the screen again.

"Here," he said, coming back out onto the porch, a steaming cup of coffee in one hand with a piece of paper in the other. "The cable and internet guy left this. The password is at the top. I just had the internet installed last week. So far, it hasn't been too bad."

She took the small paper, swearing she saw a spark when their fingers brushed. She knew she felt one. The password was definitely the original generic one from the cable company. She wondered if he knew how to change them and make the passwords a bit more secure. Maybe she could help him with a few things while she was here. Ya know, in return for her staying. Not that it had gone so well last night. But she had always had a knack for technology. Fixing lots of things, really, like her Pop had taught her.

"My aunt makes her own loose-leaf tea mixes in her shop," she said, taking a sip of her Earl Grey. "My grandparents raised us all on tea. They are from England, ages ago. But coffee is good too," she said, giving him an appreciative glance—appreciative of the coffee he sipped or his just woken, heavy-lidded eyes she wasn't so sure. His t-shirt had "The Academy Rugby" on it, with his sweatpants, and she wondered if he had played. Her Pop talked about Rugby sometimes, her father had supposedly played a lot in college, and his father had as well. She didn't know much about the game, other than it was popular in England and that it played rough. *She wondered if that was where she got some of her inclinations from.*

"Yeah, I don't play." He seemed to have noticed her focus on his shirt. "My uncle did, though. In his college days in Europe. And my father." Well, there went her fantasy of him liking it rough. She noticed his expression had soured. "I'm definitely more of a sit-in-front-of-a-computer kind of guy than sports. But I get the tea thing. My family is from Europe as well. I was born here, though, in the US. New York, actually."

Tucking her hair behind her ear again, she breathed a sigh of relief as the wifi connected and web pages started to work more normally. Clicking on her class page, she checked her exam grades. "WOOP!" she yelped a bit louder than she meant to, jumping a little in her seat. "YAY!" she exclaimed. "I got an A on the exam yesterday," she explained a bit further as he eyed her, a brow raising. That brow could raise at her any time. It seemed to zing, again with that direct line to her clit.

"Mmmmm..." he almost purred low. "Good job." How had she heard *'good girl'* in that? She really needed to get some. Well, soon. Not necessarily from him, although she could *so* imagine that if she let herself. *This was getting ridiculous.*

It had been a minute since she had had time to really relax and explore sex. Jenny had been her last relationship thing. But Jenny had graduated last year and moved back home to where her parents were in Seattle. They had had fun for a while, not exclusive and open to others, sometimes even playing with others together. But when Jenny was offered a position with her father's rival law firm after graduation, she'd decided to head home. Maggie totally wished her well, but neither of them were interested in anything long-distance, other than friendship. And Maggie had been focusing on her thesis research this year.

Her phone buzzed, and she checked the text from her aunt. Pictures of the homemade cinnamon rolls she was missing this morning made her mouth water.

Morgan had gotten up and grabbed a hoodie from inside the doorway. Pulling it over his head, he mumbled something about taking Xander for a run. "I'll check on your car, too," he said. "Is there anything else you need from there?"

Shaking her head, she didn't trust her voice, as when he put on the hoodie, it had inched up his t-shirt a bit, and that dark trail of hair that narrowed at his waist, where his sweatpants settled low on his hips, made her mouth water. Maybe even more than those damn cinnamon rolls. Maybe she should take up running. This energy building in her needed to go somewhere.

Watching him take off down the long driveway with Xander at a steady pace, she watched his ass as he headed on his run. *DAMN. It was going to be hard to focus on work.*

She picked her phone back up. She had a few calls to make to arrange to work completely virtually for the next week or so anyways.

Morgan

That energy between them was definitely real, but Morgan wasn't sure what he wanted to do with it. She was a bit younger than he usually dated, although, to be honest, it had been a hot minute since he was in any kind of relationship. He did have a slight penchant for younger women, enjoying having them leaning on him a bit for guidance, especially in bed. But he had struggled with those girls and had never really developed relationships there, as they had limited in common. And then there was the leaning-too-much kind. He liked a little spitfire. Independence and knowing herself. Or himself. He did lean towards women in relationships but had explored some over the years.

The last few years, though, he had mostly focused on his writing, other than something quick here and there for release. It had been so easy to hole up in his small apartment over the coffee shop post-college. Beautiful views of northern New York City, writing, coffee, and food all easily accessed with a quick break. Small market within walking distance. The little coffee shop below him had even expanded its small selection of tea offerings thanks to him. He'd mentioned the brand he liked from London, and they had eventually tried it, selling out of their selection quickly to locals.

He'd met a few people here and there, especially if he ventured out to parties on the rare occasion, but it had definitely been a while. He tended not to need frequent sex. Not that when he did engage in it, he didn't enjoy it. Witches had a tendency towards a passionate nature. But he preferred the more patient, stable side of his personality, rather than when the smoke intensely billowed in him—and sex, especially with fellow mystical folks, brought out his intensity. And he could sense the ashes stirring within her. But he wasn't quite sure he was ready for what he sensed could happen between them.

He would rather refocus that energy on his writing. If only he could break his writer's block. Get his creative energy flowing again.

He jogged past her car, feeling the endorphins rising in his system. He had hoped a run would get her off his mind. Noticing her bralessness had not helped his morning frustrations. Brought on by both her and the young naked witch in his dreams. Maggie's small but pert chilled breasts made his fingers itch to pluck. UGGH. Maybe a cold shower would have been better. Or a warm shower and rubbing one out.

But now, all he could think about was pulling the young witch-wanna-be into his lap and congratulating her on her hard-earned grades in a way he probably shouldn't. Or maybe she wasn't a wanna-be 'cause he wasn't sure yet why she didn't know she had powers. He sensed them in her energy signature. But he had learned from Xander last night that her familiar, or her mother's familiar really, knew she wasn't aware of them. There was a curious story there. He hadn't decided if he wanted to uncover it or not.

Witches generally knew at a young age about their developing energies. It was impossible to miss. At the latest, by the time hormones rage and one explores sex, they would find themselves popping off with spurts of electrical discharge from their energy signatures. Each witch different in nature and how it was expressed. He knew his energy was more of a dark blue when it radiated, billowing with smoke when it intensified. Her energy had a purplish light, as he'd noticed before, with a radiance to it. It was extremely strange that she would make it to her twenties and not know. He wasn't sure how that could be. He would have to be careful while she was here, to not allow his magicks to show and scare her if she wasn't aware of the supernatural.

He had a moment of imagining educating her on all kinds of things. But that just made him begin to harden again, which wasn't very comfortable for running. He didn't stop, though, figuring he deserved the pain in his groin due to his wandering thoughts. He wasn't afraid of a little pain. Giving or receiving. But he really needed to reign in the wandering thoughts, or this run would be pointless. He pushed himself harder. As he felt the intensity rise in his calves and lungs, he pushed again even harder to distract himself from the rising violet energies calling to him from behind.

Chapter Five

Maggie

Maggie had called home to check in. Auntie assured her things were fine and they would be there when she finally made it. She mentioned the writer's name she was staying with, and Auntie had thought the name sounded familiar, but she couldn't place it. Maybe she had read some of his books? Maggie hadn't read for pleasure in ages. All her time reading anymore seemed to be work related.

"All work and no play makes Maggie a bored girl who has no fun," her aunt reminded her laughingly. While Maggie knew Auntie meant to read for fun more, she also knew her Auntie would encourage her to play with a man as handsome as Morgan. It was an understated sort of handsome, with a dark edginess if you didn't pick up on his random shyness. He didn't seem to care how he dressed, well, for the less than 24 hours that she had been here. His hair could use a trim, and he seemed not to love to shave. But the dark brooding in his blue gaze would definitely be a place she could get lost. And his mouth. And that little trail of hair down his narrow hips...

But she hadn't told Auntie about that part. Yet.

Maggie wasn't one to initiate very often. She had come to understand that about her more submissive sexual nature. Like, when her first boyfriend hadn't been much of a starter, that had fizzled really fast. She knew Jason was much happier now, though, with his wife and kids. They owned the small cafe in her grandparent's neighborhood, having taken it over from his own grandparents when they retired. Both being raised by grandparents had brought them together. Sex had not kept them together. *But who stays with your teen boyfriend anyways?* She wasn't sure if Sarah, his wife, knew they had been in that kind of relationship when they were younger, but Sarah always waved welcomingly to her anytime she would stop by for coffee when in town.

Morgan had put out some cereal when he got back from his run. Maggie had done her best not to jump his sweaty balls on his return. She could have sworn she felt a frisson of something between them but grabbed a bowl and sliced a banana to add to her raisin bran instead of stopping to breathe in his pheromones. He had grazed by her to grab the milk, and she was almost positive she had felt his hardened penis graze her hip. But he had turned away instead of doing something about it. For a second, she had thought he might pick her up and set her on the kitchen island, pull her tank down and have his sweaty way with her—but that was probably just wishful thinking.

She might need another shower. A cold one. Or to rub one out on her clit. *Something.*

She had shifted back out to work at today's temporary workspace on the porch. This gave her some room to breathe, away from whatever was developing between them. Maggie had always been fairly intuitive—of others, of energies, of what she herself wanted. Auntie had said it ran in the family, that Esme was intuitive too, as had been her mother. But her grandmother didn't like talking about emotions, so they didn't discuss it much with her. Maggie figured it was because Nan didn't talk much about her mother, always getting sad so quickly.

Maggie also felt like she was always missing something. A piece of herself. She knew that must be the loss of her parents. But some days, it felt like that wasn't all. She'd tried to bring that up once to her aunt, but she'd just told her to have fun and enjoy being young.

She wasn't sure why she was thinking about all this so much since being here.

Morgan

"Max," Morgan frustratingly replied. "I told you I'm working on it, I promise. I've delivered 12 books that have generated near the top of both the mundane and magickal society's top sellers lists. I think I've earned a little grace period here."

"Hey, Morg," said Max. "I get it, man. Your uncle died. I know you were close to him. But you were already behind on getting the next concept to the publishers before that." He sighed. "But I will hold them off again. We need something soon, buddy. You need to spark some ideas, somehow."

Morgan hung up. He knew that. No one needed to tell him that much. He leaned forward from his desk chair, face in his hands. He breathed. Counted his breaths backward from 5, then another 5. He knew the more he tried to force things, the more stuck he would likely be. He rubbed the scruff on his chin. He should probably shave. It was getting thick.

Nope. Who had the energy for that?

He had come back from his run and eaten a quick bowl of cereal. Xander was worn out enough that he had stopped chiding him for the girl wearing his robe last night. It was a good thing Xander couldn't hear the shit he had been thinking in the kitchen about jerking her up by her armpits onto that kitchen island and tearing that thin tank top off her tits and—well. Let's just say it's better that Xander couldn't hear everything he thought; Morgan had to send his thoughts to the pup intentionally. Not that Xander hadn't been with him through all his dating years and seen more than his fair share of too much. He had ironically learned more about the animalistic side of sex, and also the soft, nurturing side—from his familiar than he had any of his male adult figures. I mean, Xander wasn't just any canine. He had the heart and mind of a wizard. Until coming to live with his uncle as an awkward teen, almost everything he had learned about magicks had been advice or knowledge from Xander.

Familiars didn't age like the average pet. While Morgan had received Xander from his uncle as a pup when he was 8, Xander most definitely did not have the typical health of a 25-year-old German Shepherd. He actually tended to age much more like one year per human decade. Which meant he still had some young pup energy for a Shepherd. Morgan was ready for that part to pass. But the running helped keep him somewhat fit and got him up and started each day.

Even when he had nothing to write about.

Now Xander lay quietly on his goose-down dog bed on the other side of the office here at The Hollow. He still couldn't quite think of it as his home, but he knew this could eventually be a fantastic place to live and work from. He had chosen to use his uncle's office space today, just off the library. It was down a corridor on the 2nd floor, so he did have to go upstairs and down the dark and dusty hall to the space his uncle had often disappeared to when he would "work."

His great uncle had been a wizard—and a powerful one at that. Morgan had learned a great deal from him in the four years he lived here. He had advanced Morgan's skills far beyond what Xander had introduced him to, beyond the typical lights and flashes and basic spells. Had taught him how to hone in his energy intuition that was his strength, had started to teach him how to control and release the intensity of his own smoky energies and powers, and they had been slowly working their way through his uncle's well-developed spell book. It had been passed down through multiple generations of witches and wizards. And he supposed it was his now, wherever it was.

But Xander had never really known what his great uncle "did" for a living in order to need to work every day. He almost hadn't wanted to use this room. It felt like it disturbed the dead, being here. He wanted things to remain as they were when his uncle left them. He hadn't been meant to die just yet, Morgan knew that without a doubt. He could fully sense the disruption of time and space in this room. His uncle's things waited for him, as though he would return, he could feel it.

But they had made room for him when he came. He had shifted only a few of his things into the space—making room on the large old mahogany desk for his laptop and adding a printer nearby. His old trusty Webster—leather-bound, a gift given to him by his uncle as a graduation present—sat on the printer table against the wall behind the desk. While his uncle had upgraded the house phone in the kitchen to one with all the bells and whistles, he'd left the old, rotary phone in here the same. He still remembered calling a girl for the first time from that phone. The gold was partially worn off the dial, and the black scuffed a bit on the handle from decades of use.

He'd changed as little as he could at this point. He hadn't even had the cleaners come up here just yet, dusting some of it himself when he first began to use the room. The windows were fine here, not broken like a few other closed-off areas, although he had turned off the vents to the rest of the unused parts of the home to save on the massive electric bill. He'd have to figure out something soon, though, about those windows, as it was getting chilly. There was a fireplace in here, and the light from the fire he'd started when he came in glanced off the corners of the room in a way that whispered stories of the many things this room must have seen through the years.

A large old painting of witches in a seasonal gathering around a fire was hung over the fireplace. A full wall of shelves ran along one wall, filled with hundreds of books, pots, and jars of various sizes and colors filled with old spell ingredients. The center of the long room held a long wooden conference table with a dozen chairs, its thick legs curling like the feet of a lion. A vast, antique chandelier that Morgan rarely turned on hovered over the table, almost watching the room. He faintly remembered his uncle hosting some sort of board meeting for the council at times. But his uncle would usually send him away from The Hollow on some random errand until he finally got a job in his teens. Castian had attempted to shelter him from the not-so-pretty parts of witchcraft, like the politics, while also educating him on aspects he felt Morgan needed. He would often say, "If things were the way I wish they could be, witches and wizards could come and go freely amongst mundanes, not afraid of having their magicks taken for granted." His uncle had been the one to teach Morgan to be open to his mother choosing what magick she wanted in her own life. And incidentally, eventually influenced Morgan to pull away from much of what the council stood for, preferring a more solitary lifestyle as a witch. Morgan hadn't agreed with many things the Wiccan council had made policy over the years, even with his uncle's dissent. He didn't want any part of it.

But he knew they called on that old phone. Their ring was different somehow. He knew that they knew Castian had passed. The voicemail had grown more and more full as each week passed by and he didn't check the messages. Morgan had little interest in calling anyone back to discuss his great-uncle's death. He was having a hard enough time sorting it out himself.

If he had only come down that weekend as he had planned. Maybe his uncle wouldn't have wrecked his car so unexpectedly. Maybe Morgan would have noticed whatever it was that caused him to run the car off the road into the ravine. Maybe his uncle would be here, resting by the fire in the sitting room, beckoning him to a game of magick chess, each piece a different position in the supernatural world, representing a political game of different sorts. At 72, his great uncle had been aging, but Morgan knew it hadn't been his time yet.

The lights in the room flickered. Morgan felt the small surge of energy rise and fall. He had called the mundane electrician two weeks ago about the periodic electrical surges the house seemed to experience, but he had said it would be a few weeks before he could get out to see the place. Morgan suspected that after last night's storm, other emergencies might end up putting this old mansion even further down the list, as emergency repairs likely would have cropped up as a priority. So, he held onto his patience. Although sometimes, like now he noticed, as his computer disconnected from the cloud, surges would overwhelm the router, and the wifi would go down.

He got up to turn it off for a little while and allow it to reset. Usually everything would start back up okay. Eventually. He looked at these moments as opportunities for breaks.

Well, breaks if he were actually writing. As of now, all he did was stare at his blank document screen or search for ideas and research potential topics that just didn't inspire him.

And he'd add to his list of repairs that this old place needed. He'd eventually get to things. The list was already longer than he'd like to think about. Even in the last week, he definitely hadn't gotten as much done around The Hollow as he would have liked to. He just wasn't really a handyman. But he could Google and YouTube like the best of 'em. Research was his forte in writing, and he wanted to honor the history of the building.

"Helloooo?" He heard her young, sexy voice from a distance. Shit, it's a good thing she didn't put a foot through the old stairs. He'd definitely be liable for that. He got up, Xander running ahead of him to greet her in the hall. The pup didn't have to tell Morgan how much he liked the girl, Morgan could tell.

"Hey," he said, probably a little too gruffly. He closed the office door behind him. "You really shouldn't be up here." Her eyes flicked up to his from petting the pup. Maybe he should peddle that back a little. "I mean, it's such an old building. My uncle didn't keep up with it very well, and I'm not even sure how rotten the wood is on the stairs. I keep meaning to have someone come out and look at that for me," he said, wincing as he admitted his lack of follow-through.

"Oh!" she said cheerfully. "If that's all you're worried about, I could take a look at that." She peered up through her natural, long lashes and those glasses a tad shyly. "I mean if you want me to. My Pop, er—my grandfather, taught me all kinds of stuff about fixing things. I'm pretty good with my hands." She blushed. "I mean, er—you know what I mean," she rushed through the last part.

He chuckled. *Uh-uh. He wasn't going there.* But he nodded his head reluctantly. He really didn't want her getting tetanus from an old nail on his watch, but she wasn't his to say no to. And he had already decided she wasn't going to be, even if her energy called to his. "If you think you know something about carpentry, feel free to take a look," he said. *He never had felt very 'manly' in his inability to fix things.* Generally, he threw off gender norms, but today he somehow struggled. At least he could afford to hire someone. *But he wasn't going to be able to for long if he didn't get to writing a goddamn book.*

This place was going to need a lot of work.

"Ummmm..." She looked around a little curiously. The hallway was dark and musty. The lights flickered again. "Oh yeah, I was going to mention that too. I was going to ask if it were okay to look at your electrical board. But that can wait. Do you have any tools or flashlights or anything? It's a bit dark on this level," she said. *Kind of sounded like she might know what she was doing,* he admitted to himself.

"Well, yes," he began, "there are flashlights in the kitchen, but we are going to need to check the cellar for the tools, I think." He had hardly been down there, even when he was a teen. It was eerie down there like you could feel the millions of souls who had passed through. And his uncle had generally seemed to want him to avoid it. A friend had dared him to go down there one night when his friend stayed over. They had made it into the third room, seen chains, and that had been it. Morgan had gotten his friend out fast—and had never invited a friend to stay the night at his uncle's home again. *Way too much to explain.*

He had already tried to repair the electrical work with magick, but that didn't work. He couldn't quite get to what was wrong in the wiring. But he couldn't explain that to her, and he knew his uncle's workbench for the actual repairing of mundane things was in the first room of the cellar, so not too far in. He led the way back down to the kitchen, and out a side door that led through the greenhouse walkway, aged with time and moss on the outside in sections, to another door about 30 feet from the kitchen. The greenhouse passage had small piles of gardening items, pots, bags of dirt, two old rickety garden benches, and a rusted, tall metal shelf filled with jars. Glancing, he thought they were all empty. He hoped not to have to explain some unusual substance his uncle might have left there.

Uncle had explained that a previous generation had decided to encase the walkway between the house and the cellar in glass, creating a greenhouse. A green witch from a few generations back had been reportedly powerfully skilled in herbs and plants. Morgan had a touch of that skill but hadn't had much of an opportunity to explore or nurture very much to life, well, since he'd left his uncles at 18. Other than a few herbs he would keep handy in his small apartment anyways. He liked mint, basil, and oregano the most. Mostly to cook with.

He clicked on the electric lantern he had grabbed from the entry of the passageway. Her eyes widened in amazement behind her glasses.

"Oh wow!" she said. "This is so awesome!!" She turned in a slow circle in the greenhouse as she waited for him to unlock the double cellar door, partially grown over by a few hungry vines.

He wasn't sure how she wasn't freaked out. Who goes with a stranger into a dark cellar like this? Definitely not cautious mundanes. Wise ones anyways. He unlocked both old locks, his uncle had always been very careful about who might enter this area. He stepped back, making room for her to enter, mentioning the old cement stairs down into the space had a few cracks, and not to trip. He directed her immediately to the left once they made it down into the dark space, his lantern lighting the immediate area where they were until he reached the sconces on the wall. Her eyes lit up when he turned the knob beneath one and then another and electricity brought the room into a low glow.

"I'm not quite sure who installed the electricity in this place," he said. "It's definitely faulty and old in places, but they were smart enough to run it out here too."

"Oh my gods, this is so completely fantastic," she gushed. He had never, ever met someone who might love a dark and dank cement cellar, even one as large as this. She began to quickly move through the space, noting the workbench and tools against one wall. But she moved into the archway, glancing into the next room. "Oh," she said, disappointed.

"I can't see very well. I bet this is a great old space with lots of stories." She turned to him, face lighting back up like a schoolgirl. Oh gods, he needed to get his head out of his pants. She looked so eager, like a young puppy, eager to please so she could get what she wanted—which he read from her so clearly as wanting to see the rest of the lower level.

But she was cute enough that he decided to appease her, at least some. He walked towards her, brushing alongside her back as he moved through the doorway she stood in. Time stood still for a moment as he moved past her, smelling the lavender and amethyst soap he knew his uncle had had shipped in from London. His hips and cock just barely grazed her pert backside as he moved through the archway behind her. He thought he felt her energy heighten as well, as his had.

But he turned into the next room, holding the lantern up a bit, to shine the light into the dark corners. This room was a bit like an old kitchen, but thankfully mostly empty of the spells and items for spells that he knew would have been kept here decades ago. His uncle hadn't used the space much, the hearth no longer holding the cauldron that would have been there many moons ago. The wooden and glass shelves that lined the walls were mostly empty, except for a few with some remaining dried herbs and sticks in them. An island similar to the one in the updated kitchen stood in the middle of it all, an old oak and stone space in which to work and prep the spells and potions of old.

Thinking she would be satisfied with the space and return, he turned back. But her eyes were alive, and she was moving forward toward the next archway.

"Wait—STOP!" he barked, louder than he probably should have. She immediately halted, eyes wide. "I mean, that room is just old, and no one wants to see that one," he said. Or at least his friend hadn't. And he was fairly sure a dewy-eyed, young college student who liked to read and play with computers might not view things the way a witch might. Especially if she knew nothing of her heritage.

"Oh," she said hesitantly. "Is that all? Cause I really like to see unique places, like even old horror ones, cause—" She stopped. Having moved into the archway, her eyes were wider than before. "Hooooly shiiiit," she mumbled under her breath, standing frozen in place.

Dammit. "What?" he asked hesitantly, moving behind her, and holding the lantern at her shoulder. He knew what she saw. There was a crude cell, the metal-barred door hanging open, broken at some point during the years. Inside the cell, there was a chain looped to a stake in the floor, with the other end holding a broken cuff that might have been attached to a prisoner at one time. Outside the cell, on the rough cement wall, were two old metal cuffs clearly meant for a prisoner's wrists, and two closer to the floor that were meant for ankles.

He could only imagine what she thought. His friend had been freaked the fuck out. Had Morgan known what was here, he clearly would have not brought him back all those years ago. Although Morgan wasn't scared of them. Not anymore. He was more intrigued by the history behind the need for them, for the various mystical beings he could sense they held at one time. And the pleasures.

"Did you see that though?" she asked, breath coming in short little puffs in the chilling air, as night was settling outside and the dampness thickened inside. She turned, looking at him, eyes still wide. And he sensed that her energy wasn't fearful as he once thought, more anticipation... and he dared to think, did her dark energy just reach out to stroke his?

She looked back towards the cell area. "Did you see the women—the women in white?" she rushed on. "I don't know, maybe she wasn't wearing white. She may have been a ghost or something. She had on a short flowy dress. She was young—maybe a little younger than me," she said, turning back to him.

But all he could feel was her.

Her eyes glazed over in heat as they looked up at him.

He slowly moved towards her in the archway, giving her time to retreat. But instead of retreating, her eyelids fluttered closed, waiting. He tucked a piece of her hair that was stuck to the corner of her lip behind her ear. Tracing her jaw, his finger ran down the curve of her neck slowly, tracing the strap of her tank down to the rise of her breast.

"I know you feel this as much as I do," he grated out. Gently pressing her through the doorway behind her, back against the wall, his hand came up to cup her neck, his fingers moving to both raise her chin to him and press ever so gently against her windpipe with his thumb. Just enough. He sensed his smoke as it began to tangle with her slowly burning kindling. His teeth grazed her jaw. He gently kissed the path he took, inching closer to her mouth. Her berry-swollen, fucking mouth that had been beckoning him for what felt like ages, centuries even, when it had really only been less than 24 hours.

He took her mouth, inhaling her essence, as his smoke engulfed her and brought her to flame. She writhed beneath him, eager for more. His other hand came up to cup the back of her head amidst long burgundy locks, twisting his hand just right, to pull her head back gently and still her movements.

He looked at her, dripping with violet wanton. He had never seen anything more beautiful. Or more complicated. She had no clue how their energies combined, she likely didn't see their energies fusing as he did. This wasn't just some college girl he could play with for a little while, even both fully consenting. There was no way they could fuck where she would not experience her hidden magicks—not with their both being witches. Whoever had warded her gifts had taken great care and likely hoped she would never consummate with another supernatural. The energy explosion between them would be magickal in and of itself.

He eased his hand from her hair. He didn't want to hurt her—not by exposing her magick to her, nor by rejecting her. Her magick was so pure, so light. Her sex dripped off of her energy right now, he could almost smell it, taste it in his hands.

"This—" he said gently but firmly, "shouldn't happen." And he took a step back from her.

"You are beautiful. And while I know it sounds trite—it's not you, it's me," he said. Hoping he could play on sarcasm and joke. He really had enough on his plate, with not being able to write and managing his uncle's estate and mourning his death. Yes, he'd blame it on that. Her eyes had opened and begun to clear. Why did he feel such an intense loss when her essence began to separate from his?

"Seriously though," he said, "this whole situation," he gestured around him as he walked back towards the front room, "should scare the fuck out of you, little girl." There it was. He saw the fire. Better the fire than the sadness she had started to feel. "The last thing you need is to be fucking an old copyright in his dirty cellar."

"Fuck that," she said, her chin coming up in defiance as she stormed past him to the workbench. Selecting a few tools and a flashlight, she spun back around on him. "You aren't *that* old. Plus, I'll fuck whomever the hell I want to, wherever the hell I want to." She shrugged. "Your loss. That shit was gonna be good." And she stomped right on past him and up the cement stairs like an angry teenager. *But he wasn't gonna tell her that, 'cause it was actually kinda cute.*

And she wasn't wrong. That shit could definitely be good between them. But it would likely fuck her sideways, as learning one has supernatural powers is life-changing.

People died for having that gift.

Chapter Six

Maggie

Thankfully Maggie had gotten a significant amount of work done earlier before deciding to *be all beneficent and shit* and offer to check out the lights. Which of course led to checking out these damn stairs.

If she couldn't focus her frenetic energy on fucking the hell out of him, she would focus her energy on these damn stairs. Looking at them closer, maybe two of the boards should be replaced, but even those weren't horrible. *He had made a big deal over her being careful on old stairs that were really mostly fine.* She threw her hands up in the air irritably. Not even a single damn thing she could do about it right now either, not a piece of wood in sight to drive a nail into. No two-by-fours anywhere in sight.

So, she stomped on past him, went through the kitchen and out the door into the greenhouse area again, looking for the fuse box to check something for the lights. When she didn't find it, she stomped back in and stood in front of him, knowing underneath it all that the petulant attitude was too much, but not really wanting to stop. *What was he gonna do about it?*

Huffing and blowing a strand of hair out of her eyes, she said, "Where the hell is the electrical panel, dammit?"

His eyes chilled and he looked at her a moment before answering slowly, "Try that again." He'd reigned in his tone with a quiet edge. That was not going to make her stop. She had better start interacting like an adults, not like a brat he might turn over his knee and give a good swat to. A swat she knew would not only reset her attitude but also stroke the fire her clit had become earlier. *Gods she wished.*

But he turned her chin up to his steely gaze anyways. "Again," he said firmly, not raising his voice. The stillness in his voice stroked over her soul like molten lava.

Her eyes automatically dropped. She definitely was not new to this. "I'm sorry," she said softly, responding to the limit he set at the moment. She took a breath. "Where is the control panel?" She asked much more calmly. Like it or not, she had needed that reset. Like it or not, and she did not—he was not going to be stroking her clit tonight. Or probably any night.

He regarded her for a few moments more, his eyes deciding his next step far less impulsively than she had. He quietly walked around her and guided her to a small closet off to the other side of the kitchen, where a pantry was, with a wall of cleaning items and the control panel.

He nodded at the panel, not saying another word. She moved past him and began to assess what she was working with. He moved quietly out of the kitchen, to where, she wasn't even sure. Probably anywhere to get away from her. She knew he had felt it too, so she wasn't misguided in thinking he wasn't attracted to her. But clearly, he was not going to fuck her. Not tonight at least. *Maybe never.*

She sighed.

Something within told her this could have been a life-changing connection. Like when the fuck of your life presents itself and then says, "Nah, bitch. Not tonight." It kinda pissed her off, but at the same time, she was a huge proponent of consent, especially with this kinky shit. It was too dangerous otherwise. So, if for whatever reason he was not feeling it tonight—or ever—she had no qualms. She could always rub one out herself to get rid of this frustration he'd left her with.

Everything her Pop had taught her about the multimeter she had recognized in the workbench, told her that the electrical fuses were fine. Everything she could tell anyways. Morgan may really need to use an electrician to check lines and everything. The surges were few and far between, but they definitely occurred. When the wifi dropped earlier for the second time—she had thought it would be helpful to look at things. She definitely hadn't expected all that to happen.

Walking back into the kitchen, she decided to act like nothing had happened. No need to keep hashing this sexual tension out. He could decline in any way he chose. She provided a brief update on her findings from the electric box and then he went on to mention that the bridge was reportedly open and he had sent an order for Chinese to be dropped off by Uber. She was amazed he got delivery way out here, being at least 30 minutes from town. But he insisted that he had a delivery guy that pretty much brought him anything with enough notice, and enough tip. He mentioned he had ordered a small array of options, but it would be at least an hour before it would arrive.

"M'kay, thanks," she said. "I think I'm going to go relax, maybe take a bath or something. Don't wait for me, I can always find leftovers in the fridge."

She ducked her head, hiding behind her hair as she went by him quickly, feeling a little embarrassed that she had acted bratty earlier. Not even sure which felt more vulnerable—knowing he knew she wanted him to fuck her and he didn't want to, or the moment of somewhat offered submission. To this man that she hardly knew.

He was clearly a good guy. Intelligent. She did have a thing for smart men. They clearly had a connection of some kind. He was a little older than she usually had a thing for, but he did put on the dominant vibe in a way she had never sensed before. It had a softness somehow to its hard edge. It beckoned her closer, stroking her sometimes brash fire. It threatened to at once burst her into flames, and yet intensify her heat for her own pleasure.

GAH. She turned on the water in the tub when she got to her room. The waxing gibbous moon was brighter than the night before, casting its light on the water with the flickering of the candles she had lit in the window. She threw in some dried rose petals and a few drops of an essential oil mix from the wooden basket. She hadn't remembered seeing those this morning, and she wasn't sure what the oil mix was, but it smelled lovely. The aroma only seemed to enhance her sexual frustration, as she stripped, standing in the light of the moon and the low candlelight.

Glancing in the full wall of mirrors at herself, she knew she didn't look bad. Sure, she was a bit small—everywhere really. Short, smaller-breasted, a gentle small natural curve of her belly, the indentions at her hip bone, and her ass was often one of her best qualities. It definitely helped her get more spanks when she needed them. And the Poison Ivy vine tattoo right above her ass that said "eat me" often got surprise responses that she usually enjoyed: laughter and sex. Two of her favorite things. After books. And autumn. And her family. Well, no need to always be so serious anyways.

Out of the corner of her eye, she could have sworn she saw the ghost girl again. But looking, she disregarded it as a sliver of moonbeam playing tricks on her. The water had pretty much filled the tub, the steam rising off the water in the chill of the night air, the rose petals floating luxuriously.

She hadn't noticed the chill earlier... Maggie shivered.

Sinking into the tub, a deep sigh releasing from her as she was wrapped in the warmth of the scented water. She wished she had brought her little pocket vibe. "Easy to travel, but noooooo..." she mumbled to herself. "Too awkward at home with the grandparents right down the hall." *I mean, it's not like they expected her to be a virgin or anything.*

She had dated a lot as a teen. Her aunt was pretty forward-thinking and had started talking to her about sex, safety, and consent at a pretty young age. Auntie was both poly and pan, and Maggie tended to be more open as well, with a tendency to value all people in different ways—even sexually.

She fingered the pendant at her throat.

She had never taken off the pendant either. Not even during bathing—or sex. Her aunt had talked to her about that at a young age too. Auntie Esme loved her new-agey things, and ironically Maggie connected with some of them a lot as well. So, if it meant a lot to her aunt and Nan to wear the damn necklace—when her aunt was always so chill about rules and people—who was she to judge. Or take off the necklace.

The moon glinted off the pendant, casting a brief flash into the mirror. Her grandma had given it to her when she was really young, like when she started Kindergarten. She said it was to always remember her mother by. But the trouble was, she didn't remember her. She had been so young when her parents disappeared from her life. The endless grief of missing someone you couldn't remember was unfathomable.

And the idea of taking off the only thing that connected her to her mother was unfathomable.

She rested her head back on the tub, wet tendrils falling around her face and back from the tub's ledge. Everyone longed to be loved. *Some of us loved to be loved a lot—and so what if that might be because she had lost out on the love she needed the most when she was little? What if she would rather not be pitied but fucked?* When people found arousal and orgasm together, in a state of enjoyment and genuine caring, Maggie thought she felt the most loved in those moments. Most wanted and needed. And especially most cared for and needs met when it was within a Dominant/submissive, trusted relationship of some kind.

Maggie didn't feel like she owed anyone an explanation for her sexuality. She knew and owned who she was, and fuck anyone else. Including Morgan Smithe.

Imagining his dark, sexy gaze immediately had her clit tingling again. She gently flicked it a little as she remembered his teeth on her jaw, his hand at her throat. Eyes drifting closed, hands sliding through the water, over nipples petulantly craving teeth but willing to settle for tugs and twists. She smelled the roses as they intensified, the smell of something else in the oil mix as well, something she couldn't quite put her finger on. Patchouli maybe.

Her gaze slid open, heavy with desire. In the faint light reflecting the moonlight and candles off the wall of mirrors, she saw herself in the bath, wet, hands sliding on wet skin. For a moment she imagined Morgan was behind her in the water, his hands beginning to roam, chest bare and wet in the reflection. As she watched, his hands began to flicker and were replaced with pure white, ethereal ones, as she watched them stroke her wet breasts. Gentler hands. More feminine lines to them, but not her own. The long fingernails began flicking at her nipples, circling the tight peaks, and eventually scraping down her skin and smoothing the building tension on her thighs. Fingers stroked closer and closer towards her warm center, teasing in the slow build up. Eventually, as Maggie groaned, she felt a fluttering sensation at her hardened clitoris.

"Oh, my goddess…" Maggie groaned out, the intensity of her arousal twisting higher and higher in her gut.

Maggie's eyes flew to the mirrors across the room, where she saw her ghost girl was now behind her, replacing the once-imagined Morgan. Unsure if this was imaginary or more, she was too turned on to even care. The ghost seemed to recognize her assent and she quickly flew around her, drawing Maggie's hips up and out of the water with pale narrow fingers. She encouraged Maggie to spread her thighs, hooking each leg over the sides of the ornate bathtub, splashing water over the edge carelessly.

Maggie, now spread wide, her breath heavy and shallow, watched as the pale-haired girl's tongue flicked her most sensitive area. Maggie wasn't sure how she could feel the girl's long locks in her hands, but she did as she clenched their silky lengths tightly, eventually coming in waves as the beautiful, blond-haired girl gazed tenderly into her eyes, flicking her tongue in repetitive movements, at times firmly and others just the tip, softly.

Maggie saw depths in the girl's eyes, swirling colors, and sadness, so much sadness. Her hand came to rest on the side of the girl's face,

Maggie wanting to give in return, but the girl's light fluttered, becoming less tangible, and she slowly faded from view, only the ripples left in Maggie's bath to remind her of what had just happened.

Maggie slumped back into the cooling water, her thoughts clearing more, with the orgasm fading. *HOLY SHIT. Had that really just happened?*

Maggie had had experiences through the years, where she had thought she saw ghosts. But not really interacting much with them. Well, other than the young girl her aunt had said later must have been an imaginary friend. But Maggie swore she had been a ghost. Milly had told her of how she had died in their home when she was a little girl—from scarlet fever. Maggie had felt her sadness too, missing her family—but they had been great playmates for a few years before Maggie had wondered where she had gone.

But she definitely didn't think this had been a grown-up Milly with her pigtails all grown out.

This girl had looked to be around Maggie's age, maybe a little younger. Her dress strangely didn't even seem to get wet in the bath, it had been a cotton slip of some kind, something like she imagined an old thin petticoat might have been. It had laced up the front, pushing her bodice up a bit, with fairly decent cleavage. Maggie regretted now, not unlacing that before she had disappeared. Maggie wondered at being able to touch and be touched at times, but not others—but Milly had been the same way when they pushed each other on the swings.

Maggie raised out of the now cool bath, water dripping from her long hair. She thought she'd shower really quickly and wash her hair. Then find a way to clean up the water that had splashed all over the dark tiles in the wake of her erotic visitor.

Morgan

He probably shouldn't have seen that.

Morgan now sat at his desk in the office, wondering what to do with the energy doubly pent up in him from his much earlier interaction with the young witch, let alone his more recent glimpse of her and what must have been Althea in her bath.

He really hadn't intended to see anything, he preferred voyeurism to be fully consensual with any exhibition he was granted. But Xander had gone outside and had been intently calling him, and it took a moment for Morgan to notice the presence of the ghost in the area. Xander had quickly run away from the view of the large expansive bathroom window that they had followed the presence to. The moon and the candlelight glowed, and the ghost's own light reflected off soft, wet skin, like a mirage calling him as they reflected off the floor-to-ceiling wall of mirrors across from the tub.

Bless the ancestor who installed those.

The way she had given herself fully over to the moment, knowing she likely would have done that with him, had made him rock hard, making it difficult not to pull himself out right then and there in the dark, amongst the trees edging his property. Let alone the beauty of what was occurring between the two young women, the fire from their both physical and spiritual encounter.

He had sensed Althea's energy signature, as well as her eternal sadness, rising from her in waves at one point and merging with the young witch's purple passion, but also her reprieve from that sadness through offering this moment of release to this witch who yet did not fully understand herself.

But now he sat here at his desk, his fingers itching to write if they could not stroke either of their soft, beautiful forms. Ideas exploded from his fingertips as he began to click away at the keyboard. He brainstormed furiously, the ideas that had risen, unbidden in his psyche. His kindled smoke flowing at his fingertips in small wisps, fueling his energy and intent into his writing rather than exploding in intercourse.

His cock slowly receding, mostly anyways, as his mind began to fill with the plot his protagonist would take, rather than the images that had once flitted through his mind in the woods of the three of them, naked in the leaves, hands and mouths uniting and bringing pleasure under the blessing of the glowing moon. While he knew that could make fantastic erotica, that was not his usual genre, and he was just glad it had sparked some kind of kindling to his once burnt-out creativity.

No, he shouldn't have seen that, but it would also fuel his dreams for many nights to come, he was sure.

Monday, he slept in much later than normal, having written most of the night. Xander wouldn't leave him alone about having gazed at the sensual moment playing out on the other side of the windows for so long. He should feel guilty, really, he should. But the image of her with legs spread wide across the bathtub, dripping with both water and sex, likely wouldn't leave him anytime soon. Or of the young woman pleasing her, as he wasn't really the jealous type.

He could appreciate good things in multiple small packages.

Instead, he warmed the leftover Chinese food, not having eaten very much last night when the food arrived as he had wanted to get back to the flood of inspiration occurring in his exploding brain. He and Maggie hadn't run into each other at all last night, but he could tell she had eaten some of the Chinese food, as the Kung Pao Chicken and the white rice were definitely reduced from when he had last left them, and an eggroll was gone as well. He heard her rustling around out on the porch again and took his plate and his cup of warmed-up coffee to stand in the screen doorway. She had moved the side table in front of her on the porch swing, cross-legged and busily typing on her laptop, having made a makeshift workstation of sorts.

"I can find a desk or something and set you up with a workplace while you're here," he offered as he moved out onto the sunlit space, settling in an Adirondack chair. The early afternoon sun had warmed the gray wooden porch planks where Xander lay at the top of the stairs, basking in what remained of the sun's warmth. With autumn settling in, it was getting chilly at night, but it still warmed a bit during the days.

'Uh huh,' Xander cocked his head at him. *'You'd miss the views too much.'*

The pup wasn't wrong.

"Oh, I'm good. Really!" she assured, glancing up. Her dark cherry-cola hair was twisted up into some kind of sexy thick topknot, with small pieces escaping. Her glasses on the edge of her nose, slipping 'til she pushed them up with a knuckle, studying her work. He wondered if she even realized the innocent but sexy picture she made.

"Seriously though, the autumn trees and falling leaves on the mountainside are probably the prettiest I have ever seen," she gushed, "it's kinda inspiring." She glanced at her phone next to her laptop. "I did however get a call early this morning from your car guy. He really does seem to know his stuff about the classics. But he said the part the old engine needs is in Plattsburgh." She looked at him inquisitively. "Are you familiar with that part of New York?"

Glad they seemed to be back on better terms than the day before, and trying not to view her through the dense fog of the erotic bath memory, he responded with his own short backstory. He'd grown up in New York City before coming to live here at The Hollow with his uncle for his high school years. Then returning to New York for the literature program at Columbia, he remained there after getting such a quick book deal.

He wasn't sure why he was chatting so much or why she was so easy to talk to. That was definitely out of character for him.

"Anyways, yes, I am familiar with Plattsburgh. We could take a day trip up there tomorrow if you need?" he offered. He wanted to go over some of last night's work today and edit a bit. But a break tomorrow after such an intense writing session would be great. And maybe get his mind off of last night, as there were too many gods-damned beds in almost every direction in this fucking place. Or chairs. Or walls.

Heavens forbid there be walls in a damned house.

Or mansion, fuck this place was huge and would take forever for him to renovate. He shook his head.

Yeah, they needed to get out.

Maggie

She agreed to the trip tomorrow, thankful to have a way to get the part for Margot. She had thought about the fact that Nan would ask why he could take her to Plattsburgh and not to Essex, but she sure as hell wasn't leaving Margot here. And if she was honest, she wasn't done with this place either. Not Morgan, nor her ghost girl. She was too curious not to wait around and see what would happen.

Something about all this felt like she shouldn't miss it.

Morpheus was content to chill in her rooms most of the time, but sometimes snuck out and was who knows where in the grand old building. Maggie could almost imagine the huge mansion being made over into some kind of humongous bed and breakfast or event facility. It would be so busy during spooky seasons—the way it seemed to fit into old-world imaginations. And she had only seen some of it.

Morgan had slept in today, so she took the opportunity to explore a bit. She knew he told her not to, but she was careful. Curiosity killed the cat, but she swore she had been one in a past life, and she had a few lives left to kill. She had ventured onto the second floor, leaving his office space alone though, as she didn't want to intrude on his work.

She had found countless other small suites of bedrooms with their own bathrooms, a few even with small kitchenettes, and a grand entertainment space on the third floor that led onto a rather large balcony off the back of the house. Large enough to entertain on, far larger than the narrow one running the front of the house. Sure, the place needed a great deal of work—many broken windows, a few loose boards, even a bird's nest or two. And it needed a mega cosmetic overhaul—hopefully, Morgan would honor the early English gothic architecture style that ran seamlessly through the place. The exaggerated, pointy arches of the black, gray, and white stained-glass windows mirrored the points at the top of the towers on each side of the home, and the buttresses built into the balconies were gorgeous, even if more for beauty than effectiveness. The stone was crumbling in places outside as well, she remembered, and likely needed tuckpointing and possibly some repair.

Maggie could imagine this being the site of some famous old black-and-white movie, maybe of some wizardry school or something. There was something magickal to it. Dark and beautifully foreboding.

She had been peeking out onto the large balcony when her aunt had called her this morning. She had excitedly chattered about the amazing building and how Morgan was supposed to be slowly rehabbing it. Auntie had seemed more curious than normal, asking for his name again, but Maggie hadn't thought too much about it. She was sure she just wanted to make sure she was safe. She didn't tell her about her encounter with the ghost girl. She wanted to hold on to that just a little longer before it was dismissed, like Milly.

Gosh, she hadn't thought about Milly in such a long time. Her disappearance had hurt as a child, more than one might expect. She had really grieved that.

Her body vibrated still with a touch of the mystical energy she had encountered the night before. Everything felt more alive today, somehow. She wasn't sure if it was all in her mind or not. Her senses were on overdrive. Her nipples responded even against the texture of her thin, cotton bra. Morgan being near also seemed to cause her to feel similar mild vibrations. *It was the strangest feeling, not bad though...* But she did her best to pretend everything was normal.

Thankfully he had slept a good chunk of the day away, it was now just past 2pm.

She mentioned that she had taken Xander on a walk of the property when he had nudged her hand earlier, standing together at the top of the porch stairs and watching the sunrise. The large pup had seemed to show her the way, the autumn colors shifting and changing around the gray building, enhancing one another's beauty. At one point, gently nudged by Xander, she had noted how well one might be able to see in her bathroom windows from the side of the building, just as easily as many of the other large, arching windows so artfully worked into the layout of the home.

She had sworn he was warning her or something, but she just laughed and told him she didn't care. Nature had made her the way she was, and if the birds wanted to look on when she showered, they could enjoy the view. Joking that it turned her on somewhat—not the animals, but being watched. "As long as they ask before they touch," she said.

Ha! Like animals even cared about the sexuality of humans. Xander didn't have a clue what she was saying, nor did the pup probably care. There was no way he had seen the night before. But he seemed to be happy now, loping along beside her on the walk, bringing her small gifts from the treeline.

He had also reminded her his food was in the kitchen closet when they returned by scratching the door repeatedly. She'd figured it out, noticing yesterday that Morgan usually gave him a full scoop at breakfast and dinner. She could have sworn he said 'thank you' when he licked her hand in appreciation.

Morpheus, meanwhile, looked at her vindictively from the kitchen doorway, like she had betrayed him or something.

"Of course I'm not replacing you," she swore to her pet. But he wasn't listening. He went on to the doorway leading to the greenhouse, chattering to get out. She had set up his food bowl out there to keep Xander from getting it, setting it on one of the higher shelves in the metal cabinet. Morpheus found it easily. He clearly liked the warmth of the sun in the glass room and had spent a lot of time out there yesterday and today.

Morpheus

'*Old dogs, old tricks is what I say,*' the cat said to the large, hairy Shepherd from his place in the sun.

'*See, I tried to tell you something is up with them, I say,*' the dog returned quickly, his attention on his master. '*Your girl sure doesn't know what she is, but you know if they truly connect with one another, there is no way she isn't going to figure it out.*'

'*You better believe I'm counting on it,*' responded Morpheus. He was 100 years old, this being his 3rd generation as a familiar for this family. He was ready to get this show on the road. Life was horribly boring with a mundane. At least when they had been with her grandparents, he would find one of them sneaking magick when the girl wasn't looking. Morpheus reveled in magicks.

Why they thought she would be safer *not* having access to her gifts was beyond him.

Humans.

How was she going to find out who killed her parents if she had no powers?

Chapter Seven

Maggie

It was an absolutely gorgeous day for a road trip upstate. The sun was shining, the leaves were brighter in color, she swore, than even the day before. Maggie didn't know if it was her penchant for old cars that made her love road-tripping so much, but doing this from a '67 Impala—red instead of black like *Baby* in one of her old favorite tv shows, *Supernatural*—couldn't have been a better way to do it. When Morgan had pulled the classic around the front of the house from the car barn, the large, detached old barn that housed his uncle's multiple old vehicles, Maggie had almost wet her pants in excitement. She felt like she was riding with Sam—'cause he would have been the writer—for the day, investigating to find the old car part. Only they already knew where it was, Morgan responded when she blurted her excitement. But he smiled a little at her, softening the blow.

She rolled her eyes, telling him he wasn't any fun. He lasered his eyes in on her and snapped his mouth shut. She could have sworn he was going to say something about her eye roll. He hadn't.

His loss.

Maggie had planned ahead and packed them lunch in a cooler. Digging in Morgan's cabinets, which were fairly decently stocked actually, she had made a quick pasta salad the night before, with some chopped veggies and dressing, some roast beef and swiss sandwiches, and packed some watermelon—already freshly cut and packaged. A few frozen water bottles to keep things cool, napkins, forks, and a tablecloth to sit on in case there weren't any picnic tables anywhere. She hoped they found a beautiful place to stop, it was the best time of year in the northeast in her opinion.

The awkwardness ebbed and flowed between them during the 2+ hour road trip, moments where conversation flowed, and moments where they both ignored the awkward sexual tension between them. Sitting next to him in the classic Impala, she very much appreciated the updated red and white leather upholstery. But the more she thought about how pretty it was, the more it made her consider how easy it would be to simply slide across the front seat, without its modern center console, and slide her hand on his warm lap, her fingers grazing along the hardened ridge she had noticed earlier.

At least he was as miserable as she was if his avoiding her eyes after that meant anything.

Morgan

This was fucking miserable. Why was he abstaining again?

She had worn a ridiculously short plaid schoolgirl skirt with that college hoodie she liked. The Doc Martens gave a 'what the fuck' attitude, and she knew it, never mind those two ponytails with messy buns. Buns did not make the ponytails more adultish really, but they *were* fucking cute. She was 'cruisin for a bruisin' as his father would have said. He hadn't really liked that saying before, not really liking the idea of spanking kids. But consenting adults? That took on a whole different meaning.

And oh, how he wanted to give it to her.

He kept his eyes straight ahead, rather than look at her legs again. He could barely keep himself in his pants and calmed down. He knew she had noticed, and he could literally feel her think through the possibilities of this old Impala's wide front bench seat. He really wished he had thought of that before they brought this beauty on the trip. He had just thought about how her eyes would light up at the classic car, and he hadn't been wrong.

But now his dick was lit up, and it was all he could do to dampen it back down. The skirt hardly covered her pert little ass, and he wondered if her wetness was rubbing against the classic leather. He could think of some other leather things he'd like to kiss those wet lips with.

Dammit, there he went again.

Math? Science? His next book. Tearing down all the damn wallpaper in that big 'ole house strip by strip, and then updating it. Wallpaper was supposed to be boring. Didn't they talk about watching wallpaper drying being the most boring thing one could do? He ran through a list of almost anything he could think of to bring his dick back under control.

FUCK. She brought her right foot up on the seat beneath her, lifting her skirt a little in the process, had he only been in front of her to glance beneath. He wondered what panties she was wearing, or if she wore any at all. He imagined sitting in front of her, instructing her to take them off if she were. If they ever moved on this shit, he would have some seriously pent-up discipline for her sassy ass. He knew she was drawn to some of that play like he was. He had seen it in her eyes, felt it in her spirit when she had cast down her eyes, acquiescing to his lead when she had been overwhelmed on Sunday. These were not vanilla vibes between them.

15 more miles to Plattsburgh, his phone showed on the screen.

He thought about taking an ice-cold bath, his rock-hard cock feeling the pain of the ice chips against it. As painful as that would truly be, it would cool his passion. He thought about the parts store they were going to, and the multiple people they would pass on their way in and out. Cooling his pants was a literal need right now. He had no interest in the humor of others at his discomfort once they got there.

By the time they reached their destination, thankfully involving some complicated turns and traffic that forced his attention fully on the road, he was in a much better place. Maggie had turned the music up at some point, playing around with some of the old 8 tracks found in the glove compartment. Some Joplin, Hendricks, and some old-school Motown helped distract him and boosted her mood. He couldn't wait til she saw his uncle's vinyl collection if she hung around for a while.

He realized he *wanted* her to hang around for a while.

Having shaken off some of the defiance he'd felt radiating towards him, she genuinely seemed excited to get the part for her car, which he learned she called Margot. She was definitely primed for having a familiar, even if she didn't know she had one yet. He had learned her intuition was high as well, at least for a mundane, not fully attuned to their own frequencies as strongly as witches were usually. He began to find himself wishing she was fully released to know her true self—not for his depraved cravings of course, but for herself. Truly. And that sent him spiraling a bit down a road regarding his lack of embracing his own gifts fully. *Sometimes we take parts of ourselves, our gifts, for granted.* He should practice more. But he couldn't imagine ever being fully disconnected from that part of himself. The concept was depressing.

Their time at the classic auto parts dealer took a little longer than he expected, especially as the owner came out to look at the Impala, whistling at the upgraded upholstery. When he had mentioned it was his uncle's and answered the expected question of who his uncle was, that led to a whole other conversation regarding the stories the shop owner had to say about his uncle—whom he had known of course. Why Morgan hadn't expected that, with seven classic cars sitting in the car barn, and this being the nearest rare auto parts dealer, he didn't know. Uncle Castian had liked to tinker, doing some of the easier work himself.

They spent a few extra minutes exploring his facility, which looked much more like a thrift store for cars in the front half. Parts of old cars lay around haphazardly, as if some of them weren't worth thousands of dollars. They got a tour of the back as well, where he did some repairs and installations himself.

Thinking about how his uncle had done so well building networks of relationships with so many—including mundanes like Fred, reminded Morgan that there was an old bookstore his uncle liked to visit while in Plattsburgh, had mentioned it a few times. He knew the store was owned by an old wizard, a friend of his uncle's, but Morgan hoped the wizard would intuit the situation accordingly and stay in a bookstore owner mindset, especially if Morgan didn't mention who he was. But he thought Maggie would like it, being somewhat similar to the store she mentioned her aunt owned, with teas and other assortments. He suspected her aunt was a witch from what she had shared, but for some reason, her aunt had kept that from Maggie.

There had to be a grand reason to keep witchcraft from the next generation. Witches were a proud and passionate bunch, and family tight. *'His spidey senses were tingling,'* Xander would have said to him. That dog loved the Marvel comics craze Morgan had gone through when he was younger.

Yeah, 'his spidey senses were tingling.' There was definitely a bigger story here.

Maggie

The sun was getting higher in the sky, Maggie figured it was somewhere around 11am. It took Morgan a little bit to figure out where the bookstore he wanted to check out was, but it was just a few blocks from the vintage auto parts store. He'd said his uncle had loved the place, and that the owner also carried lots of little "hippie" stuff like her aunt had in her shop. So they walked down with the weather being so nice.

Maggie had tried to stop thinking about how much Morgan's black hoodie brought out the dark, smokey glints in his eyes a long time ago. Sometimes she was successful. Sometimes she regretted wearing this little plaid skirt with her hoodie and Doc's. Sometimes not. The wind was catching it at times, and she had to be careful or at least pretend to be. She truly didn't always care if someone saw her panties. If it distracted them, it gave her a delicious thrill. If it pissed them off, it also gave her a thrill. She suspected her inner defiant, bratty self liked that one.

Honestly, she had only packed the skirt because it had been a part of last year's Halloween costume, and she had wanted to put it in storage. So, when the idea came to wear it as a little revenge for his denial or avoidance or whatever of what they had between them, she thought it would be fun. The joke was on her really. Obviously, she hadn't thought that one through. Wearing it, and his constant avoidance of looking at her, just made them both a little miserable. Plus, jeans were more comfortable anyways.

But she did normally wear the two messy buns, those were just fun and frankly, easiest to do when getting up early for a road trip.

The bookstore and trinket shop was just on the other side of Main Street. When they walked in, Maggie could totally feel the vibe in the place and knew her Auntie would love this. The lighting was softened by multiple different long, colored scarves hanging from the ceiling, crisscrossing at times, and the light bleeding through. Rows and rows of stacked old books and packed shelves of crystals, oils, dried herbs, and various trinkets of all kinds in every direction. There was little room left for more things, the space was overflowing so much with a peaceful, soothing energy. And the place *felt* like knowledge. Snapping a few random pics, she began to send a text to her aunt.

"Young lady, do you *know* who you are?" With a deep and booming voice, a rather large older man stepped out from the back room and assessed her in a way that just felt like he knew her, really *knew* her. He radiated with energy toward her, it was as though she could see it coming off of him in waves. Everything around him dimmed. He had

3 earrings in one ear, the last a dangling amethyst that seemed to glow as he watched her, his long, wavy gray and white hair and beard just reached his chest. He wore a long purple robe, with a long black jacket of some kind. He walked with a thick black and gold staff, a cane of sorts, as he had a small but notable limp in his slow steps.

He felt like *power*. But curiously safe. Not soft, but protective. Yet, she had no clue who he was.

"I don't think we have met..." Maggie began, uncertain in a way she had never felt before. Without thinking about it, she touched her pendant. His eyes burned through her fingers, and it almost seemed like the pendant warmed from his gaze. Something about him seemed familiar though. The memory was just out of her reach...

She continued to walk slowly from shelf to shelf, picking up a few crystals to test their sensitivity. The man hadn't said anything since she responded, just continued assessing her as he slowly forward, making his way toward the front of the store.

She felt Morgan behind her. Like really felt him. Expecting to turn and see him angry or defensive, his face had gone still, flat. He was staring at the gentleman, and if she was reading him right, he seemed to recognize the man. But she wasn't sure how she knew that since he was so expressionless. Maybe the older gentleman had been talking to Morgan...but he had said 'young lady.' He *had* to have been talking to her.

Suddenly, she felt a tug at her neck. Like someone was yanking on her necklace, and *hard*. It came to mind that her necklace had never been lost. Never broken, never even had shown wear and tear—and she had worn it for almost 20 years straight. Suddenly, the cord snapped and flew off her neck, flying through the air and directly into the older man's palm. She gasped and reached for her neck, suddenly feeling like she couldn't breathe.

Gasping, she bent over at the waist for a moment, her vision going gray, then blurry.

She felt Morgan step in front of her, like a wall of muscle, saying curt words she couldn't understand. She blinked, looking up. She could have sworn there was a wall of gray bricks, only you could see through them, as though they were invisible, between her and Morgan and the older gentlemen. But then she blinked again, and the wall was gone like it had never been there in the first place. She shook her head, hand flying to her forehead. She must have imagined Morgan speaking in some other language with the man.

She tried to catch her forgotten breath.

"It is time. She has the right to know," the older gentleman stated firmly, in his deep, bass voice, nodding his head only once, and in his palm, he closed his fist—crushing the glass of her pendant.

Maggie cried out, reaching toward the pendant, but her vision suddenly dimmed everything around her and she stumbled.

What did she have the right to know?

Why were there sudden images flying at her from every direction, one right after the other like blow after blow to her psyche. First of a young girl—she herself, she instantly knew, being given a necklace—her necklace. Then, she recognized her grandmother coming to see what looked like a younger version of the man before her, receiving her necklace from him, and exchanging money. Her stomach jumped into her throat.

So many sensations, so much flooding of emotions as she felt every-thing, saw everything, remembered everything.

"What is this??" cried Maggie. Falling to her knees, tears flowing down her face. She saw images of a young woman who looked very much like her, and a young man with Maggie's eyes, with his arm wrapped around the young woman, both standing over and looking down at her, and realized she was in a crib, and yet a babe in the memory. She saw them kiss lovingly, saw sparks of literal electricity light up between them, followed by more and more images of the two of them in different situations—often caring for a young toddler version of her or lovingly touching each other. Or Morpheus.

Morpheus? Morpheus, laying with her for a nap, rubbing up against her mother and purring his contentment, or her mother talking seriously to Morpheus like she might receive an answer.

The Knowing had come.

Morgan

If he could take her grief on as his own, he would. Oh, how he would. But he did what he could, sending her emotional comfort, warm like a blanket, to surround her, with a significant amount of protection added in, in case what was happening was more than he thought.

At first, he blamed himself, as they might not have come here today had he not thought of it. He knew that all things occurred as they should though, generally. *'As above, so below.'* He nodded, closing his eyes as he joined with her in her loss, as she gained her memories and began to reconnect with the totality of who she was.

Initially, he had wanted to send the older gentleman to the fiery pits of hell with a blast of an angry protection spell. It was rare that he acted on impulse, so he did catch himself, demanding angrily that she be given the room to choose the next step. Instinctively defaulting to Latin, his uncle's secondary language he had tutored him in, must have been an internal automatic protection of Maggie, not fully understanding what had been happening yet.

But his soul told him the time had come, as painful as it was. Mangus, the bookstore's wizard, had been a close friend of his uncle, going back to their time at The Academy. His uncle had trusted him, and really his power far overshadowed Morgan's rusty skills anyways as he quickly dismissed the wall of protection Morgan had thrown up defensively. But in the end, he realized that Maggie wasn't actually being harmed, rather in the long run, helped. Maggie had quieted, but he could still feel her soul—shattering into pieces. He took a breath, gathered her in his arms, picking up her slight form. She tucked her head under his chin like a small child, her breath ragged against his neck.

Mangus invited them to his back room, offering privacy in case someone were to enter the store in the middle of everything. Morgan waited patiently for Maggie to decide if she was okay with that, not even needing to speak aloud, she seemed to already intuit his question. Nodding her head slightly, he brought her into the small space. An old tattered but clean couch and a massive walnut roll-top desk were on one wall, and a small refrigerator and microwave against the other wall with floor-to-ceiling shelves holding overflowing books and various items.

He sat on the couch, gathering Maggie closer against his chest, her bare legs curling up under her and her arms wrapping around herself. Rocking ever so slightly to soothe her, he offered her soft words of safety and reassurance. Not what he couldn't promise, but that he had her, would protect her at all costs, and that she was safe here with both of them.

When her hiccups finally quieted, he then shared quietly that Mangus was an old friend of his uncle's, and that he did trust him.

Mangus interrupted with a slightly lowered boom still in his voice, "I was a friend of *her* grandfather's as well. Her father's father. And know her mother's parents of course. But she knows that now, don't you?" he asked, looking at her knowingly. He wasn't giving an inch. He was fully aware of her Knowing.

Maggie sighed, lightly squeezing Morgan's hand in thanks, she shifted herself over and next to him. Her eyes on Mangus, she asked, "Is all this true?" She knew that he knew what she asked.

"Yes child, every memory," said the wizard, his eyes filled with solemn truth.

Mangus rose, moving to the shelf over the microwave, and pulled out a small tube. He opened it, using a small stopper from the lid, and he dotted his fingertip with the oil, pressing it to each side of her forehead, near her temples.

"Just a little something for the headache that rises," he assured, voice rumbling. He also took what remained of her necklace, the pendant, now missing the glass that surrounded it, and handed it back to her.

"'Twas your mother's dear, the smoky quartz was what protected your memory, and your spirit. But now the obsidian will continue to help protect you as you face what is ahead." The older man nodded as he placed it firmly into her palm.

Mangus returned the tube to the shelf and pulled out a book. "You are going to want this, I recorded it when your grandmother came to me, almost 2 decades ago. Try to remember that she sought to protect you, not harm you. But there *is* one who seeks to harm you, and you will fight him yet." Morgan's back stiffened, intuition heightening, wanting more information, but the look in Mangus' eye told him he would not get it, not tonight at least.

"I think that is enough for today, child," the wizard boomed, rising. "There is plenty to uncover in that book right there when you are ready." He looked at them both knowingly. "I will give the two of you a few moments alone."

The room was silent after he left.

Morgan wasn't sure what to say. What do you say to someone whose life has turned upside down? Who finds out they weren't who they thought they were? Morgan may not know all the details, and he was fairly certain Maggie didn't quite know yet either. But she would. He knew without a shadow of a doubt that she would.

And whoever was seeking to harm her would have to go through him first.

Chapter Eight

Maggie

She had just needed to get out of there.

She watched as the colors drifted by her window, staring unseeingly at the trees and skyline, curled against the door. The images and memories continued to come, unbidden, overwhelming, but mostly welcome, as she had lived so long without the memories of her parents. Her mother's softness, her father's laughter, their love for her.

A solitary tear slid down her cheek and she didn't even care to wipe it away.

She still wasn't sure she even knew how to breathe with all the new sensations added to her chest. The Knowing, the awareness, the feeling of everything around her was so *real.* It was so much more than the memories even. She had decided to call Aunt Esme once safely ensconced in the car, Morgan driving.

Bluntly she had immediately said, "What the fuck, Auntie??" And broke down crying again. Her aunt hadn't even seemed surprised that she was calling, or what she would be asking like she had known it was coming. *Of course, she knew. Her whole god damn fucking family was full of witches.*

And all Aunt Esme had done was just try to deflect, avoiding talking about most of it, the why's and the how. Instead, she seemed to want to focus on who Morgan was, that he was a nephew of a friend of her grandfather's, and should be able to be trusted, and oh how they were glad she had found him when her car broke down and that he was there for her in all this. *Of course, Morgan knew too.* Not like they did, but he sure hadn't seemed surprised back there.

So many fucking things made sense now. The way they connected. The way they didn't connect—his holding back from her. The way he stepped in front of her, the brick wall, the broken Latin. She recognized it as Latin now, her father had spoken the language often when she had been young. Even his uncle's old mansion. His uncle must have been a witch too. So was Morgan. She could sense it.

Pieces from so many aspects of her life were adding up in ways she never could have imagined. Remembering the spiky electrical currents she had struggled to control in Kindergarten. Her grandparent's faces when they had realized they needed to protect her. The previous wondering she had done at how sometimes Pop fixed some things that people had truly thought were not fixable. Getting called a "witch bitch" in junior high, and the knowing look between her grandparents as they tried to comfort her from the bullying. Not understanding how friends didn't seem to have the same level of intuition about things as she did—all so pale now in comparison to The Knowing.

It was all just *so* much. Her ears were ringing, her stomach rolling. She was going to throw up.

"Let me out, I have got to get out of here," she suddenly insisted, 30 minutes out of town. Hyperventilating and grasping for the door handle in the moving Impala, she felt Morgan immediately bring the vehicle to a halt, pulling quickly to the side of the road. She flew from the car, barely realizing her feet hardly touched the ground. Racing across a field toward the forest of trees, she suddenly felt his hands clasp her arms firmly from behind her and bring her to a screeching halt just upon reaching the treeline.

"Just wait—" he started firmly, but she swung around and slapped him. *Hard.*

"Fuck you!" she cried, not knowing how to reign in everything swirling around her. "*YOU KNEW.* You god damn fucking knew and you—"

And he kissed her. He ravaged her. And she needed it.

He grabbed her hands that were hitting him in the chest, bringing them behind her back, drawing tension through her arms so she couldn't pull away. Well, she could have, but she trusted him. Even though he *knew*, she trusted him. Roughly grasping the hem of her hoodie, he jerked it up and over her head, but left it behind her, trapping her arms. Using it to hold her immobile for him, he grasped her face firmly with both hands, jerking her to him so he could breathe in her air, and offer her his.

Lips devouring each other, he tugged gently at the makeshift tether he had bound her in, reminding her that he had her securely held. She felt her crashing, chaotic world begin to focus a bit. The overwhelm within focused in on him, this man, seeking the intense grounding sensations that he offered.

He set her against a large fallen log, the bark biting into her thighs beneath her too short skirt. The pain only heightened her senses. Arms pulled back, chest rising in short gasping breaths from her run, from this moment—she didn't know. Feeling the cool, autumn air against her bare skin. Her thin, lacy purple bra cupped her small breasts that were turned upward toward him, her nipples already tightened, crying out, practically begging for his attention.

"Shhhhhh... I hear them," he said, his finger tracing down her cheek and then her bra strap. "I hear them. I hear you. I've *got* you."

Whimpering in response, she swallowed her begging. She realized she had stopped thinking of everything from earlier, she was only thinking of the now. For that she was grateful.

His finger traced down the center of her bra, missing her pleading nipples altogether and tracing the waistline of her skirt instead. Teasing her. Teasing the top edge of her lacy thong panties, the purple rising just above the low waist of the twirly, impossibly short skirt.

"I have thought about goddamn this, all fucking day," he said, finishing his statement with a hardening of his eyes, and a jerk of the top of her panties, pulling the front urgently up between her vaginal lips, *hard*, almost making her come on contact as it rubbed and pulled so quickly against her throbbing clitoris.

"Oh, no you don't," he said firmly. "That would be all too rewarding, kitten." His hand came beneath her skirt to graze his thumb slowly against that clit through the thin, tightly pulled lace. But too slowly. Way too fucking slowly. He was driving her *insane*.

She might have to beg. She squirmed against the log beneath her—adding to the sensations. Her legs spread wantonly, arching towards him. He wouldn't give her the pressure she needed, inching his thumb back each time she inched forwards.

"You know what I am waiting for," he grated out, his teeth slowly grazing her nipple through the lace. Lightly flicking her clit again, having moved the soft material aside.

"Okay, fucking *please*, just do the thing," she got out, begging for me. And just as swiftly, his middle and ring fingers slammed into her, his thumb grazing against her again and again, soaked in her wetness. Clenching her nipple between his teeth, he bit gently, and she went tumbling over the edge.

And oh, my gods, did she go over the edge. She cried out, sending a short array of purple fireworks shooting into the air around them, knowing they were on the side of the road, although they had gone a good 100 yards at least from the car, and were at the edge of the trees that were overshadowing them. Anyone who drove by might glimpse them if they looked. Surely the purple-flamed magickal sparks drew some sort of attention. Morgan, of course still fully clothed and standing partially in front of her, arching over her. Maggie, the hoodie behind her as a makeshift bond of sorts, her see-through bra barely covering her breasts, his hand beneath her skirt. Knowing she was on display only added to her orgasm just about as much as the bite from the bark on the back of her thighs.

As she rode his hand and forearm down off the flames, gripping him by the shoulders, the faint gray smoke gently billowing around his hands and feet made it through her foggy mind. Strange. But with everything she had experienced, that was likely the least strange thing she had seen today. Somehow, she recognized it as his energy and hers must be the mini purple firework display.

She slumped against his chest for a moment. Nuzzling his warm hoodie. He stroked her hair for a moment.

"Better?" he murmured, his stubble rough against her forehead as he kissed her there.

She breathed. Yes. Somehow, the overwhelm had settled, more than she could have hoped. She breathed him in. His steadiness settled her chaos. For now.

"I'm hungry," she blurted. A tad embarrassed, but not really. Not for the sex. More for the falling apart.

"Well, it's a good thing someone thought about food this morning," he said, one side of his often pensive mouth coming up in a half grin. Winking at her, he took her hand and led her back toward the car.

Was the sun brighter? This *Knowing* shit was rough. Tiring.

They ate their picnic lunch back at the log he had finger-fucked her on. The juices of the watermelon led to a little more licking and playful petting between them, including a little humping of his thigh in her little skirt, panties removed and rubbing his cock through his jeans, although he refused to allow her to make him come. But he seemed to know that she didn't have the energy left in her for sex on a blanket on the side of the road. Wise man. But by the time they had gotten back in the beautiful old Impala for the rest of the ride home, a few orgasms had led to settling her mind a bit and she slept, snoozing most of the rest of the way home.

She had snuggled a hand in his hoodie pocket, scraping her short nails softly on his lower abs, teasing him a bit over the top of the zip of his pants. But she had fallen asleep that way, and he had let her, not encouraging more, despite their earlier tension in the car.

She knew that he offered her grounded rest right now, and for that she was thankful.

When he woke her upon their arrival home, she had tears wet on her cheeks. He lifted her, carrying her into the house, not even worried about their picnic mess that needed to be brought in. While he sat on the large couch in the waning light of dusk, snuggling her close to his chest, she told him about the dream she had had on their way home, about the ghost girl she had seen in the cellar's small cell.

From what she remembered of the dream, her girl had watched her family home be burned, her family stuck in the flames that had been started by vicious townsfolk, seeking to kill the coven of witches. Her girl had had a basket on her arm filled with bread and herbs and cheeses, as she had gone that early morning into town for supplies, not returning in time to save her family.

She cried for her own loss of her parents as she also cried for the young ghost's pain, her loss, and her guilt, as she blamed herself for her family's untimely death, for not returning earlier to be able to save them. She had stopped in the flower shop unexpectedly, distracted by the beautiful new sunflowers out front. *'If only I hadn't stopped,'* she could still hear on repeat from the young woman's lips.

Morgan told her he thought her ghost girl was Althea. He shared what his uncle had told him about her, and how he had learned years ago about the coven burned on the property here, many centuries ago. How his uncle had talked about hearing her crying, often around Samhain, which they were drawing closer and closer to now that it was mid-October.

He warmed the remaining leftover Chinese for them for dinner, and they ate by the fire, streaming an old Halloween movie in the background, but enjoying being close together and chatting about college experiences, her thesis research and writing, and his writing work. She learned that he had made a pretty decent fortune off his first 12 books, more than enough to rehab this old mansion and live contentedly for a lifetime if he wanted to. She admitted she had snuck a peek around, not in his office of course, and that she thought he should turn it into a spooky old bed and breakfast with the rehab, generating a steady income for when he was older.

Morgan was so interested in her idea that he seemed to welcome her advice regarding all kinds of things after that, which was a refreshing take on older guys. She had experienced all too much passive (or not always so passive) misogyny, especially by male dominant figures over the years.

After her admission of sneaking around his house, he admitted he had seen her and Althea in the bathtub. Rushing to tell the story so she didn't freak out, he seemed worried she might not like his voyeuristic moment. But truly it just turned her the hell on all over again, and she ended up climbing on his lap right there on the couch and they began to make out all over again in the firelight.

This time, he allowed her to pull his hoodie over his head, and for the second time, she was breathless at his strong shoulders and the light smattering of hair on his chest. He had his own witchy pendant hanging from a leather strap around his neck, a pentacle and some strange symbols—runes he told her—that she wasn't familiar with. She ran her fingers tentatively over his skin, his nipples, and down his slightly defined abs, playing hesitantly with the button at the top of his jeans.

He had taken off her hoodie and bra when they started, her breasts getting lots of attention, but she was still wearing the little skirt. Her panties had disappeared somewhere back at the picnic, she still wasn't sure what had happened to those. She had already been rubbing against him, the roughness of his jeans feeling good on her inner thighs and wet pussy, leaving a light trail of wetness on his pants.

"Can I...?" she hesitantly asked, glancing down at his pant button and zipper.

"You know the word I'm waiting for..." He waited patiently.

"*Please?*" she begged softly. He didn't have to remind her twice.

Nodding his head, she moved down between his legs, kneeling on the carpet in just her little, short skirt. Unbuttoning and slowly unzipping his pants, she drew out his cock from his boxer briefs and open jeans. It smelled like him, so heady, precum already dripping.

Licking from base to tip, she allowed her teeth to graze the length of him gently after her tongue. She met his gaze, his eyes had turned as dark as his smoky gray energy. She wondered if hers changed colors ever. She used her fingers and her mouth, hoping to give him back even a little bit of the pleasure that he had already given her today.

She had just taken him as deeply into her throat as she could when he interrupted her with a hand to be back of her head and a *"Fuckkkk..."* and he pulled her up to him with a gentle grip to the back of her hair.

"I hadn't planned on this happening here, but my gods..." he murmured, as she climbed back up on him on the couch, taking him in with a sigh, sliding onto his cock. The firelight played over both of them, the movie credits playing softly in the background. He was still mostly wearing his jeans, she still wearing her skirt, her small, upturned breasts bare to his gaze as she rode him. His hand continued holding on to the back of her hair with just enough tension, just like she liked, pulling a little harder as she began to come. Riding him faster, she begged him to come with her.

Both rose towards the top together, his hands releasing her hair near the end, as he grasped her hips and pumped faster and faster into her, eventually exploding in her with a guttural cry and release of smoky energy. She slowed but didn't stop riding him for a few more moments, milking him for the last of her rolling orgasm. Then falling to his chest, her head resting there, she basked in the mixing of her purple haze and his dark gray fog that blended on the floor around them, both released and spent, together.

Barely moving, she held her hands in front of her, gazing at her fingertips, a tinge of purple still releasing. Curiously, she grasped her own breasts, tweaking her nipples. She grinned at the purple prints left for a moment on her breasts as she watched them fade.

She caught him silently laughing at her, but then he caressed her cheek, and said, "It is going to be so fun, watching you find yourself. I'm here for it, whatever you are comfortable with."

She slowly stilled, looking deep into his eyes that were paling from the dark smokey color back to his normal steel blue. She felt his truth, his intent. No promises for tomorrow, but a desire to explore today. She smiled. "I would love that actually," she said, snuggling into his bare chest, still connected, despite his softening. She sighed. She needed to go clean up, but she wanted to stay here just a moment longer, as she watched their magickal smoke slowly fade away.

Chapter Nine

Morpheus

'The humans have copulated,' said the Shepherd to the cat.

'Why, of course, she is connecting to her powers,' said Morpheus, haughtily, like he knew everything. Which he usually did. He had just been alive longer. Also, he was okay with tonight's arrangement. The big furmonger's bed was far softer than that pitiful little couch in Maggie's room.

But he had noticed the necklace was missing. He had had no premonitions of her having been in danger, so he could only imagine this was a good thing. It was so difficult being a familiar to a mundane—or at the very least, a witch without her powers. It was hard keeping up with them, the connection wasn't nearly as strong.

'At least they remembered to feed us last night,' Xander grumbled, reluctantly dropping his chin back into his forepaws, waiting for someone to get up and remember to take him out.

But Morpheus knew the Shepherd was just jealous, man's best friend and all. As a superior being, he, the cat, saw the brighter side of the picture. Maggie coupling with someone, or someones, usually meant he was fed well. Good moods meant good manners, which meant better fish. Also, there was that whole 'people might die' thing. Maggie's coupling with another witch meant that her powers would enhance in battle. *He'd wondered how long it would take for that writer witch to get his head in the game.*

Well, sounds like maybe he finally did.

Morpheus lazily got up from the goosedown featherbed that smelled like the mutt, taking his time to stretch in the early morning sun streaming in the expanse of windows. He wanted to try that window seat where the sun looked nice and warm, but he didn't want the dog to have his bed back quite yet. Taking his time leaving the dog bed, he lazed his way across the stretch of carpet protecting the wood floor and jumped up to the velvet seat in the window. *Yes*, this was what he had wanted. *Ahhhhh*, the warmth.

Last night, despite the two young lovers being so besotted with one another, Morpheus had sensed the connection to Maggie as being much, much stronger. Between that and the necklace being shattered, it was just a matter of time before he could speak with her—let her know his theories regarding her parents. He would give young love a bit more time to flush itself out, and then they really did need to get down to business.

Lives really were at stake here.

Morgan

Morgan woke, his body a slow ache, as he wasn't really sure how much sleep they actually got last night. After they chose his bedroom, at least for now, he had tumbled her into the covers and that had just started things fresh between them again.

And then there had been that time in the middle of the night when he'd wished he'd had the straps for the bedposts from his old bed. He'd have to work on that.

He blamed the previous days of avoidant temptation for the urgency and frequency, along with the witchery at brew. Not that anyone had set them up or anything, but when two witches coupled, especially with a soul connection, the sparks literally were just much hotter, brighter, and more intense. And often, they were far less hesitant about things. Just more accepting of the mind, soul, and body connection than mundanes often were.

Realizing he was alone in the bed, he rolled out, pulling his sweats on, slung low on his hips. Glad to not have to dig out any old t-shirts anymore. He padded barefoot down the long hallway into the kitchen. She was pouring a cup of coffee at the counter, her back turned to him. There was his t-shirt with her sexy bare legs calling to him. He walked up quietly behind her, and couldn't help it, he wrapped his arms around her waist, hands immediately running down to the apex of her thighs, to check and see—nope, no panties. Just as he thought.

His mouth went to her neck and bit gently. No panties and already wet took his mind straight to the gutter. He was already half hard when he woke, and that was before seeing her. She arched her back, moaning in response, and he could feel the purr in her neck as he followed up the bite and suckled hard. That would be purple before he was done.

Her ass arched backward while his wandering fingers explored. She rubbed intently against his stiffening cock with her ass. Slapping that ass once, and when she jumped, a second time. He spun her around and lifted her roughly onto the island, her coffee spilling onto the counter.

"Leave it," he grated out, already spreading her thighs. She was already so wet, her clitoris ready to play. He suckled there too, only much more gently than he had her neck. For now. One finger, then two entered her wetness. She had pulled up the thin t-shirt and started to play with her tits. He hadn't told her she could, but for now, he was going easy, till he began to understand her limits and interests better. Plus, she was so sexy playing with herself.

They'd have to work with that more.

She began to mewl like a kitten, eyes closing in ecstasy as she pinched her breasts tighter and he licked her clit again. Flicking with his thumb as he continued to insert his fingers over and over.

"I...fuck Morgan, I..." she began, gasping for breath as she writhed on the counter.

Shucking his pants down his hips, he jerked her towards him and entered her swiftly. Fucking her there, harder, faster, the counter catching her when they went too hard. She wrapped her legs around him and hung on. She began to contract in orgasm, and he exploded in her, the kitchen filling with a low-grade haze of purple and gray.

Breathing, was all they could do for a few moments.

Coffee, he came in for coffee.

'Dear gods, isn't that enough between you two??' Morgan heard from Xander as the pup uncovered his eyes with his paw from where he lay, curled up in the corner of the room. Oh, hell no it wasn't. It might take a few weeks for his need for her to even think about receding a little.

'You wish,' he shot back.

Setting her slowly back on her feet, he gently tucked one side of her long, burnt scarlet hair back behind her ear the way he knew she liked it. "Good morning," he said softly, kissing her forehead as she slowly pushed her glasses back up her nose.

Maggie

She yawned. "Yes, it is," she chuckled, definitely feeling more awake than before, despite having had no coffee in her system yet.

She turned around, ruefully looking at the spilled cup on the counter, her t-shirt wet in parts from having sat in it. Ha! She hadn't even noticed the heat or wetness at the time.

She pulled the t-shirt over her head, throwing it towards the laundry room, giving little thought to her nakedness, until he slapped her ass again.

"Xander's seen a lot this morning," Morgan laughed, the dog putting his paw back over his eyes at the sound of his name.

"Oh, they are just animals," she giggled, but took her newly filled cup of coffee from his hands, and headed down the hallway to find something to wear.

'Why are humans so caught up in nudity being so unusual? You don't have fur, so you need the warmth, but you creatures are the only species that wear clothes.' She heard clearly in her head and jumped.

What the hell? she thought, head flying in every which direction. The only living thing she saw nearby was Morpheus.

'Yes, darling girl,' the cat inclined his head towards her, pausing to lick his paw and clean his head for a moment. *'It's about time you could hear me. I have been waiting a ridiculously long time for this.'*

"You, what the hell, you can talk???" she gasped out loud. Eyes gone wide, feet rooted to the floor in the middle of the hallway.

The cat just looked at her pretentiously, as he always had. *'Of course. Felines talked long before humans did. Mundanes just aren't intelligent enough to communicate with us.'*

Morgan had come to the doorway. He leaned against it, far sexier than he probably realized in his low-slung sweats, bare feet, and his messy, dark hair hanging low on his forehead. Eyebrow raised and glancing between her and the cat, he sipped his coffee and said, "So, you finally heard him, huh?"

"Yes, oh my gods, the animals can talk??" she exclaimed, flabbergasted. "Can Xander??" Still naked, she cocked a hip, hands fisted on them, eyes ablaze with excitement.

Morgan's eyes scanned her, and she noticed his pants tenting again, but he just stood there, appreciating. "Yup," he said, sardonically.

Her nips tightened again, and her lips pursed. "I mean, so they know we keep having sex like rabid animals?" Giving him a come-hither look through those lashes with her glasses slightly tipped down on her nose, he began to stalk her intently backwards into his bedroom.

He slammed the door on the animals for now.

"Yup," he said again, his voice going darker. "Not that they really care all that much. Animals fuck like crazy, after all."

God, how could she be so turned on again when they had just fucked in the kitchen? But his eyes ablaze with smoke, he backed her intently towards the bed. Reaching down, his arm swept beneath her knees, lifting and depositing her onto the bed with a thump. She leaned back on her elbows, her clit beginning to butterfly again at the dark look in his eyes. He walked purposefully around the bed, reaching out and grasping her by an ankle and pulling. Immediately separating her legs, drawing the ankle he had grasped towards the other bottom post of the old iron bed.

"Stay," he said firmly. His tone caused her to grow wetter. She stayed.

His smoke began to filter out in his wake as he moved from the bed to the nearby heavy dresser, opening the top drawer and digging, searching for something. She saw him take out a few long black velvet ropes. "I thought I remembered these being in here," he said, nodding at the long, heavy curtains on both ends of the sizable arching windows in his bedroom. They hung loosely, and she realized the ropes were likely the tiebacks used to pull the curtains away from the windows. But the windows were so large, like the one in her bathroom, that the curtains were pulled to the ends of the rods and lay pooled loosely at the floor, leaving plenty of space for the sunlight to pour through, without the ropes.

He walked towards her, his eyes growing darker. She hadn't moved, not an inch, as he'd requested. His hand trailed her calf, grasping her other foot and pulling her toward the end of the bed firmly. He took one rope and looped it underneath her leg, right above her knee, and tied it securely at the other end to the loop on the low iron post. Looking at her, pausing to give a moment for her to back out of where this was going if she so chose.

She gave a slight nod of acquiescence, her eyes dropping in submission. She wasn't going anywhere.

He ran his fingertips from her knee and over the rope, trailing them up her thigh and across the heat of her sex. His fingers then trailed back down the other thigh, grasping her knee and pulling it taught toward the nearby post. He looped the rope around her other lower thigh and brought the end to secure at the other iron post. Her ass was just at the end of the bed, her legs pulled apart by the ropes. She had just enough give in the rope for some wiggle room, just enough for some movement when he fucked her, she realized.

She had always loved bondage—both watching and being made to feel secure. It was strange how being unable to get away from someone you trusted felt steadfast and heightened the senses.

He had moved towards the side of the bed, and he held out his hand, his eyes indicating he asked for her hand. She offered it, and he trailed his fingertips from her wrist up her arm, his fingertips coming to circle her breast once, pinching tightly at her nipple, causing her to gasp and flinch in pleasure.

But he didn't stay there. Returning to her wrist, he wrapped an additional soft velvet rope around her wrist, wrapping multiple times before he secured the end of the rope to the loop down on the side of the bed frame. Testing the rope again to make sure she had room for circulation and that the rope was secure, he moved to the other side of the bed. He didn't disappoint her other breast, pinching it as well before securing her other arm.

The whole process was incredibly sexy, and Maggie found herself breathing heavily, noting her purple haze already blending with the smokey path he had walked as he moved around the bed. Her arms were much more taught than her thighs. The tension was a stronghold for any resistance she might offer it. Her calves dangled over the edge of the bed, her sex wide open to his gaze. He stood back and appreciated his knots, his gaze taking in all of her.

"Beautiful," he breathed, looking deep into her eyes.

He moved to stand at the end of the bed, his hands grazing her thighs. One hand came up to twist and tug at her breast again, followed by a gentle slap. When her eyes rolled into her head a little, and she sighed, he slapped her breast a little harder. Testing her likes and dislikes, she suspected.

"We should probably get a few things in order," he said firmly. "I like to keep it simple. Red stops immediately, yellow is caution, or I'm starting to near a limit. Green is fucking go." His fingers slid along the wet lips of her pussy. "I don't fully know what you like. I can guess, and our intuitions as witches are much stronger than the average mundanes, so I may think I even know sometimes—especially when you share your thoughts. But I prefer to check in now and then to make sure, and I will *always* respect your limits. They are yours. Understood?" he asked, pausing in his movements, his eyes on hers.

She nodded.

"Talk to me, kitten," he said firmly, waiting.

"Y-y-yes. Okay." She stumbled a bit on her words, "I-I-I'm not sure what I should call you in moments like this...?" she hesitantly asked.

His fingers ran softly up her thighs. "You'll figure out what works for you. There's no rush."

He walked around the side of the bed, his gaze intent on her eyes. Their intuition melded, and she swore she heard him say, '*There is plenty of time for this, for whatever is here—both within you and between us, to develop in its time.*' His finger traced her jawline, pausing down below to circle where he had sucked on her neck earlier. The thought of him marking her in such a sensual way only turned her on.

He gently kissed her sideways, nipping at her bottom lip. She reached out her tongue to fully kiss him, but he pulled back.

"Mmmmmm...not yet," he dismissed.

He moved his attention down a bit, focusing on her small breasts once again, pulling and then slapping a small, pink-shaded areola tipped up to him, tweaking the darker reddish nipple matching her natural berry-bitten lips. Especially when they have been handled roughly.

Using both hands, he pinched the very tips of both at the same time, twisting tighter, gauging her reactions. Her hips came off the bed a little in response, and he smiled slyly.

One hand began to twist on a nipple again, and his other went to her sex, his middle finger inserting as his thumb began to play her clit like strings on a guitar. She rose up, her hips rising towards him, feeling like she was floating—maybe she was a bit, who knows anymore. Her thighs tied down kept her grounded where she was, her hands gripping the ropes as they pulled blessedly, biting into her wrists.

He added his ring finger to her pussy, his thumb playing the music he heard inside him faster and faster on her clit, playing her nipples with different tensions, sometimes soft, and then surprising her with a rough pinch or slap.

She came, and *HARD*.

But he wasn't done. He moved to the end of the bed, ridding himself of his sweats quickly. He jerked her knees the little they would move, bringing her hips to the edge of the bed, the rope biting into her thighs. He had her hips just far enough that he could enter her, standing at the end of the bed. He pushed his hard cock into her channel quickly, filling her to where she almost thought she would come again. But then he stopped. Just filling her, his eyes closed, chin tilted to the sky. Savoring their joining. He began to rub ever so softly at her now overly sensitive clit, judging its reaction to her recent orgasm.

He pulled out slowly, then rammed back in quickly, slapping her clit at the same time. She nearly came up out of the ropes. He paused, gripping her hips. "You still with me?" he checked in.

"Green, fucking green, oh my gawd..." she gasped, her hips moving the little she could, her hands gripping the ropes tightly. And he moved, beginning to pound into her repeatedly, and she felt herself building... Reaching down, he flicked her clit another few times, and she felt like she was flying.

Maybe it was just her spirit, but she swore she was floating on the ceiling in a cloud of gray and purple mist. Eventually, she began to feel sensations again as he soothed her thighs where the rope had been and eventually removed them from her legs. They continued to be connected, so she brought her ankles back around his back and held on for just a few moments more.

His hands slid soothingly up her body, softly stroking against the previous pain in her sensitive nipples.

"Shhhhh...that's it," he soothed, his voice low, as she dropped back into the present moment, her head lulling back. The peacefulness, breathtaking.

Pulling out of her, he slowly reached for his sweats, cleaning himself and her up as best he could. He leaned on his elbow beside her, smoothing her hair from her sweaty face. He kissed her forehead softly.

Reaching across her, he unwrapped the rope from one wrist. Looking down at her, eyes still dark, he softly murmured, "I just can't seem to get enough of you."

"Holy shit, yes," she sighed. "Thankfully." This might be the best sex she had ever had. Well, a 23-year-old could only be so experienced, but she definitely wasn't green. She knew she had likely had more sex—and more of what many would consider *unusual* sex—than most of the college students she went to school with. And that was saying something, the way they partied. She attempted to flex her still-bound hand, feeling it falling asleep on her.

He got up and unbound that one as well, helping soothe the blood back down her arm with gentle strokes. She had also never felt this cared for during sex. I mean, even as a Domme, Jenny hadn't been as careful or so caring afterward, not that Maggie had been unhappy, they were busy college students. They'd parted amicably.

"So, I want food. But," she asked curiously, "how long have you been a Dominant, and how long have you been a witch?"

He smacked her ass as she got up, pulling her hoodie from yesterday over her head for her. They meandered back towards the kitchen for a second attempt at starting the day again.

"Well, I kinda always knew I was a witch," he started. "Most witches do, actually. I was so sure at first that you were trying to play me when you didn't seem to know your powers." He got out some eggs and veggies, looking like he might make omelets. "I was both shooting stars out my fingertips and learning to hide it from mundanes before I ever started preschool. But my father is a mundane, and my mother doesn't really practice much, so it was pretty slow going. My uncle began to send me things when I was young, I thought he was so cool." He ruffled Xander's head and tossed his pup a piece of already-cooked bacon.

"He got me Xander actually," he said, smiling sadly. "He knew me so well." He returned to chopping veggies. "So, when I was tired of trying to fit in with the mundanes and wanted to learn more about my spiritual heritage, my mom sent me to live here."

Smiling ruefully, he added, "Before you think that was all good, it was really more for my mother's convenience, so she could travel more and not have to raise an awkward, 14-year-old male witch. But, that being said, it probably was the best thing that happened to me. My uncle taught me a great deal, and I probably would have turned out much more spoiled and snobby had I stuck it out with my Mom and Dad."

Pouring the egg mixture into the sprayed pan, he continued, "Now, dominance I didn't explore till college. I mean, it's nature, right, part of personality. I don't think I knew who I was enough in high school." He smiled, a twinkle in his eye. "Although there was Jessa, the one cheerleader..."

She slapped his arm when he stopped. "Why stop?? I wanna hear the story. Was she hot?" she asked honestly, just a tiny bit jealous.

He winked at her, "Yep. She had these fantastic tits and often didn't wear a bra. You would have loved her." He added the toppings to the omelet, edging the eggs with the spatula. "Although I eventually stopped trying to date mundanes. Word got around about uncle's mansion, and it became more of a strange popularity thing, and I wasn't interested in that. It got me some awkward attention from girls interested in dark and edgy guys, but they didn't really want to talk seriously, and I wanted a smart chic. Or guy, I wasn't that particular," he said, eyeing her response.

"I mean, you saw me and Althea. I'm good," she said, shrugging her shoulders and stealing a piece of bacon left on the cutting board. "I've clearly played with both, and sometimes together," she added, wiggling her eyebrows flirtatiously.

He smacked the back of her thigh with the warm spatula as she spun away. "Sounds like the potential for possibilities," he said. "But fingers off my bacon."

She wiggled her eyebrows again, backing slowly towards the door. "Never," she teased. "What if I like my hands on your meat?" Innuendo totally implied, and he knew it.

He groaned at her cheesiness but turned back to the stove, cutting the omelet in half with a new spatula from the round container next to the stove and sliding each half onto plates.

"We aren't going to get anything done today with talk like that, little girl," he teased, playfully gruff. He added some sliced fruit to the plate from a bowl in the fridge and grabbed forks, following her out onto the porch.

The big hoodie went just past her ass when standing. So, when she sat, she crossed her legs and tucked them up beneath her. She knew she didn't have any panties on and that he knew it too. But she pulled her laptop onto her lap anyways, determined to check her email at least. He set her plate down beside her on the porch swing, running his finger along her cheek and jaw. She flicked his finger with her tongue teasingly.

He groaned again. "Eat," he said firmly. "You're going to be the death of me." But he sat down in the chair nearby, where she knew he had a sideline view of her pantiless state.

She hoped not. She wasn't done exploring him. Or her own new powers.

Chapter Ten

Morgan

Somehow, they both got some work done. Morgan eventually kissed her forehead and moved up to the office. The sexual tension from watching her work pantiless had given him some motivation for his own writing. He wondered a bit at the tension not lessening but figured it was just the duality of their magickal natures intensifying things.

For now, he'd take the intensity it created in his writing. It played out well in the new mystery, highlighting ideas for him to lace into the story, building intrigue, he hoped.

The afternoon came, and he decided to take Xander for a run. There was some mild chastisement from the pup for jumping in so deep when he had only known the girl for not even a week now. But it honestly didn't feel like that. It felt like they had known each other awhile.

'I do agree with you, my boy,' said his faithful pup, *'You do know more about her at this point than any mundane you have ever dated. But that's not very surprising, considering how hard it can be for you to let people in.'*

'I know,' Morgan thought in response quietly. There were reasons, and he didn't like talking about them.

'I know,' replied Xander gently. *'Not everyone will hurt you, though. Sometimes you have to let people care about you.'*

Xander knew better than to bring up the past. They returned to the house, both sweaty. Morgan stripped off his top when he entered the laundry room, dropping it into the basket, then decided to start a load of laundry. Kicking off his shoes, he thought about a shower so he grabbed the stack of clean towels from the other day, and took them with him.

He turned on the shower, thinking he had never quite realized how kinky his great uncle must have been at some point, or someone had been anyways. Between large windows in certain frequently nude places like the bathrooms, the loops in the iron bedposts, and the velvet straps that had been clearly set aside for a reason, he also now realized how sexy the damn shower was. One wall was a full fogless mirror, the wall the multiple shower heads were on was black tile, and the other two were transparent glass. A black tile shower seat was on the far end, away from the shower heads. Two could easily fit in here, hell, a small party could.

He got out after quickly showering, drying his face with his towel and wrapping it around his waist. He sighed. It had been a while since he shaved. He wasn't interested in growing and taking care of a full beard, and it was getting long.

He had set the stack of towels on the edge of the large, yes, enough for two people, whirlpool tub. He picked up the stack, putting them on the shelf in the walk-in closet off the bathroom.

His uncle had loved antique shaving items, and after moving in, Morgan realized he had been missing out all these years. He hated to shave, but at least it was with this old lather and antique razor. It had taken him a little while to research and find the brand and how to replace the blades.

The sunlight from the expansive window, much like Maggie's bathroom, sent a ray of warmth across him as he scraped the soft foam he had lathered off with the grain of his thickening scruff. For a moment, he could have sworn he heard, "Mooooorgannnn…" in the wind, and then the lights flickered.

It clicked. The lights flickering had to be connected with Althea. Maybe that was why uncle hadn't been worried about it. Something to think about for sure, maybe see what Maggie thought.

For a brief moment, he paused, realizing how much he had begun to value her perspective.

He smoothed on some after-shave moisturizer, threw on a fresh pair of boxer briefs, and found some black jeans and a soft, blue v-neck t-shirt.

Making his way back to the office with a quickly made ham sandwich, he returned to his work. But it wasn't long before he felt a shifting spirit in the house draw him out of deep concentration. Sometimes he got so lost that he missed what was happening around him. But he could feel her searching.

Recognizing Maggie's essence rather than Althea's, he waited it out. She would be exploring who she was for days and weeks to come. But the feelings grew sad. He sensed her grief, so while she wasn't calling to him, he decided to go to her anyways.

He found her in her room, the door already cracked. He knocked gently as he entered, seeing her sitting on the floor against the dark loveseat, the cat by her side. She was surrounded by her laptop, papers, and the leather-bound book from Mangus.

She had a few trails of tears down her face, so he lowered down next to her, joining her quietly. His shoulder against hers, he waited till she decided what she wanted to share. She didn't say anything at first, sniffling quietly, petting Morpheus every now and then.

"Morpheus told me he thinks my parents were killed by whoever also killed my father's parents." She sniffled again quietly. Looking up into his eyes incredulously, she added, "Morgan, they were all killed by car accidents—all of them! Into ravines!"

His gut twisted. He sensed the cat's assuredness. Xander had followed him into the room and added to Morgan, *The feline thinks it was an old acquaintance of the girl's paternal grandfather. Something about how the mother and father were investigating him, and the girl's mother was afraid of him. That's why they traveled without her at the time they were killed.'* The dog settled on the other side of the spread of items, resting his head in his paws, whimpering softly at Maggie.

She leaned into Morgan, and he pulled her onto his lap. Tucking her into his arms, he brushed back the hair from her forehead, kissing her softly.

"My uncle was killed in a car accident as well," Morgan said apprehensively. This didn't feel like happenstance—despite being decades apart. "It hasn't set well with me, his death. He was a very skilled driver. He loved his old classics far too much to drive recklessly, even in his 80s." He would have believed a heart attack or even dying in his sleep before he'd think he would drive off a ravine. But the old roadster had been too mangled for any conclusive answers when he had asked.

She pulled back slightly in his arms. "I've been reading some of this old book from Mangus, though. He had collected some of my early magick here, which included some of the memories my mother had told me already when he made the memory locket." She opened the hand she had fisted in her lap, and the locket sat there, gently glowing. "This began to glow when I opened the book and started reading about it."

She held it out towards him tentatively, "Will you help me put it on?"

"Absolutely," he assured, grasping the locket from her hands, noticing it had a witch's clasp. He opened the protection ward on the old silver clasp, bringing it in front of her and the clasp around behind. "Did you read anything in there on the protection ward put on it?" he asked, uncertain about what he sensed, believing it to be a normal protection ward, but the way the necklace was clearly tied to protecting her from her memories when it was worn, concerned him for re-closing the ward.

Excitedly, she pointed to an early page she quickly turned to in the leather-bound book. The pages were older, rougher paper, and the printing was clearly not from a normal pen. Morgan suspected the old wizard had intuitively taken information from Maggie's young memory, as well as memories held by the necklace that had once belonged to her mother and infused them telepathically into the book. He wouldn't have doubted if the spell used had required other objects of her mother's as well. The essence radiating from the book had two unique signatures—one that felt like a much younger, livelier Maggie, as well as a feminine essence similar to Maggie's, but different—and much more powerful.

He read the spell information collected there and noted two different spells—one noted as *The Knowing*, which protected memories, and the other noted as an enhanced protection spell designed for Maggie after the eventual memory release. Mangus had planned ahead, and he suspected her mother had as well. Morgan felt the current ward fit the second one, and passing his hand over the clasp at her neck, he closed the ward.

"As above, so below," he whispered to the necklace and to her.

"You say that too?" she asked, sounding intrigued. "My aunt would say that at times. I like it. It has big energy to it."

Morgan explained the actual meaning behind the words and the wards that had been cast, showing the descriptions in the book and explaining what he had sensed between the two. "Mangus had mentioned this would continue to protect you from danger, so I think it's important to keep the second ward active," he said. He really couldn't bear to think of something happening to her.

"Speaking of spells and stuff," she said, eyes brightening a bit, "watch what I can do!" Flipping the book to an early page, she held her hand in front of her, and she brought a small round ball of purple flame to life. "I mean, I didn't even mean to do it earlier, but it just happened. I thought the word 'ignus,' which I learned here is Latin for fire, and it just happened!" she said, amazed. "It does it with 'flamma' too," she said, bringing her other hand to life, showing him she had learned the word for flame.

"I think I remember my dad teaching me this when I was little," she said, cupping her hands together to douse the flames. "See!" she said, pointing to the page.

He smiled, enjoying watching her delight in her powers. This was how it had felt for his uncle, huh? To enjoy watching him learn and grow spiritually. He had mentioned as much. He showed her quickly a few different ways to bring light and fire, his base flame blue. And a few ways to carefully put it out.

"Things like fire and smoke for us don't always work the same way as mundane fire. Ours is naturally more spiritual unless we put intent into it for burning," he said, showing a small rolling ball of his gray smoke versus a small, hot blue flame. "But even spiritual flame can be powerful, so be careful. I wouldn't really leave it unattended."

"Oh my goddesses, I have so much to learn to catch up," she said, anxiously flipping through the book, glancing at a few. Looking up seriously, she added, "But I want to go into town tomorrow. We need to take the engine part for Margot, and I want to visit a library if there is one. See if we can access any info on your uncle's death or on who the person might be who knew them all."

"Dammit, I forgot about the car part," he said, slapping his forehead. That was irresponsible of him, he thought, feeling bad. But a girl who liked a library? One after his own heart.

'You seemed pretty busy the last 48 hours.' Xander reminded him sardonically, letting him off the hook. Xander often reminded him that he had a tendency to carry blame or responsibility too easily.

'Yes, yes we were,' Morgan laughingly agreed with the pup.

Xander

After they had finally been fed, their masters snuggled on the couch watching an old black and white horror movie in honor of the season. Both familiars found separate comfortable places not far from the fireplace.

'Stop discouraging him,' Morpheus chastised the black Shepherd.

'Whatdya mean?' asked the yawning Shepherd. He liked Maggie. She snuck him treats, plus she woke up earlier than his Master did, so he got to go out earlier in the morning. He had just seen way less of his Master than normal since she came around.

The older black and white cat wasn't the worst to hang out with, though. It was nice having another familiar in the house to share the responsibility of raising the impulsive human witches with.

'Can't you see that the two of them are meant to connect—at least right now?' asked the cat, shaking his head. *'Look at them. He is helping her figure out her magick. And one day, whoever killed her mother and his uncle is going to come looking for them. They will need all the magick they can muster,'* he grumbled, sighing. *'Ahhhhh... Young love.'*

'There is definitely no need for more deaths,' Morpheus went on after a moment, sadly. *'After all, who would feed us?'*

Chapter Eleven

Maggie

Friday morning, she called her grandparents and told them she would still be here until at least the next week due to taking the car part into town today. Auntie Esme had filled them in on what she knew, and while her grandparents had texted a few times to check on her the last couple of days, they had given her space to think. Pop told her he just wanted her to know he loved her, and he hoped she knew that. Of course, she did. But making the decision for her to keep her heritage from her hadn't been okay—she felt sure of that. She had so many feelings to sort through, and while her Nan wanted reassurance that everything was okay between them, she told her she couldn't honestly say that yet. But she did love them. She always would.

Having memories of her parents had made such a drastic difference the last few days. Knowing, really remembering how loved she had been, was so different from all the uncertainties she had carried around in her heart for so long. When she finally went home, she planned to demand that they allow her to explore some of her parents' things. She knew her grandmother had stored them in the attic, but they refused to talk about them...and she had never seen them.

Grief wasn't meant to be silent or alone.

She wanted to know *everything*. Every hair from a hairbrush, every photograph, every word from a diary or old box. Last night she had poured over the memories and words kept in the book, reading late into the night as Morgan had slept. Maybe it could help them solve this mystery of her parents and grandparents and maybe even his uncle's death. She wondered if they had known it wasn't an accident. It could only make sense to her that they did somehow, that this had been the grand reason that led them to make such a drastic decision to hide her powers from her.

Auntie Esme had texted her a few times, offering to help with re-connecting to her gift. But Maggie was just so furious that she had participated in the lies and secrecy that she had left it on read. All 4 times.

They headed towards Rochester after 10, getting a slightly late start after not getting much sleep again last night. It's not that Morgan's bed wasn't comfortable. It was. Maggie had finally been convinced to admit that his bed was better than hers. It was king size, after all, plus it had those loops in the old iron bed frame. They hadn't used them again just yet, but Maggie hoped they would.

Despite the late discussion, Morgan told her that she likely wouldn't need the birth control she was on. That witches didn't get pregnant without intention. But they did talk about both of them being tested recently, or for Morgan, at least since his last partner. He mentioned it had been a year or so since he had been active with anyone. Maggie thought that was probably why the intensity between them wasn't dying down yet, but she was happy to be along for the ride.

Last night, before her reading fest, he had shown her how to play with her smoke to enhance the intensity of her orgasms. Damn, it was like she had a built-in personal massager in a way. She had smiled pretty wide at that one. He had sat back and watched her play, content to stroke himself now and then until she just couldn't stand it anymore and finally pounced on him.

She sipped her coffee as he drove. Today's old vehicle from the car barn was a classic 50's Chevy pickup. Like all the others, this one was in beautiful shape, with robin's egg blue shiny exterior, with a beige interior. Morgan maneuvered the old beige and silver stick shift like a master, Maggie even having a moment of jealousy for that old shifter.

Morgan mentioned wanting the truck bed to bring stuff home in, and that they might stop at the local home goods store and pick up some supplies.

They got the engine part to Mike, who showed them around his old shop. Morgan checked in on the old Ford truck Mike had been working on for a while. He also asked Mike if he thought Morgan might be able to talk to the examiner in town about the old roadster from his uncle's accident.

"Why, son?" Mike asked, looking concerned, "Ya think someone mighta messed with it?"

Morgan nodded, adding that it was just a hunch he had, but nothing really to go on. Mike told him that he was old poker pals with the examiner and would see what he could find out at their next poker game. Morgan had said that Mike and his uncle had been friends, although Mike was a mundane and likely unaware of anything unusual about his uncle.

They went to the home goods store, picking up some two-by-fours, more nails, and Maggie talked Morgan into a nail gun. Morgan had Maggie look at the wallpaper with him, talking about working on the sitting room that had all the dark green wallpaper, but some of it was peeling at the edges it was so old and fading. She pointed out a few that honored the style, with deep tones that modernized the space just a little bit while accenting the scrolls and arches of the gothic period. Morgan picked one for the sitting room, and another for the hallways. Maggie also pushed for some supplies that would make taking down the old wallpaper just a little easier.

They talked about Morgan's theory regarding the electricity surges, that they might be occurring when Althea was active and communicating in some way. Maggie wondered at his uncle knowing and why no one had considered asking Althea if she wanted to be released from whatever kept her there. *Surely that was an option?* she thought. Morgan knew it could be done, but he had never thought to ask his uncle about it.

She also wondered at the fact that there had been a few electrical surges when they had been having sex. She smiled a little at the thought of Althea watching them and somehow getting her own kicks at their play. The surges had never felt negative in any way, and she had just accepted them as part of the house at this point, as it wasn't very often.

They stopped at a local coffee shop, grabbing some sandwiches for lunch. Choosing to sit outside in the cool autumn weather, they were far enough away from others that Maggie asked Morgan all kinds of questions about growing up as a witch. She hushed her voice at one point when a server walked by, sweeping the area. Morgan smiled and told her not to fret, he had drawn a sigil in the salt he had sprinkled on the table earlier, and others couldn't hear them. She hadn't even noticed. He teased her, saying rather loudly while the server was walking by that he could even play with her through her panties right there outside of the cafe, and no one would even notice if he added their not being seen to the ward he set—unless she wanted them to see of course.

She fanned her face...it wasn't supposed to be warm out here, fall and all.

But Morgan just stood up, trailed his finger along her jaw, briefly kissed her stupefied lips, and then ever so normally, carried their trash to the nearby container.

He pulled her to her feet, kissed her forehead, and then lightly slapped her ass as she went on by, heading towards the car. Laughing, she said, "Uh huh, they didn't see that, did they?"

"Oh yes they did," he said with a wink. "They just can't hear us. I said I *could* add to the ward." The little old lady nearby on the street who dared peer at them over her little wire glasses was smiling knowingly.

They went to the local library, both reminiscing about the importance of libraries in their childhood and college years. Maggie had wanted to stop by and do a little local research regarding the history of Althea and her family, and Morgan wanted to see if he could dig up anything regarding his uncle and any old cronies, or adversaries really, he might have had.

The old microfilm and microfiche storage and readers were in the library's basement, a dark and dank space that was filled with rows and rows of shelves and crappily lit hallways. As one might imagine with their raging lust for each other, Morgan eventually dragged her down one of the long hallways and deep into some tall shelves, to fulfill an old steamy fantasy of making out in a library. Well, that's what he told her. She figured sometime during his college experience he had to have gotten head in a library. She hadn't actually made out in a library before, but she would today, he said when she told him that.

He had her by the hair, and she was gagging a little on him when they realized they had a friendly mundane voyeur two rows over, searching for some lost archive. They heard the person stop their movements, and Maggie figured they must be listening, as she kept right on gagging and slurping, not trying to be the least bit quiet. Morgan was leaning against the wall at the end of their row, his jeans unzipped, just open enough. He had pulled her tank down beneath her braless breasts, having played with her bare nipples before she went down on her knees in her jeans. She didn't look, but she really didn't care if someone might be trying to peek through the shelves at them. They could be masturbating for all she cared.

Glancing up at him, she saw his eyes glancing behind her and to the right, and realized he could probably see someone. She slid back up him, turning, and facing outward from him, she bent at the waist, and he slapped her ass. Peering the same direction Morgan had, she saw a dark-haired guy, probably in his mid-twenties, two rows over. Nerdy, with glasses and a side part, he was staring at them, leaning on one hand against the shelf. From his movements, she could tell he likely had his cock out and was furiously stroking.

Deciding to play with the moment, she slid back up Morgan, grasping at her own breasts and tweaking her nipples, she glanced to make sure the guy could see her. Morgan reached around her, as she ground her ass on his cock, unzipped her pants, and finally noticed she had failed to wear panties today. Growling in her ear, he pushed the pants down her hips and slapped her ass again, neither of them really caring anymore if anyone else heard. She ground against him again, as he pinched and slapped her nipple.

Maggie was sure Morgan was getting as much out of the guy watching as she was, if not more. She intuited to him, *'If that guy were to come over and begin to suck on your cock, I'd be okay with it...'*

He must have understood, because she heard his quiet voice say, *'Would you?'* in her ear.

But Morgan continued what he started, sliding his finger inside her moist pussy, rubbing his palm back and forth across her clit. One hand at her sex, the other pinching her breast, she heard their watcher start to grunt. She imagined him coming all over the shelf in front of him, thankfully likely only metal boxes of archives, although she laughed to herself as she considered how he was going to clean it all up.

'I should have you lick every last bit of his cum, like the sweet little cum slut you are,' she heard him growl telepathically.

'I would if you told me to,' she answered back, rising into euphoria as she rode his hand, his holding her up in front of him.

Giving her a moment to ride that wave, he eventually turned her to face him, gently pushing her to her knees in front of him again. *'Drink, like a good kitten. There's no place else to go with it,'* he instructed as his smoky gaze drilled deeply into hers. He came, closing his eyes and leaning his head back against the wall, and she swallowed every last bit of it greedily and obediently.

Morgan's eyes eventually opened to look at the guy still standing a few rows over, staring at them with mouth agape. He winked at the young guy, sliding his zipper back up.

Pulling her to her feet, he zipped hers for her as well, as she licked her lips and gathered herself back into her tank. She picked up the flannel that had dropped to the floor at some point, tying it around her waist. She knew her nips were still hard, that had all just been so hot between them. Ah well. People could look if they wanted to or not, she shrugged.

He pressed a kiss against her lips. "We should do that again sometime," he said quietly in her ear.

Now, where was that microfiche?

Morgan

Fuck that had been hot. If that guy had wanted to, he would have definitely let the young college student join in. He wasn't gender-biased when it came to sex. And honestly, some of his best head had been from guys—likely because they knew how it felt or gave how they wished they were sucked. But there hadn't really been time for that. And he preferred to play with strangers when they had been properly vetted, like at play parties.

He tucked his hand into the back pocket of her jeans, as they stood by the microfiche reader. He was going to do what he could to keep her little nipples as hard as a rock for him today, as that was what had started the whole thing. Braless at the library. There should be a special place in hell for little girls like that, and he would happily join her there.

But she had also found the story about Althea, thankfully easier to find since they had the first name and knew her family had died by a fire somewhere near his property. Reading together, they learned that Althea had been alive back in 1852, and her Coven had died in a fire at the riotous hands of the local community. A previous news article just a week or so before had ranted about "the witch coven being a den of iniquity" and "kidnapping young women for virgin brides." But it seemed they had thought Althea had been kidnapped by them when they found her crying near the long driveway of the home. He figured someone had made that assumption because she looked so young and innocent, her face cherub-like, but he noted she had just turned 20 years old. It seemed the local church had taken her in after that, and she had become a seamstress. He wouldn't have blamed her for running with that story in order to survive. At least if his uncle was correct in somehow understanding she was a witch. He had never come to know how his uncle knew her name or about her family dying on their property.

The article noted that none of the members were actually related to one another, so Morgan assumed they were her coven rather than her family, as his uncle thought. Maggie was curious about how Althea survived after that, but they couldn't find any other trace of her name in the archives other than the one article from the town gazette.

Morgan looked but had little luck finding much about his uncle here. He had suspected that the person responsible for the deaths, if there was one, would likely be a powerful wizard or witch who had gone rogue, and there would be minimal traces of them in mundane spaces. If there was any trace at all. Like his uncle and most other witches, they were careful to keep clear of records as much as possible, other than as property owners and voters in the area. He knew he could find more online, which he could do from home. He would have access to the virtual witchcraft and Wicca spaces online, as well as some of the migration records for when his great-uncle came to the States. Morgan had been born in New York, and he knew The Hollow had been in the family for generations, but as far as he knew, he and a few of his cousins were the only ones with natural-born citizenship here. The rest of his mother's generation and some of his grandparents' and great uncle's generation maintained dual citizenship while they were alive but were all born in the United Kingdom.

His grandmother and another uncle and his family were just outside of Lancashire, but the story was that their bloodline had come from Belfast, Ireland, a century or so before that. Morgan had visited the old home in Lancashire a few times, but his mother and grandmother were not close. His Mum had had a falling out with her parents when she decided to marry a mundane, but especially when she had decided not to cultivate her craft. Morgan, having no real relationship with them, thought it was shitty that they hadn't allowed his mother the freedom to choose for herself. Once he learned that, he had never really sought to build a relationship where one was not.

For many years, his great-uncle had been the go-between in the extended family. Morgan had seen many of them at his Uncle Castian's funeral, held in Lancashire due to the family mausoleum being in the area and it being his uncle's wish to lay with family in the end. But he had only minimally engaged. After all, they had abandoned his mother for choosing not to live their lifestyle.

They definitely wouldn't understand him, especially when he didn't follow all the Wiccan practices.

Morgan had honored his uncle's wishes, setting everything up and participating in the funeral formalities. But when everyone realized most of everything his uncle had owned was left to Morgan, suddenly they had wanted to be close to him, and he wouldn't have anything to do with it. There was a reason his uncle left it to him, he figured. Although there was that tidy sum left to care for his grandmother, that required he see to her eventually. He wasn't in a rush. She continued to be taken care of as she always had.

Chapter Twelve

Morgan

They headed home as the sun was just starting to set, the colors framing the autumn leaves in all their glory. Morgan wasn't even going to focus on the fact that he hadn't known her very long, and yet he had just thought of it also being her home. The intimate intensity between them burned hot, but so did the spiritual connection, likely influencing each other. And grocery shopping together, as well as the home goods store where she had offered him advice on The Hollow's rehab, didn't help with all the domesticity either. He could almost picture them together and running this Bed and Breakfast she mentioned.

He felt himself pull back a little as she said she'd prep something for dinner, and he disappeared upstairs to the office to work on his writing a bit more. But pulling away only seemed to affect his writing, as often, when he cut himself off from his natural emotions and inclinations, his writing suffered too. Eventually, he allowed himself to lean back in the chair, gazing out the large window on the wall behind him at the desk. He opened himself up to the universe and allowed his mind to wander, thinking of her so uninhibited today in the library. Imagining the young man joining them, his mouth on Morgan's cock, and his hand going to Maggie's bared breasts as she shared him.

Morgan's cock stiffened. Giving it a few strokes through his semi-opened pants, he turned back to the desk and felt the words begin to flow. This time, he began to add in some pansexual inclinations for this new protagonist, a vampire named Devonshire, who was assisting his primary lead, Sigmund, the head of the Witches Council. As the story flowed from him, he felt his energies rise and fall with the storyline. By the time he felt Maggie enter the office, he had laid down some solid narrative, infusing intrigue and sexual passion together for the first time in his published work. He sat back, pensive about this new addition to his book. Unsure how the mundane world would accept it—they weren't as open and flexible about sexuality as witches often were.

Maggie entered the office, glancing around and taking in the massive space, her eyes settled on him at the desk. She brought a bowl of stir fry with a fork, steaming and smelling wonderful. Setting it next to him on the desk, she perched beside him. She noted his undone jeans with a raised eyebrow but simply asked, "How ya doin'?"

Turning towards her, he drew her closer, setting her on the desk in front of him. He ran his hands up her thighs, pulling her feet into his lap and rubbing his thumbs against her arches. He sighed. "Sometimes I just get all up in my head." Her feet came to rest on his thighs, and he continued pensively, "Sometimes I wonder who might accept all the unusual aspects about me." Rushing on, not meaning her, he quickly added, "As an author, of course."

She slid off the desk and onto his lap in the chair, straddling him. Brushing his hair off his forehead, she kissed him there, much like he had her. Her knees on each side of him in the massive leather office chair, he felt the contact of her jean-covered pussy with his still-hardened cock in his open jeans. "I think all kinds of people are awesome. Kinda like I thought today was awesome," she said quietly.

He looked into her eyes, their souls intertwining softly. His hands came to rest on her legs, brushing her inner thighs softly with his thumbs. "You did? I'm glad. You were a very good girl after all," he said, his voice dropping a bit as his thumb tip grazed the crease of her thighs over her jeans. Her nipples were tight in her tank, peeking at him through the open flannel she wore.

She groaned a little. He leaned forward, licking the faint purple spot where he had left a mark on her neck the other night. Her head dropped back a little, her hands resting around the back of his neck. "I like it when there's more than one person sometimes. It's hot," she whispered breathily.

"Me too," he said, gently biting her neck.

"...and I like being watched," she trembled. He ran his finger along the edge of her tank, so close and yet so far from where he knew she needed him.

"I know," Morgan said. "I noticed." He noticed *everything*. Like how open she was to everything, not even just sexually. How quickly she was picking up on her craft, studying the leather-bound book whenever she had a chance. How empathic she was, attuning with him fairly quickly when he reached out. How sad she was about her family right now. He noticed because he *felt* her—everything about her.

And if she let him, he would keep her safe.

"I get the feeling you are familiar with polyamory," he said softly, his finger tracing her lips softly. She nodded.

"Honesty is important to me," he said thoughtfully, "and loyalty." His fingers smoothed her hair back softly. "As well as communication."

He filled his palm with her long, dark hair, pulling her head back further, scraping her tank down below her tits with his teeth, biting her hardened nipples—first gently, then harder. He would need to try clamps with her one day. She was nicely responsive.

The lights flickered.

"One day, she will join us and stop teasing," Maggie murmured. He chuckled low, as he hadn't considered that option before. But it made sense. Sometimes Althea seemed to be communicating some type of engagement.

"Sometimes I like to play together with others. Sometimes I like to play separately. If there are going to be metamours, we agree to use protection with regular health screenings to keep everyone safe," he said. His scruff growing in was leaving rough, reddening trails along her skin.

"And we communicate when we don't like something or when we've had enough," he said, his hand cupping her sex through her jeans, gripping harder than the average vanilla mundane might enjoy. Maggie only groaned with pleasure. "No holding resentments when we can be open and talk about things," he added.

"I can...I can agree to all that for sure..." Maggie whispered with her head lulling back as he licked her neck all the way up to that little place behind her ear.

He slid her zipper down, his fingers finding their way to her wetness. Scooting closer to the desk, he lifted her back onto the edge again, easing her jeans down and dropping them on the floor. Pantiless, like before, she sat in her lowered tank and open flannel. He parted her legs and gently bit her inner thigh, working his way up slowly, teasing her.

He tucked one of her legs over his shoulder as he eventually delved in, tongue grazing her clit as she shuddered against the scruff on his jaw. She leaned back on her hands while he ran his fingertips softly down her inner thighs and then slapped the soft inner thigh skin as he delved fully into her with his tongue.

"Oh, my gawd..." she gasped.

"Thanks, but not a god, that's for sure," he smiled cheekily against her wetness as he slapped her soft inner thigh again. He would need his riding crop at some point, maybe the flogger as well. They were going to need to get into New York and pick up a few things.

Reaching down, he pulled his cock out, stroking the hard length a few times as she watched through lowered lashes, languishing back on her hands on the desk. Pulling her back onto his lap, she sat right where he wanted her. She sighed deeply as he lowered her onto his rigid cock, her toes barely reaching the floor on each side of him. She rocked forward and back a little, tipping her head back with a moan.

"Mmmmmmm...kitten," he said, stilling her hips.

"Yes...Daddy?" she asked tentatively. He had a feeling she might go that route, having lost hers. But it had needed to be her choice.

He softly cupped her face between his hands, bringing his mouth softly to hers, letting her know how much he approved and was honored with the gift. He would take care of her any way that she would let him, as long as she would let him.

He began to move her hips as she rode him there in the chair. Controlling her movement for the moment, going slower than he knew she would have probably chosen.

"Gah! PLEASE..." she whimpered, "I just..."

"You just what, kitten?" he asked, nibbling her jawline so perfectly turned up to him.

"I...just...need..." she continued breathlessly as she tried to urge her hips against his hands.

"What?" he asked, his voice growing firmer. "What do you need?"

"I...I...need you to fuck me, dammit!" she grated out as she clenched her cunt around his cock, urging his movements. He smiled at her frustrated cry. Another time he would address her impatience, but today was not for lessons. This time he felt himself chasing her orgasm.

Steadily building energy between them, he eventually came first with a powerful thrust, and she let out her own cry, their eyes locking as their smokey hues fused together around them. He reached between them and slowly began to flick her sensitive clit while she was still wrapped warmly around his cock. He watched her writhe and, more quickly than he expected, she came a second time. She slowly rolled her hips against him, riding the orgasm as long as she could, her fading sounds like the mewling kitten she presented as.

He still remembered hearing the mewling sounds from her when she came that first time, thus his inclination for her pet name.

She limped against him, resting her forehead against his chin, making it all too easy to kiss her there. His fingertips brushed softly up and down her quivering thighs.

"I brought food," she muffled against his chest as she kissed him there.

He laughed. "Yes. Yes, you did." She remained there on him, warm and wet and still wrapped around the softening evidence of his arousal. He reached for the bowl, still slightly warm. He offered her a bite from his fork.

"Mmmmmmm, yummy, Daddy," she said, languid and still in kitten space. She curled her legs up in his lap, staying right there and snuggling against him.

He chuckled. He was going to want to keep her if this kind of stuff continued. Watching her delight in the moment warmed his heart more than he had ever experienced with anyone else, even in this older/younger, nurturing space.

Daddy/little space wasn't always his thing. It was more that the overarching dominance was a natural inclination to take care of and nurture. But he had taken that on in various forms for others before. He knew his own shit likely influenced it, with his mother being so flighty, unattached to him, and chaotic. Many folks were drawn to their various kinks out of subconscious inclinations to heal themselves. Meanwhile, Maggie was very much a consenting adult, with a 23-year-old's body that seemed to fit his slightly older one well.

He continued to feed them both small bites as they chatted. A tiny piece dropped. He wasn't so sure she hadn't intentionally let it as he licked it off her chest. Her nipples had remained hard most of the time, and hell, he had been half-hard most of the time since being around her. Her toes came to play with his open zipper, and she peered at him shyly.

"Is it too soon again, Daddy?" she asked, her voice small.

"Absolutely not, kitten," he said, setting aside the bowl and picking her up. Carrying her to his bed—their bed lately, he admitted to himself—he deposited her. Leaning on her elbows, still wearing the open flannel and lowered tank, his eyes couldn't get enough of her as he stripped off his jeans.

The lights flickered.

"Althea...!" Maggie flung her head back and crowed. She lay back in the bed, excitedly calling the ghost again, "Come out, come out, wherever you are!" She giggled, eyeing him again. "Is that okay, puhhhlease Daddy?"

He felt the temperature drop a little in the room. He certainly didn't mind. Watching them before had been unbelievable. "I definitely don't mind, kitten," he said. "Whatever you want."

She settled her eyes on something behind him, "I want you both," she said softly.

He felt a slight tingle up his spine and a soft flutter at his belly. Looking down, he realized Althea must have come up behind him as ghostly hands reached around him, grazing down his stomach. Pale fingers played softly, trailing down to his already hardening cock. He couldn't have imagined how it felt to be touched by a ghost, but the tingles themselves were small intense vibrations leaving a trail of goosebumps on his skin. Not quite as strong as the vibrations from a cock ring he had experienced in the past, but alluringly better, as she slid her hand up and down the length of him.

"You look a bit like him when he was younger," the lilting soft voice said. *Shit, she talked! Him? Him who??*

"Your uncle," she said as if she could hear him. Moving around him, eyes sweetly appreciating Maggie's bare chest and bottom half but focusing back on him a moment later. In front of him, both of her hands reached out and grasped his cock. Sliding her fingers up and down him felt like a suction of tingles, a bit like his teenage fleshlight but with added vibration. He had a flash memory of when he had tried that with his friend when he was younger. Only this was *much* better.

"Your uncle and I had an agreement. He pleasured me any time I needed, and I promised to leave you alone. You were a handsome young man, exploring yourself," she said, shrugging, eyes batting a little flirtatiously. Her nipples were hard points beneath her thin slip of a dress, the ties partially undone, offering voluptuous cleavage. He wondered how well one could feel them. He glanced over her shoulder, wondering how Maggie was doing with the loss of attention. But she seemed riveted on Althea. She slowly reached down and began to play with herself a little while she watched Althea stroking his cock. Seeing her finger's part her wet folds while her eyes were on the ghost bringing him pleasure almost made him explode.

"That's okay, you can," Althea assured, seeming intune with his thoughts without him impressing them her way. "Don't worry. You're young enough. We can bring you to full energy once again later."

The young ghostly witch reached up and pulled the string to her dress, and it fell softly around her. Her young body was on the curvy side, thicker in the chest, thighs, and ass. Bending at the waist, she took Morgan's bursting cock into her mouth, using her fingers as well to bring him pleasure. Winking up at him, she inserted a small finger into his ass, pressing slightly, and he came almost immediately with a "holy fuck!" *That prostate move got him every time, but never so quickly.*

"Holy, I am not, but the minister said that one, too," she said cheekily, licking her lips. "He didn't want to let me leave the church, even after he caught me doing a spell. I think he would've missed my mouth too much." Turning, she glanced at him over her shoulder with flirtatious eyes. "Your uncle was quite good at this too, and he couldn't withstand that part that you just liked either."

Walking over to Maggie, Althea gazed at her. Maggie had continued to stroke herself softly, her hand at times at her breast as well. Althea trailed her fingers along Maggie's inner thigh. "You, my love, are so beautiful doing that. I couldn't resist you the other night. You remind me so much of one of my Coven sisters, Causette. She was rather lovely to pleasure as well."

Spreading Maggie's legs, Althea knelt between them on the bed. Using her tongue and fingers, she began to explore, bringing Maggie higher but then edging her back down again. Morgan wondered if Althea's cunt was wet, and he wondered if he would be able to feel it. He figured he could, as he could feel her fingers and mouth on him in her magickal way. Approaching her, he ran his fingers softly down Althea's long, wavy locks, thinking they must have been very pale blonde before becoming a ghost. He paused for a moment, allowing his fingers to lightly graze Maggie's sweet thighs as well, watching her delight in the young witch's offering.

After a few moments of watching the two, he trailed his hand farther down Althea's back, his fingers sliding between the thick curve of her ass, feeling the wetness there.

"Mmmmmmmm…" Althea murmured, wiggling her ass as she continued to pleasure Maggie. She spread her thighs a little wider, inviting more. Morgan moved behind her, leaning down, and licked her honeyed drips. As a ghost, her taste was unbelievably sweet, and it was no wonder his uncle hadn't minded their little deal. Or hadn't married. But Morgan had known he had dated and had an active sex life with both men and women.

Hearing Maggie coming, with Althea's long fingers inside her, tongue flicking Maggie's clit, Morgan reached below Althea and inserted his own fingers. As she seemed to welcome him, he then pushed into her slowly with his cock. Gods, it was like when her mouth was on him, there was some sort of magical vibration, possibly spiritual. He had just become hard again, but he already wasn't sure how long he would last.

Maggie decided to help him from the other side and reached out to Althea. One hand at the curvy girl's breast and the other reaching below to the ghost's sex, she began to flick at her clit. Her fingers periodically grazed Morgan's cock while he entered the ghost, over and over again. *FUCK.*

Maggie must have felt him coming, her fingers softly caressing his balls to let him know she was with him. She bit softly on Althea's large nipple, the tip already darker from being manipulated by Maggie. The ghost reared her blond head and gave a small cry, coming all over his cock, taking him up with her.

Althea slumped on top of Maggie's now naked body, and Morgan lay alongside the two of them. Their breaths remained heavily entwined. Hands, who even knew whose were where anymore, softly ran along various limbs and soothed after the interaction. Ghostly kisses rained down Maggie's arms as Morgan soothingly stroked Althea's back.

Despite all his years of experience, nothing had ever compared to sharing sex with a ghost and the most beautiful woman he knew.

Maggie

Maggie had never experienced anything as intense as that before.

She'd never been a witch before, either. *So maybe having sex with a ghost was common among the supernatural folks?*

She had had sex with multiple people before, though. She wasn't sure if it had ever been with someone she had begun to care about as much as she was feeling lately for Morgan. Dear gods, it had only been *one week.* It felt like eons.

As she caught her breath, she felt a wet tingle fall on her arm—*what the hell is a wet tingle?* She realized it was a ghost tear. Althea was sniffling softly.

"Oh gods," Maggie rushed in, "I'm so sorry if that was too much... I'm too much sometimes..."

But Morgan kissed her forehead and pressed a gentle finger to her lips. He looked at Althea knowingly. "Tell us about them," he said reassuringly, seeming to know what was coming.

He settled next to her, wrapping an arm around Maggie and leaning back against the headboard, and they listened as Althea told them vividly about her Coven family. Two men and three other women, one widowed with two children, had all found each other through the years and made a family. All consenting witches and one wizard, they were all happily raising the woman's children together, carefully staying out of the eye of the town.

"Our small cabin wasn't anything like this majestic mansion, but it was here, on this beautiful land. We didn't have much, each of us with a few skills that supported us, a garden, a few chickens, and a cow to help feed us, with some meat now and then when one of us would risk going into town. But we had our love between all of us, and it was enough," she explained.

"Anna and Causette had gone into town one weekend but found a hurt little fawn while on their way home. They truly thought no one was near, but as they were magickly healing the fawn, a local townsperson saw. They ran crying back to the village that we were witches. The townspeople wouldn't leave us alone after that. They wrote such horrible things about us in the paper. They screamed at us and commanded that we deserved to die. *SO* many hated what they feared or didn't understand—much like it is even today, it seems," the ghost added sadly.

Turning away from them both, she continued softly, "After we thought the fear had died down, I went into town early one morning to sell eggs. I took them directly to the general store, where we barely received pennies for them. I had promised to return right away, but they had the most beautiful sunflowers for sale outside of the store. I got distracted. By the time I made it home, the cabin was in flames, and they had been blocked inside with wood hammered over the front and back doors."

"I could hear them screaming from so far away," she barely whispered. "I hear them even now. I cannot ever stop hearing them." A tear slipped again from her wide eyes and down her cheek. "It was only fitting that after the year with the minister in his church, he brought me back to this very place and burnt me on that cross of a stake, all in the name of his god. I thought surely that might release me to where they were, but I have never been able to leave this property."

"Althea," Morgan asked quietly, "why has no one ever released you to them?"

Althea looked at him, eyes wide. "That is possible?" she asked incredulously.

He reached for her hand, "I think so. I have heard of it but have never seen it. I knew a wizard once who said he had participated in a releasing ceremony. And I know Samhain is the best time to do it."

Which was less than two weeks away, thought Maggie.

Well, she would most definitely be staying.

Chapter Thirteen

Mulligan

He was sure he had sensed the shift in the power dynamics in the Universe. A very powerful young witch had awakened. A power that felt familiar to him. He searched his glowing celestial orb, the light and shadows shifting and merging as he probed the universe for where the power was emanating. Mumbling incantations, the dark navy-blue smoke of energy rose in the room as his power focused on the ball, intensifying.

Mulligan glanced to the antique scrying mirror on the opposite wall as he worked the spirits, noticing the handsomeness of his own reflection. He had worked hard to maintain the prime of his life. As he approached his late 70s, he appeared much closer to one who might be in their late 50s, full of wisdom and prowess. He knew he had benefited from various aging spells throughout the years. He relied on his appearance, especially when engaging younger men and women in trysts or leading the power dynamic parties he would host periodically at his dark mansion in the hills, just outside of London.

He often didn't realize he hadn't needed to look as handsome as he was, as it was his nature, his depraved personality, that generally drew many to him. With his powerful body, raven dark hair now glinted with silver at the temples, still hanging in wavy locks to his shoulders, and his dark and silvery goatee framing his mouth. A mouth often pulled into a dark, sinister line, usually intent on inflicting pain on his next prey.

There had always been someone, somewhere, open to the magnetic but sadistic qualities in him. But what drove his intense anger always continued to be the jealousy for what he felt he never had. Despite now swimming in riches, owning his various affluent properties, and having his magnate hand in the sordid affairs of the witchcraft community in his own silent ways anytime that he desired. Well, he preferred things silent and sordid—at least the politics he engaged in. Power was to be taken, and he was the one who would take it, every damn time. He would never be the one at the mercy of the powerful again, as he had been so long ago—a young child, dirty and running beneath his mother's cloak, as he watched the influential businessmen of London use their affluence, and their ability to fire her, to bring her under their cruel thumbs.

What he hadn't recognized until later was how they had wielded their power to get her beneath them at their desk, as she would oft send him on errands to distract him. Now he was the one who held the power to both humiliate and yet benefit an underling witch as they crawled to him beneath his office conference table in the midst of a meeting, sucking his engorged cock at his demand while he finished an important merger.

Sex held power, as did money, and he owned them both. It was rare that he would even need to stoop to magicks to ensnare a new young intern when they caught his attention. Between his power in the local and international Coven business world, his now deep pocketbooks, and his ravenous appetite for fresh young magick, he had little difficulty keeping his bed and cock warm when he wished. He took energy from the young developing witches, of course... They owed him. Their power was fresh and invigorating, keeping his magicks—and his health—as alive and even more potent than when he had been young. Being so near The Academy, his connections kept a fresh flow of interns in his business practice and beneath him whenever he wished. But lately, he had been getting bored with this current Generation Z. They were too smart for their own good and thought they deserved their own independence in the workplace. It made their lack of consent a bit more thrilling if he wanted, but he preferred his slaves not consider lawsuits against him, having just escaped a difficult one. Thankfully he had an excellent law team that represented him. Money or magick really did solve almost everything.

The clouds began to sift apart in his magical orb, his strengths of divination and scrying having assisted him many times in his power search over the years when he needed them to. Long ago, shifting from using his gifts in ways that brought unity to the earth and all its inhabitants, as The Academy taught magick was for, he had grown more and more powerful in using his skills to divine his own manipulations and need to feed on the power of others.

His attention settled on a young, burgundy-haired witch who was pouring her sensual energies over a naked man and a young female ghost. As much as he wouldn't mind tasting the other two, the man having a fine figure with a healthy sized cock that the ghost had just taken into her mouth, it was the young witch on the bed watching them who drew his attention. He noted the intense violet smoke that filtered around her, uninhibited. He recognized that energy signature somehow...and he found himself grasping for the memory. He watched her stroke her own pert, small breasts and insert her own petite finger inside her wet and soaking pussy, moaning as she watched the dark-haired young man orgasm into the ghost's fucking mouth. The memory came to him as though petitioned of a young, similar-haired witch and her handfasted young Talon, the son of his old friend William. After having seen to William's demise many years before, he had kept his eye on the young man.

Mulligan had made sure there was a space available to him at The Academy, and conveniently assured he accepted a position as an intern with Mulligan's own developing company at the time.

Back then, Mulligan had appreciated the lithe lines of young Talon, much like his father's had been. While Mulligan and William hadn't had any sexual interaction, it wasn't for lack of Mulligan noticing the fair Wil's then firm lines in the locker rooms after rugby games. The outline of Wil's firm cock often had made Mulligan's mouth water and fed just a few of his thoughts when he would later take a pounding out on a Welsh rugby fan's youthful ass. So, when Talon drew closer to Mulligan's power and business leadership during his year interning with him, Mulligan had begun to have fantasies about the young man's servitude and how well his collegiate mouth might feel around his cock.

But Talon had been besotted with that young witch at The Academy, Allegra. Mulligan had allowed the developing romance, not pushing things quite yet with Talon. Allegra had been beautiful in her thick burnt rose locks, her fine cabernet eyes ensnaring him once or twice, making him pause to consider if the two of them might join him together sometime—both in bed and in business. In the end, Allegra seemed to somehow see through his goals, and Talon left Mulligan's business practice. Mulligan didn't even consider that his own controlling nature or lascivious patterns might have been at fault. So, when a few years later, he learned that the young couple was investigating him for the previous death of Talon's father, he didn't think twice about ending their supernatural journeys on this earth. He hadn't imagined that they had produced offspring already, but he sensed as he watched her that she carried the elevated power of the firstborne of two very powerful witches—whether she realized it yet or not.

His gaze observed her, his scrying eyes narrowing in as in her nudity, he saw flashes of her youth as well as her future. She would understand and know great power, this daughter of the divine. He wanted that power. He would taste her youth as well, this sensuous vixen. Multiple generations of untasted virility by him through her sweet but powerful scent. He could almost taste her now.

And Mulligan began to plot.

Maggie

Maggie awoke the following day alone in bed. Althea had disappeared shortly after their assurances that they would research and find a way to help her join her family on the other side, which Althea viewed as Summerland—a haven for the Wiccan.

Talking long into the night, Morgan filled her in on some of the Wiccan traditions his mother and uncle had shared with him over the years. He also shared why he didn't practice, with concerns for the leader, as well as various politics and the limitations he didn't like. He still held some original things from centuries of witchcraft as important, like celebrating Mabon right now. Before her arrival, he had created a small altar outside under the full moon this month to thank the Earth Mother for her blessings and to consider what he would let go of this year. He shared that he had realized he held onto isolation out here, and he had known that wasn't good for him. And the gods and goddesses had seemed to have sent him her.

She sent up gratitude for that.

Maggie was sure he didn't realize how sweet his words were, but he did write words for a living. She lay in the warmth of the memory of them now, covering her head with the down comforter for a moment. He had continued to tell her a bit about his uncle, and how many things now made sense, other than why his uncle had never sought to release Althea to be with her family.

"He was one of the wisest wizards I have ever known. If anyone could have figured it out, it was him," he had puzzled.

She took a quick shower in his bathroom, using his soap. Instead of the lavender and amethyst soap, as she had, his was cedar and cypress and appeared to contain bits of smoky quartz and tiger's eye. Smelling like him was somehow so sexy, like feeling his hands running along her limbs with the soap suds. So was lathering in that shower mirror. But she quickly finished and dressed in a hoodie and leggings. Throwing her hair on top of her head with a scrunchy and a headband, she grabbed a cup of coffee in the kitchen and roamed to find Morgan. She was usually the first up. She guessed he must be writing.

He was in the joint library/office, but he was pouring over books from the shelves. With books spread all across the conference table, he seemed to have been at it for hours. Researching she knew well.

"Sheesh, did you even get any sleep?" she asked.

Distracted by what he was looking at, he said, "Yeah, some. I got up a few hours ago, though."

She came to stand behind him, her hand on his shoulder, as she looked at all he had spread out before him. He seemed to have a pattern or something going.

"Yep," he said, not even looking up. It was like every time they had sex, they became more attuned to one another. "The ones to the right are the greater possibilities for the spell we need. The ones to the left are the ones we may need to be familiar with if something unusual occurs. The ones right in front of me are the things that have gone wrong in the past with these types of spells."

She rubbed his shoulders for a moment, feeling his tension. He really cared about what happened to Althea, and she did too. She sat down across from him at the conference table and began to review some of the past concerns for time, death, and world-shifting spells. Curses, hell, and dismemberment in the afterlife, among others. And that could be both on the individual being released as well as on those casting the spell. Damn, these powers had some serious consequences.

"And ye harm none, do what ye will."

She saw it on repeat, it was at the front of her leather book as well. Her mother seemed to have really cared about that quote. From what she gathered, magic was supposed to help others, not harm them. What they were pursuing wasn't going to harm anyone, only help, so she didn't know how it could go wrong. But she guessed playing around with changing the afterlife might anger some sort of demon or god.

But she couldn't bring herself to believe that Althea being kept from her loved ones was meant to be, so there had to be a way to release her.

Her Auntie owed her.

She thought about a plan and ran it by Morgan. They could take a few days and do a quick road trip. Swing up to her grandparents'. She wasn't sure what she was going to say to them, but she wanted to look through some of her parents' things. She felt sure she might find something to clue them in to what was going on. Then they could head down to her Auntie's shop in New Haven. It was quite a drive but pretty this time of year, and her aunt lived on the water. But she felt she needed to see her and run some of these releasing spells by her. See what she thought. She trusted her aunt, even if she hadn't been honest about the necklace. But she suspected her grandmother was really the one in charge of all that.

Morgan was open to the trip, but since they were considering New Haven, he wanted to run by his condo in New York. He had a few things he wanted to check on.

So she called her grandmother and texted her Auntie. She told them both briefly that she had started a relationship with Morgan, but they owed her, and she didn't want any questions about that. Really, she wasn't sure she had the answers where he was concerned. She was just winging it at this point. But she planned to share a room with him while at her grandparents' and wasn't sure how long they would be at her aunt's. They weren't prudish, so it wasn't a problem, she just wanted them to know.

Chapter Fourteen

Maggie

The following day they packed up the very standard Chevy Suburban that Morgan pulled around from the car barn. Morgan said this one had already been his, and he had a reasonably comfortable dog crate installed in the back portion of the vehicle for Xander. Although he said sometimes he let Xander ride in the front, so she gave Xander extra belly rubs, knowing he was giving up the front seat for her. She added Mr. Morpheus' cat crate in the back as well, and they made sure they had everything they needed before loading each of their bags, including their laptops.

Morgan had wifi in the vehicle, and satellite, which was fantastic. Maggie had never had that, what with her classic car only having a cassette player, not even from the factory. She tucked in her Bluetooth earbuds and worked while Morgan drove. She had some research processing to catch up on.

It was only about an hour and a half drive, so as they approached the area, Maggie tucked away her stuff. Taking a measured breath, she quickly told Morgan she hadn't really talked with her grandparents yet about things. They knew she knew, but she had avoided the hard conversation by phone. She knew she was going to have to talk about it before she left. Her grandmother only had so much patience. She knew Esme had recently left to go home and check on her shop and that her grandparents supposedly had fallen into a routine around Pop's physical therapy and staying on top of other things. They had mostly retired anyways, Pop only tinkering at the store now and then. Maggie didn't know what always kept them so busy, but they were.

They pulled up to the small, English cottage-style home, with its archway stone and maple wood porch cleared from her grandmother's usual pots and various greenery that filled the space during the late spring and summer. Auntie must have made sure things were put away and ready for winter before she left, as the cold nights were already too much for the herbs and flowers so often used in Nan's potions and elixirs. Forget calling them lotions and balms now, Maggie knew better. Something magickal definitely kept people returning for her grandmother's famous soothing mixes.

The vines scrolling along the porch and down the sides of the home seemed to cry out in welcome to Maggie, and she wondered if maybe she really did hear them, as she did Morpheus. She had let him out immediately upon their arrival, and he had run to his favorite place where the sun always warmed the porch. At least now she knew why he was always allowed outdoors and he never ran away. She had always wondered about that as a child.

The door opened before they reached it, and Maggie almost cried out when she saw her Pop on a walker. Hugging him gently, she got on to him for even being up, forgetting the drama of the moment in distress.

But he tsked her as only he could do, saying, "I'm not a fragile, senile old man. I can greet my girl at the door when I haven't seen her in ages." His thin, older frame folded a little over the walker, but his eyes were alive with the light and energy she had always known him to carry. Nan came to the kitchen doorway, drying her hands on a towel at her waist. Her eyes overflowing with anxious love, she waited as Maggie approached her, and they hugged as well.

Her grandfather introduced himself to Morgan, who nodded respectfully, clasping hands, and she heard him say, "A lightworker, I believe?"

Maggie spun around in time to hear her Pop respond affirmatively, his eyebrow raised. "Can't pull a punch with you, huh, boy? When did you begin your practice?"

"I've always been attuned, sir," Morgan said respectfully. "But I began to focus more in my teen years, under my great uncle's tutelage."

"He was a good man, Castian," said her grandfather honorably. "I was sorry to hear about his passing. I knew him actually, you know, but I was two years behind him at The Academy, so he likely wouldn't have remembered me. But I followed his work in the community. He tried to keep things in line. It's an uphill battle some days." He shook his head sadly.

"What the hell is a lightworker?" Maggie broke in impatiently. *And why didn't she know?*

"Lightworkers," said her grandmother, "are spiritual cousins of sorts to witches and wizards. They have innate powers to heal and repair—often both spiritually and physically."

"So, his shop?" She looked back and forth between them questioningly.

"Yes, he often used his powers there, carefully so none would know. Just as I also enhance my lotions and balms," her grandmother answered.

Uh-huh, lotions and balms. "Potions and spells, you mean?" she asked, a bit more sarcastically than she probably intended. She didn't often lean into being disrespectful, even at the height of her teenage years. *But oh, her sarcasm sometimes.*

Morgan had walked up beside her while she was speaking a few moments before. He put his hand at her elbow, and she noticed his firm grip, bringing her a bit back to her senses. She was angry. Hurt really, but not really about their work in the community. They were struggling to adjust after her Pop's injury, and right now probably wasn't the right time.

"I'm sorry," she uttered. "I haven't worked through all my feelings about this yet. It's still pretty raw." She saw her grandfather's sorrowful eyes and her Nan's proud ones. Oh how that told her so much and confirmed what she had thought all along.

She turned, carrying her backpack into her bedroom. Morgan had followed her, setting the rest of their bags down to the side of the full bed. He took her by the chin firmly, bringing her eyes to meet his.

"What do you need?" he asked her softly.

At first, she wanted to say a good smack on the ass. But then she folded herself into his arms, snuggling in. Sighing. Maybe she needed both. But for now, this would do. He kissed her forehead and reminded her that everything in the world didn't need to be solved tonight.

He was right.

Maggie knew her grandparents loved her and meant well. That would have to do for now. They had bigger fish to fry.

They ate a small lunch and took a quick nap, resting together on her much smaller bed, listening to the sounds of the autumn breeze and the birds in the trees through the slightly open bedroom window. Her senses seemed so much sharper now with this witchy business.

She woke when his hand slipped inside her leggings, his finger and thumb bringing her to a wriggling orgasm while his other hand covered her mouth to keep her quiet. *They would have to talk about some of her consensual nonconsent fantasies one day,* she thought. Maybe they could work something out. That hand over her mouth stuff was *fire.*

As the blend of their sensual smoke dissipated around them, he pulled her panties and leggings back up over her ass. "That's a good pet," he said, patting her pussy through the thin cotton, and got up to use the bathroom connected to her room. She flopped over in the bed, flinging her hand across her eyes. How did she get here?? No, not home, but in this overwhelming place in life?

Oh yeah, her car broke down outside of a haunted mansion. She had gone inside, literally to her fate. Everything had changed since then. But there were definitely some perks, like Morgan and his magickal fingers.

They each did a little work, working quietly from their laptops for a few hours before she ventured back into the kitchen where Nan was working on dinner. Stirring and tasting the soup while Nan folded the homemade bread she would bake soon, they worked in silence for a few minutes. Breaking the ice, she asked for an update from the doctor for Pop. Nan was very direct, telling her that they had put two pins in his hip but that with regular physical therapy, and her magickal potions infused with her grandfather's lightwork, they expected him to recover pretty well. He might walk a tad slower sometimes. They expected some arthritis to settle in eventually, but Nan was adamant that her lotion would resist that development.

Pop had come in, and rather than resisting the healing talk, he admitted it would be helpful if she might check on the shop. Looking her directly in the eye, he told her she had remnants of his lightwork in her blood, and she had begun to cultivate those skills before her parents died. Her grandmother had included that as well in shielding her gifts. Not being willing to pass up the open door, Maggie looked at them both and asked, "So is that what happened then? They died, and you decided that was reason enough to stop me from sensing my heritage? What was more important than my knowing the fullness of all that I am??" Her hands flapped as she gestured to the totality of her family roots around her.

Her grandmother's face went pale, and her grandfather grimaced. Sitting down at the head of the kitchen table, Pop told her shocked grandmother to sit down as well. Maggie sat down hesitantly.

"When your parents went on that trip, we knew they were in danger from the start. They had generally taken you with them on missions, as they had begun to work for the Coven Crown, or an FBI of sorts for witches, if you will. But this time, your mother insisted it was different. She felt uncertain of their successful return. She was a powerful young witch, your mother, inheriting some of my lightwork, some of your grandmother's kitchen witchcraft with a propensity towards spells and potions, but also, she seemed to have inherited some of your great-grandmother's divination and elemental energies as well. You, I believe, have inherited all of that from her. Plus, your father's family lineage was lunar magicks, their energies becoming more intensified when the moon is high, and I believe you hold their power within you as well," Pop told her calmly.

"They had been hunting a man your father had known well—his old boss and a close fellow classmate of his father's, your paternal grandfather, and your uncle," he said, looking at Morgan pointedly as he joined them. "Mulligan Windsor is a name that holds great fear at times in our communities, as he is very powerful and rich, in many ways a silent influencer behind our head council in London."

His voice grew very grave. "Your father believed Mulligan Windsor had killed his father when Talon was only ten years old. Mulligan, William, and Castian had been close friends and confidants once upon a time at The Academy. All three were leads together in the school's Rugby team, synching their bond even tighter. While William, your paternal grandfather Maggie," he said, "and Castian remained friends, Mulligan did not. I remember those days—the school had been alive with rumors regarding Mulligan's wandering. He had been rumored to get involved with one of the school's old wizards to overthrow the council. But somehow, all of that never came to fruition for them, and Mulligan wasn't heard of for some time."

"But he rose to power again within the ranks at some point and has held authority somehow with The Academy now for decades. Your father and mother even interned with him for a short while, while both at The Academy, where they met. Your mother never did like him." Her grandfather shook his thick head of white hair. "Talon truly gave him the benefit of the doubt as his father's friend until something must have changed that for him. They had recently found some sort of new evidence of his involvement in William's fatal car accident."

"Now," his hand went to cover his wife's hands as she sat quietly at the table. "I know it's hard to understand why we did what we did. But what we understood was that an evil wizard with great power in the International Witches Council had likely killed not only your parents but also your paternal grandfather."

"When Mangus told me he saw you being harmed one day by Mulligan," her grandmother exclaimed, "there really was no other choice. You had to be kept safe!" Her voice rose shrilly at the end, wringing her hands.

"But keeping her powers from her only put her at a greater risk," Morgan said firmly but respectfully. "Are you not able to recognize that? Her powers are her greatest defense." He took her hand, their energies fusing and radiating warmly from their joined hands. Her grandparents looked at one another for a moment. Then her grandmother looked back at Maggie sadly.

Maggie sighed. "The past cannot be rewritten, but it is passed. All I can do is move forward and hopefully prepare myself for what is to come. I'd like to see my parents' stuff if I can," she said hesitantly.

"Of course, it's in the attic," Pop assured, his voice offering penance if it could. "You are welcome to it anytime, now that you may understand it."

"Truly," her grandmother pleaded, desperate for her to understand their decision. "I only meant to protect you, my dear."

"I know," she sighed, leaning forward to offer a hug, knowing she was once again making others feel better when it should be her space to grieve all she had lost. "Now I have to find me again."

She dragged Morgan along with her to the old shop, Xander going with them. Morpheus was still lounging in the same spot in the sunshine, looking as though no mortal soul could move him if they tried.

She checked Pop's messages and his stack of repairs that had been waiting for him since he fell. Thankfully the list wasn't too long. After Morgan did a round of the small building, he found her on the 3rd repair, noting she was funneling her growing magick into the work, finding the problem faster than she would have without it, and repairing much more quickly. Morgan assisted with a broken vacuum cleaner, quickly discerning the pet hair clog and removing it the old-fashioned way.

When they returned to the house, the bread was freshly baked, and the soup was ready to eat. She worked out a plan with her grandfather to have a young neighbor teen, Christopher, who had helped a few times before at the shop, come by a few times a week for a few hours. Pop admitted that the freshman had budding repair skills, so as long as Pop correctly discerned the problem, Chris could often even repair with some direction. It was a plan to get him back into the shop at least part-time, which would make Pop happy.

After dinner, she and Morgan climbed up into the small attic. Digging through boxes upon boxes, she found a few that had her parents' things in them, one of which contained her mother's journals. Pulling her into his lap, Morgan provided some solid reassurance as she poured through the journals, noting various things about Mulligan Windsor, sometimes labeled only MW, in the journal just before their death. She had also found her mother's spell book, or her grimoire, as Morgan called it. He said each witch created their own grimoire during their lifetime, where they gathered the various spells, sigils, runes, crystals, and essential spiritual things regarding one's craft.

Maggie knew she had found a treasure. The leather-bound book from Mangus had held some things from her mother. But this, this was all the important parts of her maternal guidance, if she could not be here herself. Maggie gathered a few things that she wanted to take with her—the journals for further exploration later, a beautiful amethyst-handled bronze hairbrush with sigils inscribed on the bronze, her father's golden pocket watch, and a framed photograph of the two of them, laughing and holding one another on a hike in the mountains. It was clearly a selfie-style photograph taken by her father, his arms wrapped around her mother from behind. But she felt their love so very strongly there.

After they went back downstairs and she showed her grandparents the things she planned on taking with them, her grandmother shared with her that the framed photograph was the moment her mother had told her father they would be having a baby. "They had such beautiful plans for you," her grandmother said, her hand coming to cup Maggie's cheek. "They loved you so very much."

Morgan held her on his chest as she cried that night. Tears for her parents' lives cut too short. Tears for her own loss of love and childhood innocence. Tears for her own missed enchanted journey through her teens, recognizing so many signs of her internal inclinations that had been unable to expand and multiply as they should have under the proper tutelage. It should have been under her parents' guidance. She knew that to the very depths of her soul.

Chapter Fifteen

Morgan

The next morning, they packed up for the five-hour drive to New York City. Maggie started out driving his Suburban this time, which was a world of difference from her little Volkswagen. Mike had called early this morning and told her the car would likely be ready by Wednesday. She'd told him they were out of town and would probably get back by the end of the week. Morgan knew she was excited to get her little car back, but they hadn't really talked about her staying after the car was fixed. He needed to rectify that soon.

Morgan continued to steadily write as she drove, handling a call from Max. He had sent the first six chapters of his next book before they left The Hollow to head to Essex, and his publisher had already reviewed it. Max thought it would be a hit with the supernatural crowd. The publisher just wasn't as sure about the mundane world acceptance. Religion still drew a hard path for many, even those who had begun to accept sex as natural, and a primary gay couple didn't always sell well. But the publisher was willing to take a chance, as he had an established following, guaranteeing a baseline of preorders. But he said something about maybe being extra careful with how they wrote the preview.

"Hey buddy, if we can just get people to start the book, I know they will love the character's relationship arc as much as we do," Max had insisted when Morgan got annoyed at the censoring.

Damn mundanes and their limited tolerance.

Life was so much more when you could view it from outside of the box. When your view was enhanced by the energies around you. Even viewing nature the way that she was, one could sense her very breath, the tree's song, the flower's chorus line. Everything lived and breathed to connect, to enhance each other if you were open to it.

He'd better stop before he waxed too poetic. Instead, he funneled that frustrated energy into his work.

He was working on a scene about midway through the book when his phone pinged.

```
Hey kid. My friend said he had reported the brake lines cut in the
investigation. But somehow that report changed between hands. (Mike)
```

```
Damn. I suspected. (Morgan)
```

```
Something is def fishy son. (Mike)
```

```
Thanks Mike! I appreciate your time. (Morgan)
```

```
Let me know if there is anything else I can do. Your Uncle was a good man
and a good friend. (Mike)
```

Morgan filled in Maggie on the new information. He wondered if there might be some kind of record back home that his uncle left that might hint at why Mulligan would have targeted him only recently. He knew he had avoided going through most of his uncle's things so far, especially in the office. Immediately coming to mind were their likely opposing viewpoints on the International Witches Council. Morgan didn't know anything really about this Mulligan Windsor, but he would soon enough. Research was his thing, as it also was Maggie's.

He teased her a little as she drove, reaching over and running the tips of his fingers along the seam in her jeans—along her thigh, and up her pussy. But when she got distracted from driving, he laughed and stopped, promising her he would have her naked before the end of the night. Despite the little orgasm he'd given her during their nap the day before, they hadn't fucked since they'd left The Hollow. He was missing her skin against his too.

Later she got him back when they switched places after a brief lunch when she showed him she had taken her panties off at the little restaurant they had stopped at. Since she seemed to want to play a bit, he tasked her with tucking her little tank she loved to wear without a bra so much, below her breasts and to pleasure her tits while they drove, allowing her to decide how much she wanted them to peep around her open flannel. He knew she was exhibition bent, and he gave her room to decide just how much of that occurred. He wasn't surprised though when she allowed the flannel to fully fall away from her breasts as she played, as he'd suspected she might.

The sun's rays seem to be drawn to her, as she ran the tip of her nails softly around her small, pert breasts, stopping to pinch the nipples every now and then tightly as she liked, or licking her fingers sensually and then wetting the nipples to make them more sensitive. They passed various vehicles and a few truckers who even honked at her play as they happily watched, adding to her turned-on flush that made her squirm a bit in her seat. One man almost veered off onto the side of the highway, the woman with him hitting his arm repeatedly once she realized what had distracted him. What turned Morgan on the most was how much the exhibitionist play turned her on, her nipples harder than ever, her breath heavy and catching at times. He reached over and rubbed her pussy through her jeans now and then, eventually even unbuttoning them one-handedly and sliding his middle finger in for a few moments to flick at her impossibly begging clit and slide his finger inside her dripping wetness.

But she would wait to come, he told her. Tonight. Tonight, she would come more than she could imagine.

They had things to try tonight if it were up to him.

He looked forward to picking up some of his things from his condo for a while now. From their time together, he had gleaned that she was drawn to some mild pain play, to bondage and exhibitionism, and group play was a clear interest. Were they going to be in New York for more than the night, they would visit The Dungeon, the BDSM sex club he had frequented before when so inclined. She would enjoy the quiet room in the back designed only for supernaturals, where they infused their magick into their play as well, consensually only, of course. He knew they would both enjoy that, but unfortunately, they wouldn't be staying long enough in New York this time to stop in. *Maybe some later trip*, he thought, realizing he hoped their exploration and connection wouldn't end anytime soon. They had barely known each other a week and a half, and already he couldn't imagine his life without her. He wasn't sure how he felt about that.

Morgan had been alone more in his life than he liked to admit. Sex didn't always mean letting people get close emotionally, sometimes it was just a basic need, and you didn't really connect emotionally with everyone you had great sex with. Early on, he had thought all women were as flighty as his mother, preferring friendships and then eventual tentative exploration with boys as a young teen. His explorations with Shawn, when they would meet at his friend's treehouse in the woods just before coming to his uncle's, had been his first exploration of how amazing touching another human could be when it was between two healthy, exploring young people.

His friend had found a stash of toys his parents had used, and in trying them, they had eventually tentatively touched one another as well, at first accidentally in passing the items back and forth, and then intentionally when they realized how hard the other was at the accidental touches. They eventually learned the feel of a mouth on their penis far surpassed the fleshlight they at first thought was so cool, and their early explorations with the small vibrators likely surpassed the average teenage boy's experiences. Eventually, learning he could add magick to the mix and intensify things only heightened his experiences with sex and pleasure with anyone he explored with.

But his mother had rarely been there when he needed her—from rarely bandaging his young bleeding falls to forgetting parent-teacher conferences to apathetically guiding his witchcraft journey. He had learned mostly to take care of himself through his younger years. He had often wondered if that was why he had developed more of his witchcraft and his sexuality a bit younger than some, as he had needed to learn the connections, the powers, the herbs, and spells to cleanse and bandage his own wounds—whether metaphorical or physical. As an adult, he knew she struggled to see past herself, always seeking to find the next pleasurable thing in her life, as she had had very little attention from her own parents.

His mother had supposedly been the result of an affair her mother had with her father, and she had been told that even from a young age. When his grandmother chose to keep the baby yet stay with her husband, she had seemed to take it out on his mother, never being happy with her and blaming her, it seemed, for something that hadn't even been his mother's fault. His grandmother had reportedly treated her other children very differently. His great-uncle had often apologized for his sister's selfish behaviors but had also continued to look after her.

He would honor Castian's wishes. He had been the first adult who had shown Morgan a true level of caring and guidance in his life, starting to take him for weekend camping trips in the summer shortly after his arrival at The Hollow, even willingly including Morgan's friends at the time if he asked. Castian was the reason he had learned how to tie ropes properly, build a fire, create a shelter, and care for the earth, all things that taught Morgan respect for nature but also for himself.

Morgan knew Castian had eventually offered to take him on, not just for the witchcraft guidance, but because he saw him beginning to go down a dark and lonely path as a young teen. That first year with Castian, not really knowing anyone else in the area and not having access to drugs had literally saved his life, forcing him to get his shit together.

His boredom outside of school and their periodic camping trips pushed him toward the various classic novels in his uncle's library, starting a path that took him down a writing road he may have never considered otherwise. No, he hadn't forgotten the pleasurable aspects of sex, and his uncle had addressed him directly about safety, but his life balanced out more after that year. Yes, he would honor his uncle's wishes, but that didn't mean he would ever honor a relationship with a woman so callous as to blame a child for her own shortcomings like his grandmother.

Early on in first exploring polyamory, he had feared he was somehow just like his grandmother and mother, stuck in self-pleasure more than caring for others. Thankfully, he had explored and learned that polyamory was very different from torrid and dishonest affairs. He was far too loyal-natured to treat someone he loved the way his grandmother had her daughter or husband. But he wasn't too daft to realize that his recent isolation was leaving him far less connected to humanity than he probably should be.

They arrived in New York as the sun was setting. All done up from her earlier state of undress, Maggie hopped out of the parked Suburban. *Gods she was beautiful*, Morgan thought, the last rays of sun catching the deep scarlet in her hair and glinting off the burnt berry of her mouth. And she hadn't even learned any glamour magicks yet, although he suspected her mother's amethyst brush might be enchanted with some.

They gathered their bags and the animals, Morgan putting Xander on a leash briefly. They had an agreement—Xander didn't like leashes, but New York residents got scared of big dogs easily. So, Morgan only leashed him when he absolutely had to, in order to assure other people. He knew Xander wouldn't take off, they communicated too well. Even youth hadn't made the dog feistily chase a squirrel up a tree. If anything, Xander was the one who had talked Morgan down during his teenage years from some far worse impulsivity.

"Since we are in the city, do you want to go out for dinner, or order something in?" Morgan asked Maggie, leaving the timeline of the night up to her.

"Are you even kidding me right now?" Maggie said, indignantly rolling her eyes. "I haven't been able to jump your bones for like 72 hours, and you had me on the edge almost the whole way here with your promises," she said, flushing as her nipples peaked against her tank top again.

"Dinner in it is," he chuckled, slapping her pert little ass as she turned towards the building with her hands full of cat stuff. He would just eat her for dinner, but their stomachs might get hungry. And he was looking forward to seeing her naked and writhing in his bed.

His condo was pretty small, especially in comparison to his uncle's place. But the place had a decent small kitchen, a dining room that he had made into a small working office, a half bath and small laundry space off the kitchen, and a hallway back to a full bath and two bedrooms. What had sold him were the large windows, knee-high to ceiling almost, running along the front and back of the building. While not arched like his uncle's, it had reminded him of the windows at home, and a witch loved the sun and the moonlight. Plus, it gave him space to grow some things now and then.

They walked into his place, and he set their bags down by the leather sofa. Xander immediately crossed the room and drank from the dog bowl at the entrance of the kitchen, asking for the water to be refreshed soon as it was stale. Maggie set the cat carrier on the couch and opened the crate, but Morpheus was currently somewhat peeved at being in there so long. So, Maggie told him to do what he wanted, and she went to set up the travel litter container she had brought in the small laundry room.

Morgan walked through the place, turning on some lights and cracking a few windows to air it out a bit while also turning on the heat as the cool autumn night air was settling in. It had been about a month since he had headed to his uncle's place. He'd decided for now that he didn't want to give up the apartment in NYC, as he figured he'd travel here now and then for publishing related business. He had considered renting it out as an Airbnb, as he still had a tendency to think like he was struggling to make ends meet, despite his healthy writing income, let alone the money left to him by his uncle to assist with The Hollow.

Castian had paid for his college tuition, but back then, it had been up to him to handle his rent and cost of living, as his mother couldn't ever remember to send him money as she would often promise. He'd learned not to count on it, or her, very often. He had hated working for mundanes and worked for them as little as he could afford to, he would rather spend his hours writing more than working, so he had learned how to limit his spending back then.

Stepping into the bedroom, he turned on the small lamp beside the bed, glad he had had the cleaning people stop by the place every other week to check on it. Fresh sheets were on the bed, the blanket folded at the end, and he knew there would be clean towels in the bathroom when he needed them. This he could get used to, as he hated laundry and changing bed linen. He had a small service scheduled to come to The Hollow every few weeks as well, only now, they dealt purely with the first floor. He'd selected an agency that utilized only witches from the cleaning industry, as they knew how to care for supernatural spaces, including some cleansing spells and such—knowing what to touch or not touch, and how to manage their energy signatures. They had also assisted him with packing up his uncle's clothing, the only thing he had known he wouldn't ever need, and donated it to a good resource that helped the underprivileged.

Walking into the second bedroom, which he had turned into a library of sorts, with dark mahogany shelves lining the walls and a central island of the same dark wood to work at when he elected to use his magick here. He opened the balcony door to let in a breeze for a moment. The balcony ran from one bedroom to the other, shallow but enough to move about on, and provided shelter for the coffee shop workers below on their smoke breaks. There was a small table and two chairs out there, with a small grill between the two bedrooms' doorways. He had a planter hanging the length of the railing, the vines trailing down and continuing to do fine despite the lack of consistent care, but some of the herbs had ended their outdoor run for the year. He grew some indoors and would be fine with those but preferred the sunbathed ones when possible.

He felt small hands circle him from behind, her front snuggling against his back. He sensed her impatience, but he had thought they might call in some food first, prioritizing eating after a long day of travel. Nourishment for both of them was good.

But he felt her impatient fingers as they crept below his belt buckle, sliding along the front of his jeans, teasing him.

"Ahhhhhh..." he started, "you aren't finished teasing today, are you? Haven't learned your lesson, little girl?" He was more than half hard, had been throughout the day, really.

"Why, Daddy..." she asked, teasing still, "whatever do you mean?" She slowly unzipped his zipper, working completely from touch, as her cheek pressed closer into his back.

He didn't move, allowing her the moment to tease. She would get plenty in return later. Plus, he wasn't anti-exhibitionism. Just as in the library, he felt intensity boost up a notch at the thought of being watched outside on the balcony as well, although partially hidden behind the vines of the planter. He felt her slide his cock out of his pants, her fingernails grazing, swirling, and stroking his cock to a full hard-on. She slid around him, her ass leaning against the metal rails he had thankfully reinforced upon moving in.

He pushed back her tank straps and flannel off her shoulders, both of them catching at her elbow, immediately baring her breasts to his gaze. He turned her around, bending her over the thick metal rail, and slapped her ass not once but twice. She reared up a little, and he knew she was enjoying showcasing her bared breasts to any neighbors who might happen to look out their back windows or any alley dwellers who might quietly lurk.

He reached around her, unsnapping her jeans, and pulled her pants over her ass. "This is what happens to little girls who don't wear panties without permission," he said, slapping her ass again. He reached in front of her, sliding his fingers along the slit of her labia, already damp. He brought his wet fingers to her lips, where she sucked on them as he pinched and played with her breast for all to see.

Grabbing her hair a bit roughly, he bent her forward again over the metal rail, spanking her, counting aloud to 10. By the time he was done, she was mewling, grinding her ass back against his cock that was throbbing against her pert little ass.

He turned her to face him, kissing her forehead for a moment, and quietly said, "Things happen when you play without permission. Do you understand, kitten?"

"Promise, Daddy?" she said petulantly. Her eyes rolled intentionally, drawing a reaction from him. He'd suspected that was how she might respond.

"Just remember, little girl," he stated firmly, his hand still grasping the hair at the back of her head, "I always follow through on my promises." And he pulled her head down to his cock, pushing her to her knees there on the balcony. She immediately complied, taking his hard-as-sin cock deeply into her mouth. Holding her by the hair, he gagged her little fuckmouth on his cock. Gods, her mouth was so damned sexy. Even when he backed out to let her breathe, her little mouth just begged for him to fill it again and again, taking him as deep as he desired, gagging sweetly as her mascara began to run.

Below, down the alley, there were a handful of girls, some nearby college students, he suspected, stumbling in their slightly drunken states, giggling as they tripped their way around the corner from a local bar scene. One loudly shushed the others and pointed to them, oohing and giggling some more.

The sound of the girls just seemed to make Maggie even more into her cock-sucking job, moaning louder and begging him to fuck her face.

"Mmmmmm…" she moaned, "fuck my mouth like it's yours, Daddy." Her groans vibrating against his cock nearly made him come right then and there, she felt so good.

Morgan just smiled, though, and complied, not even sure how often he was ever in charge anyways. So much of what he did was either because she drew the power up and out of him or because they seemed to make each other so goddess-damn horny. He loved to watch the heat deepen the purple in her eyes when she felt she was complying with his lead, submitting her beautiful intelligence and stubbornness.

He wouldn't change a single moment of her sassy nature, even if she wanted to. It was what made her, her.

He ended up coming on her open mouth and tongue as well as her breasts, as she continued to lick him with one hand wrapped around him while rubbing her own pussy with the other, panting as both hands flowed with her energy, enhancing both of their experiences. He knew she hadn't come yet, but he had plenty planned for her.

"Enough," he said. He took her by the hand and led her back into the apartment, leaving the half-drunk college girls making out with each other in the alleyway. He half wondered if they were making out on their own accord, simply turned on by the show, or if they had somehow inhaled their strong witch pheromones, filled with enhanced sexual pleasure as it poured off of them and into the night.

They would eat dinner later.

He led her to his room, the space already cast in the low light of the lamp. His bed was a dark mahogany and black leather sleigh bed with built-in leather straps at each corner. Long ago, he had had to make do so many times that he had a specialist come in and add the straps in a way that was both convenient and could also be hidden away behind wooden slats if necessary. He couldn't remember the last time he had actually taken the time to hide them.

He led her to the bed and checked in. "Red, yellow, green," he reminded her.

She got up on her tiptoes and kissed his cheek. "Green, Daddy, green," she said, taking off what remained of her clothing while staring him in the eyes and crawling back onto the bed, clearly intending to be cute and sexy in her nakedness. She quickly yelped as he grabbed her by the ankle and flipped her onto her stomach, pulling her ankle towards one of the straps. After closing the soft leather buckle around her ankle, he moved up the same side of the bed, lightly slapping her nipple that jutted out so obstinately as she tried to turn towards him as he was pressing her arm up towards an upper corner strap. He kissed her lips softly from beside her, biting her lower lip as he closed the buckle without even looking.

She giggled as he stalked around her, inspecting her like a lion with his prey, as he attached the other ankle and arm strap on the other side. For a moment, he just stood, leaning against his massive dresser in his undone jeans and bare feet, as he stared at her bare body, tummy down and ass up on his bed.

So petite, so perfect, so feisty.

"C'mon, Daddy," she pleaded, tugging at the straps a little as she bounced her body around impatiently. Her ass jiggled with the movement, only making him smirk.

Noting her impatience, he took his time then, turning to the dresser and pulling out the hidden drawer at the top, wide and shallow, that wasn't just decorative. Instead, its velvet-lined space was filled with all kinds of leather and metal tools for intimate use. He picked up the thin black crop, the tip hosting a piece of soft velvet leather that belied its bite. It was a good introductory tool to pain. He didn't know her limits on pain yet, and he wanted to learn her.

Walking around the bed, he considered his options. He held the crop securely. Snapping it at her ass cheek first, she jumped a bit but giggled. "Is that all you got, Daddy?" she said, shaking her ass a little at him as she turned her face toward him.

"I like crops," she purred.

He couldn't help but chuckle as he also tsk'd at her and snapped the crop three more times at her little wet pussy that was bared to him between her stretched legs.

"Ohhhhhh... Yeah, that's better, Daddy," she groaned. "Do that one again."

Instead of following her orders, though, he reached out and ran a soft finger along her wet pussy lips, her ass arching back, clearly hoping his finger would enter her. Instead, he snapped the crop at her soft puffy lips again and began counting softly—"One, two, three, four..." making it staccato and steady to ten.

"I'll decide what to do next, kitten," he leaned down close to her ear after the end of the count. "I don't need help."

Maggie was gasping, and her pussy lips shone with her desire. He watched as she tried rubbing her tits and clit against the bed sheets, desperate to add to her pleasure. The slight humping motion she was doing against the bed with her hips at each slap only spread his grin wider. Which, of course, he tried to cover up with his serious tone.

"Trying to reach your orgasm, little girl?" he mocked gently. "Don't you know that I own that by now? At least here, tonight, your little cunt is *mine*."

He didn't know if he was going to make it much longer. His cock, hanging out of the top of his unsnapped jeans, begged for her wetness again. He stripped his jeans, now naked and pacing slowly. He stroked his hardened cock as he looked at her, the tip of his forefinger wet with his own precum. He ran the wet finger along her lower lip, and she licked and then sucked it greedily, begging for his cock in her mouth again.

But instead, he turned back to the dresser. He selected the new purple and black flogger from the drawer. He'd thought of this tool just the other day, new to him as he'd bought it shortly after the last sex party he had attended about a year ago. It was the same one used by the other Domme who had been in charge that night. Then he had thought it beautiful, but since seeing Maggie's deep purple eyes and smoke energy that seeped from her even now—he knew it was meant for her.

He saw her hips undulate against the bed again.

He added a pillow below her hips. Knowing she might want to hump against it, he added a firm, "Not yet, kitten." She was likely close.

He flicked the soft suede straps, feathering them initially across her back and sending a feathering of his smoky energy with it. She practically purred with a wave of orgasm as she undulated against the pillow. He flicked them again, knowing the tips stung just a tiny bit as the ends flicked against her ass and cunt. She tried to squeeze her thighs together around the pillow but couldn't fully with the straps holding her in place. He saw her clenching her vaginal walls then, instead, trying to come despite his command to wait. He flicked again with a steady rhythm multiple times but then reached for the thick dildo in the drawer. Moving forward, he climbed on the bed and straddled the back of her thighs. He rubbed his thick cock against her ass teasingly, but he ran the dildo along her wet pussy lips, dipping in just slightly and then pulling back out with the slightly bulging head of the jellied cock, now slick from her wetness.

Clearly, she was ready for something to fill her as she writhed on the bed, raising her ass and trying to seek orgasm. He wasn't quite ready for this to be over yet, however. He turned on the low vibration on the dildo. She arched her ass against his cock, rubbing against her tight hole, as though she would rather have that than the dildo, but he smacked her ass down.

"Not yet," he said firmly, slapping her pussy for additional threat, hearing the wetness.

He inserted the vibrating dildo between her wet and grasping vaginal walls, and she came almost immediately, clenching tightly around the pulsating dildo head.

"Ohhhhhh, fucking godddsssss yessssss..." she ground out, gasping for air as she nearly would have come off the bed were it not for the restraints. Her hips writhed on the pillow, not being able to move very far. But even with the offered release, she still didn't seem quite satisfied.

She began to pant, "Please, Daddy, please..." over and over again at him.

His cock was raging harder than ever. He had planned to wait just a little longer—so many other toys to try together. But instead, he rose up behind her on his knees, the wet dildo still in hand. He rubbed against her pussy with his own hard cock, and then gently began to push into her, in case it wasn't still wet enough.

She was still soaked.

She pushed her little pillow propped ass back against him, saying, "yes Daddy, yes..." and he began to press the still wet and vibrating dildo against her ass. She went a little wild with the vibrations against her asshole, allowing him to push it in about an inch or so before she convulsed again, coming all over his repetitive thrusts into her wet cunt. Leaning even more on his knees and fists over her, he rutted harder and faster into her raised sex, coming again himself, filling her as their smoke intermingled and filled the room with a deep haze.

She lay gasping beneath him, her hair around her, some sticking to her wet mouth. "Ohhhh myyyy godddssss..." she breathed through the echoes of her orgasm.

He needed a second... He felt like every part of him had poured out and into her.

He eventually rose back up, straddling her thighs once more, his softening cock resting in the crook of her ass. He made sure to not fully crush her, but he knew some weight would actually help a little with the grounding needed with sub drop, especially with impact play. He drew her hair back into his hands, smoothing it away from her sweaty face and out of her mouth. His hands ran up and down her back and sides lazily, soothingly, over the red marks from the crop and flogger. Eventually, he decided to softly braid her hair but didn't have a hair band to loop around it at the end, to keep it back, as it kept falling into her face. While messy was hot when his cock was in her mouth, he suspected it was not as enjoyable afterward when sweaty and struggling to catch one's breath.

"Holy shit," she swore. "That was better than any of the play dates I have ever been on." He felt his ego double in size, and smiled.

"I'm glad you enjoyed that kitten," he said. "We should discuss the idea of play dates sometime, though, for sure." Her stomach growled. He laughed, rolling off of her. He gently undid each strap, taking a moment to help the blood flow ease back into her limbs.

He sat beside her naked on the bed as she curled towards him. "I think we need to eat," he said.

"Oh, that sounds yummy," she said in a small voice, still rising out of little space. He tucked a wayward sweaty curl back behind her ear.

"I will order something, but it will likely take an hour to get here," he said. "You can rest, shower, or whatever you want." Her eyes looked sleepy as she closed them.

He pulled on his jeans, sans underwear, and zipped them, leaving the snap open. He padded barefoot to the living area, he settled on the couch as he grabbed his phone to peruse the delivery app. Deciding on the little Italian place down the street that he would have taken her to if they had gone out, he placed the order. Yep, 55 minutes till delivery. He checked on the animals, Xander grumbling that he hadn't refreshed the water yet and that Maggie had put out food for Morpheus, but Morgan hadn't fed him.

Morgan stretched and told his dog he needed to find a she-wolf or something, that clearly it had been a minute for him, and he needed to get some and chill. But he changed the water and put out the dog food, even mixing in a can of beef stew, Xander's favorite. Xander clearly forgave him, forgetting quickly in his rush to down the treat.

Morpheus had curled up on the couch and was cleaning himself, looking like he would be fine for the night. Although he looked pointedly for a moment at the still-cracked window, and Morgan took the hint, closing the open windows as the night air had chilled.

He took a quick shower, as Maggie had fallen asleep for the moment, and he hadn't showered yet today. He also shaved, as it had been a few days and his face scruff was getting thick again.

He was still just wearing a towel around his waist when the doorbell rang, and he didn't hesitate to answer it that way. The young college boy who had delivered more than food to him before looked him up and down invitingly as he answered, causing his cock to rise a bit and tent the towel. But Morgan wasn't feeling like introducing him to Maggie tonight, too many other things to explore between them, so he didn't invite him in as he would have in the past. He knew the young lad had a strong draw toward being ass fucked, and it had been a while for Morgan, but that wasn't his craving for tonight. A young blood-haired girl who was curled up in his bed was.

Closing the door, he heard her behind him. "You could have invited him in, I wouldn't have minded," she said, her eyes sparkling as he turned back. That was one of the best parts about her, they seemed to intuit each other's thoughts so well, and they seemed more and more alike in some of the ways that mattered.

"Maybe next time," he said quietly, setting the packages down on the kitchen counter and drawing her towards him. He set her on the counter in front of him. She had pulled on his t-shirt, but it was thin enough that he could see her hardened nipples peeking through. He couldn't believe how responsive she was. He softly kissed her lips, intent to eat food first before they fucked right here in the kitchen, but he got distracted by her lower lip. Sucking it into his mouth, he bit gently. Her toes ran the length of his slightly hardened cock through his towel.

"Eat," he said roughly, pulling back with some semblance of control. He got down some plates and opened the silverware drawer before going to the bedroom to swap his towel for clean dark jeans. Trying to talk his cock back down, he left the snap unbuttoned, and the zip halfway zipped to relieve the pressure a bit.

Running his fingers through his wet hair, he walked back into the kitchen and found the bottle of cabernet he'd thought he still had. Cracking open the dusty bottle of wine, he poured two glasses, offering her one.

"To a night of fuckery," she said, eyes laughing at his half-undone jeans. She had already made up a plate of salad and some of the pasta, so when he stalked towards her, glancing threateningly between her eyes and the plate, she laughed again and took off towards the couch. "Okay, okay—I'll eat," she promised.

He chuckled, turning back to make his own plate. By the time he joined her, she was sitting criss-crossed on the couch, her little naked pussy peeking out from beneath his shirt at him. He groaned internally at his ever semi-hardened state and shoveled a mouthful of the fragrant red pasta into his mouth. *There's plenty of time,* he reminded himself.

"So, I heard your car is supposed to be ready this week..." he began. They needed to have this conversation.

"Yep. Margot should be ready like tomorrow or something," she said, excitedly, but he noticed her nervously peeking through her lashes at him. Good, he hoped she wanted to stay as well.

"Have you thought about staying on at my place for a while?" he asked, trying to hide his nervousness that she might not want to. Like his mother never stayed around, came up unbidden. "I'd like for you to," he admitted honestly, vulnerably. "I mean, even if just to finish Samhain and assist with Althea's releasing," he rushed to add.

"Sure," she said softly. "For Althea then." They were quiet for a moment.

He couldn't stand the silence. Setting down his plate on the coffee table in front of him, he turned to her. Setting aside her plate for a moment, he cupped her chin and looked at her seriously.

"For us, too," he said quietly. "I'd like to see where this could go if you might want to as well?" he tentatively asked her, softly kissing her forehead above her glasses.

She curled into him for a moment, and he felt her take a deep breath. "I'd like that too," she purred into his chest.

She curled into his lap, and he reached for their plates again. They finished their food curled up like that on the couch. In the quiet, their hearts intermingled, their energies unable to be divided were they even to try. The pets rested quietly in their spaces, Xander softly snoring. He could get used to this peaceful companionship, this beautiful quiet that it brought his heart.

Finishing her food, she leaned back against him with her wine glass in hand. Before long she had dribbled a little bit of wine down her cleavage, and he was unable to avoid following it with his lips, turning her on his lap to face him. Bending her backward, he followed the wet trail down into the t-shirt, suckling her breasts and biting her taut nipples through the shirt, knowing the material added to the sensations for her, intentionally playing with that sensory aspect. She gripped his hair and began to move her little uncovered pussy against his cockhead peeking out of his slightly open jeans. He pulled her hair a bit at the base of her hairline, watching her and simply appreciating the sight of her heavy breathing as she undulated against him in his now wet-spotted shirt, her nipples peeking through, begging for more.

He knew he could assist her, that her clit would already be so reactive—right here, right now.

Instead, he picked her up and took her back to bed, shucking their clothes on the floor, and just lay beside her, trailing his fingers along her petite, lithe body. Fucking her with his eyes. Her fingers came to grip him tightly, pulling at him like she was milking him until he felt close to coming again.

He pressed her hands back over her head, holding them there with one hand and finger-fucking her milky wetness until she was mewling again, begging him to come inside her.

He joined her there, no toys, no straps. Good 'ole missionary style, which was highly irregular for him. They both came together, looking deep into each other's souls, face to face, as their smoke intermingled on the floor beneath them. He felt her magick enhance her orgasm, and thus it enhanced his, as she clenched even harder around his orgasming cock.

After, he tucked her into the crook of his arm as she fell asleep, watching her drift in and out of a state of consciousness, trusting him to be near her like this at rest. She was just so pure, her energy uninhibited in the purest of ways. He wanted to protect her from what he sensed was coming her way, but he had a foreboding sense he wouldn't be able to, that he might not be enough. He tucked away the thoughts and slept as well, reinforcing the wards on his condo before dozing off, knowing Xander or Morpheus would alert them, were anything unusual to occur.

Chapter Sixteen

Maggie

Maggie wished they could stay in the cocoon they'd built the last 24 hours in New York. But the next morning they packed up again and headed to New Haven to visit her aunt as planned, and then they would head on home to The Hollow. Morgan had told her that was what he'd called the space in the mountains that seemed to be carved out just for the dark, old mansion, and it had totally fit.

Wednesday had come and gone. Morgan had shown her around some of his favorite parts of the city, including one of the best little bookstores. They ate at a small, quiet restaurant nearby his place that night, the owner coming out and greeting Morgan, asking where he had been. He boasted about Morgan's most recent book to her, and Maggie had already downloaded the first of his series to her Kindle for the drive. She hadn't mentioned that to Morgan though.

The trip to New Haven was only about an hour and a half, so before she knew it, they were pulling into the quaint, seaside town. The drive along the water had been relaxing, although it was getting a bit too chilly to have the windows down, even with her hoodie on today. Morgan's writing was fantastic, she couldn't believe she had never heard of him before now. He had a way of intertwining the supernatural with mystery in such a way that she now totally understood why mundanes, who wouldn't think magic was even real, enjoyed the books.

She peeked over at him as he focused on the directions. He was such an enigma. One moment sheepish boy, the next, experienced sex god—or witch, she should probably say. Morgan had his Columbia hoodie on, almost passing for a frat boy today with that lock of thick dark hair that often fell over his forehead. She wished she could climb in his lap and rake it back with her fingernails, seeing that boyish light in his eyes grow dark and laser in on her, but she knew they would never get anywhere today if she did.

He reached over and wrapped his hand over hers, bringing it onto his lap while he navigated the last of the drive, rubbing his thumb along her wrist. She thought of where the straps had been before. The leather had been soft, softer than any restraint she had been in before. Hadn't even left a mark she'd need to explain away to vanilla, close-minded folks.

He parked the Suburban on a side street near a small coffee shop. She knew her Auntie's store didn't open until 11, and it was only 9:30, so she suggested they take their laptops in with them for a bit. They cracked the windows for the fur pets in the cool autumn weather, and they went in. Each got a cup of coffee, and she got a bagel. They sat and worked quietly alongside one another on their laptops until the early lunch crowd began to build.

Wrapping up for the time being, Morgan took Xander out of his crate for a quick bathroom break and to stretch his legs. He told her when he got back in the car that Xander had reported that Morpheus knew the town and that the witchcraft community had been here for many generations.

When they pulled up alongside the cute little purple shop, Morpheus insisted he needed to come in as well. He reminded her that Esme liked him and that he knew Esme even better than she did, and clearly, he was right when she hadn't even known her cool Auntie was a witch all along.

The dark wooden eaves that arched out from the grayish-purple siding had built-in spider webs glistening with sparkle, so you knew they weren't real. Maggie knew that the furry fake daddy longlegs that hung over the tall, arching porch was out year-round and not only for Samhain. She sensed her aunt's vibrant energy long before they entered the arched doorway, and she realized she would have known her aunt's signature energy anywhere—enhanced intuition or not.

Morpheus flew out of her arms once they entered the shop, and she heard, "Morpheus, darling!" come from the back of the shop as Esme flew through the swinging doors, her long gray and purple skirts swishing as she swayed almost hips-first into the open space.

"Margaret, my love!" Her enchanting essence flowed around her as she entered the room, followed by the scent of jasmine. She embraced Maggie, kissing each cheek. Turning to Morgan, who stood nearby with Xander on a leash, she leaned into him, pressing a kiss to his left cheek, and assured him the pup could be off leash. "I'm well aware of who you are, young man, and I'm sure your familiar will be fine here, as he seems to be quite the protector," she said, giving Xander a ruffle on his head and a knowing nod.

Maggie knew that her flitting around and not settling easily likely meant she was a bit nervous about the conversation they needed to have, but she wasn't letting her aunt off the hook.

"Auntie," Maggie said firmly.

"Oh, my dear," Esme started. "Do we really need to pull this all apart?" she asked, looking a bit forlorn. "It wasn't my decision, after all. I told them again and again that it wasn't fair to you. I wanted to teach you things all these years—and I did after all—you already know so much more than a beginning witch about crystals and oils and herbs and such," she insisted, looking hopefully at Maggie, eyes begging forgiveness of her.

Esmerelda was smart as a whip, but she was also a bit flighty when it came to emotions. Pops had sometimes talked about how Maggie's Mum had been the typical older child, more stable and constant, while Esme had taken to the younger, light-hearted, irresponsible way of life fairly easily. Maggie knew that sometimes, Esme used her frivolous impulsivity to her benefit—as others didn't always take her as seriously as they should, and she would whip right around and take advantage of the moment as she had already thought five steps ahead of them.

Maggie sighed. Her aunt was right though, she really had found a way to teach her a lot of things that she had already recalled as she explored her mother's books. Not offering a serious apology was her way, as she offered her love and effusive energy instead. She hugged her aunt.

"Well then," said Esme. "Now that that is out of the way, how was your trip? Did you completely wear yourselves out in New York, my dears?" She winked at Maggie knowingly.

Gods. Esme needed to keep her intuition out of Maggie's love life. She flushed.

But Morgan walked up behind her, his hand sliding along her waist and tugging her against him. "Yes," he said, laughing lightly. "But if you aren't careful, I would willingly take her all over again, right here on your polished floor," he said cheekily, playing into Esme's charm. Not many people made Esmerelda blush, so the slight red that rose to her cheeks as she fanned herself was delightful for Maggie. *GOOD! That's what she got for embarrassing her!*

"WELL," Esmerelda said, fanning herself as she moved further into the store. "Don't you two have a special connection, then? Rather scorching even from over here, I do say." But she was smiling as she selected a book from a shelf on the back wall.

"Now, I knew your uncle, you young charmer. A few times, actually," Esmerelda said rather elusively, not elaborating. "All Coven related, of course," she said, but Maggie saw the twinkle in her eye. *Oh, gods. That wasn't weird, was it, that her aunt had slept with her current partner's much older uncle?* She tried not to think about it.

"He was well...loved by many," said Morgan knowingly, chuckling.

"Well, anyways, I'm glad the two of you found each other," Esmerelda said, her tone growing serious. "Especially now. There is trouble brewing, and it's coming your way." She looked pointedly at the two of them. "I somehow knew that no matter what my parents did, Mulligan would find her. This is her journey, and only she can find her way through it."

"I wish I could stop the future from coming your way, darling," she added, wincing. "But I *can* help equip you." She handed her the book. "You will need this in the future, that I can sense." Walking intently around the space, she gathered a few other items as well, a few crystals, oils, and herbs.

"Now, let us have tea," she said decisively.

Over the next few hours, they spent time catching up in her aunt's small apartment upstairs. She had a young witch working the shop that came in shortly after they arrived, and they went upstairs to her small apartment, settling in her living room comfortably among the various plants and Auntie's cat Starla, whom Maggie quickly realized was a familiar as well. How had she missed that all these years? Morpheus' greeting to Starla definitely showed some sort of familiarity between them, more than Maggie had noticed when they had been around one another before.

"Why, they grew up together, Starla as mine and Morpheus your mother's, but he had been around long before that as our great aunt's familiar," her aunt assured her. "Did you know that Morpheus is close to a century old? He would never tell you that, of course, he's rather particular about being referred to as old."

Auntie reminded her of various things she had taught her along the way, previously alluding to them as "hippie." She shared more stories of Maggie's mother and father and mentioned some of the history regarding Mulligan that Maggie hadn't been as aware of, despite reading through so much of her mother's journals already. Mulligan had apparently been interested in both of her parents sexually at one time before they left his employment. Esmerelda filled them in some on Mulligan's known history of dark sexual escapades, including her own brush with him once at a sex party near the Coven capital. She mentioned his dark, intriguing nature and how she had almost joined his group, but her parents had called her to come join them in assisting with something emergent, and she had needed to leave the party early. And how she learned years later that that night a young witch had lost their life. The quiet word in the air was that Mulligan had consumed too much of her powers and drained her that night.

"He is captivating in his darkness," she said. "You must be careful, my love. He has ended more than one witch's life through the years, to be sure. And he is never held accountable for it, as he has the power within the Coven authorities and the local courts to somehow always evade the outcomes of his actions."

"Your parents were so close to finding the evidence needed regarding the death of Talon's father, but also regarding the early takeover attempt of the Coven," Auntie Esme said. "But I've never seen your mother as scared as she was when they went on that last trip. She was fairly fearless, your mother—a real badass, my sister," she sighed. "She still had so much life left to live. Sometimes I feel as though they are caught between this world and the next. But I have never been fortunate enough to see or talk with her to know for sure."

Maggie tentatively mentioned she had at times felt she heard her singing when she would wake from a deep sleep.

"Yes!" Esme exclaimed. "She loved to sing to you, at times, you would refuse to go to sleep without her singing to you as a toddler." Her face saddened, "It was heartbreaking that first year after they died, as you struggled to go to sleep without her sweet voice. None of us could sing as she had."

Esme took a breath and seemed to decide to cheer herself. A smile pasted on until it felt more natural—that was her Auntie Esmerelda.

They had a light lunch of chicken salad, crackers, and fruit at one point, shifting to talk a bit about Althea and the hunt they were on to get her back with her family. Esme shared some insights she had regarding her experiences with crossing between worlds, and Maggie was windblown to learn there were actual other worlds in which to explore, sort of like Dr. Strange's multiverse. Esmerelda stated she felt someone supernatural had to be contributing to those stories, even if they weren't exactly correct most of the time.

"I would happily assist in educating that simply scrumptious Mr. Cumberbatch, however, should anyone ask," Esme said playfully, batting her lashes. And Maggie knew she wasn't even playing.

Later, after Morgan had returned from taking Xander out for a brief walk, Esmerelda looked at the two of them very seriously.

"Now, I know you aren't staying much longer today," Esme said. "I want us to enhance your powers before you go back to Castian's place. Your intentions with Althea are pure, but you will need as much power as you can get. Plus, Mulligan is coming, I assure you. I feel it in my bones."

Esme invited them into the small office she had converted into a magickal space within the small apartment. Low colorful lights, hanging dried herbs, soft carpets, curtains, and scarves hung to soften the eye and the lights even more. She lit a few white candles in the room, using a selenite wand to cleanse the space first. She selected and set out a few dried herbs on the table, peppermint, basil, and a few star anise. She then invited them to sit at the small round table in the center with her.

She lit the large, deep-purple candle in the center of the table and then lit a small gray candle from the many colored small candles around the purple one. She mentioned the purple represented not only their family's core energy but also psychic abilities and powers, including wisdom, knowledge, and authority. The gray she mentioned represented intuition, femininity, and the powers of the moon, which she knew were enhanced for Maggie on her father's side.

She then lit the green one, mentioning it honored the abundant healing powers enhanced by her grandfather's lightwork, the black one for protection from negative energies, and then finally the blue to honor Morgan's energy at the table, and mentioning the blue energy also carried with it a calm, grounding spiritual protection that would be useful.

She spoke for a few moments about her intentions in the coming spell, sharing their powers with one another in order to enhance Maggie's, but in turn, Maggie's would also bless and enhance theirs. She forewarned that a great deal of conflict was ahead, and Maggie would need all the power she could access within her in order to come out successful. Looking at Morgan, she said he would need to find acceptance of himself in a way he had never accessed before.

She invited them to both center their attention on their breath, grounding to the present and then opening their mind, bodies, and spirits to the metaphysical realities around them. She held her hands out to each of them, and they joined energies, hand to hand. Taking a slow breath, Esmerelda's voice rose softly but commandingly to the Universe.

What's mine is yours, what's yours is mine

Let each of our powers cross the line

We offer up our gifts to share

Enhance our powers through the air

Wind, earth, water, spirit, and fire

Elemental energies enhance and never tire

Confusion transcends, all knots be undone

Soon this battle will be won

By the power of three

So mote it be

Maggie felt the energies rising within her, mingling with what she knew was her aunt and Morgan's energies, until she felt them begin to overflow from the tips of her fingers and seep out the corner of her eyes as violet tears that dribbled on the table in front of her. She had heard her mother's beautiful lilting voice rise, joining her sisters in the chant, and she felt a hand on her shoulder that she instantly knew to be her father's energy. She felt the authority of the early moon rising just outside the window as if summoned to her and joining the circle, feeling the sovereignty of generations before her, joining to magnify the energy of the group.

Maggie literally vibrated with energy as she opened her eyes, watching as her aunt snuffed out the candles and offered fresh lavender stems as an offering to the gods and goddesses. Morgan paused and then took the blue candle with the wax still warm and liquid, spilling a bit on the tablecloth, and writing a gratitude sigil of his own in the warm wax. Maggie considered what of her own that she might leave in thanks, and settled on an earring she had worn today, of hematite and amethyst, left in front of her space on the table.

What do you even say after something so life-changing? She hugged her aunt, who had tears streaming down her face, as she had heard her sister's voice as well. They shifted through the room with the dissipating blend of purples and gray smoke low on the ground. They quietly gathered their things and departed, heading back to The Hollow.

Mulligan

Damn witches thought they could best him.

Mulligan stared into his celestial orb, the clouds having parted as he watched the young girl access her powers in a much deeper way, enhancing not only her elemental energies and intuition but her beauty as she dripped purple drops of her spirit that only read as sensuality and lust to someone like Mulligan. He wanted that energy. There was something impressively compelling about hers that far surpassed her young parents' or even her aunt's—the frivolous wench who'd escaped his grasp all those years ago. How had this family avoided him so many times?

He was hungry for their power, *and he would be fed.*

Did they not know that he took what he wanted? Whether they willingly complied or not.

He had some packing to do. He had a private flight scheduled on the morrow.

Chapter Seventeen

Morgan

They both slept in a bit the next day before getting up to get any work done. They had arrived back somewhat late, crashing after a brief dinner and the three-and-a-half-hour drive from New Haven, to get home.

Morgan woke to an empty bed. He smelled coffee, but he lay there for a moment, thinking about his dream that was fading as he woke. He had seen his Uncle Castian from a distance and followed him through the woods, never quite being able to reach him. Castian knew he was there and had glanced back at him periodically, almost as though he wished to be followed. Morgan wasn't quite sure if Castian was trying to tell him something or if the dream was just a reflection of the journey he was on in finding out what happened to his uncle.

He pulled on underwear and some sweatpants and grabbed socks. Maybe he'd take the frustrations of his dream out on the pavement this morning. While it was almost 10, it was still a bit brisk outside with the late October morning, and he thought the cold would do him some good. He walked into the kitchen, grabbing his shoes from the laundry room. Maggie looked like she was grabbing her second cup of coffee already, and he kissed her forehead and let her know his plans. Xander was already ready and waiting by the door, even prancing in place as he laced his shoes.

The brisk morning air hit his naked chest the moment his foot hit the path, deciding to instead take the unpaved path through the woods off the property today. Xander loved this route, as he could wander more freely, away from the eyes of mundanes worried about an unleashed pup on the road.

As his feet pounded the uneven terrain, he thought through the remnants of the dream and what he knew so far. He had dug a little online the last few days since knowing Mulligan Windsor's name and the relation to Castian and Maggie's paternal grandfather. He had read repetitive articles from The Academy from their rugby days, and he understood the three had supposedly been best friends. So then, why kill William so many years ago and his uncle only recently? And why was it Maggie who was in danger now? She wouldn't have even known of the man if she hadn't recently regained her powers and found out from her family. So why would she just now be in danger when it had been nearly 20 years since her parents had been killed?

He had also read some of the Wiccan Weekly archives and seen some of the connections Mulligan had, both in the Wiccan Community and the local London community as well, close to his manor where he supposedly lived. Much of even the Wiccan archives were scrubbed of the darker side of the stories he learned when he investigated some of the darker sides of the web, where he learned of the "Sexcapades" Mulligan was known to throw, where drugs and sex abounded, but even more worrisome were the eventually silenced voices that claimed they had loved ones who went missing at the events.

Mulligan was worth a ridiculous amount of money. As far as Morgan could tell, the man bought and traded businesses like they were pocket change. There didn't seem to be anything he couldn't get his hands on—from economy to people. And, if he had been at The Academy when Castian and William were there, he was likely as powerful as they were, if not more so now if he engaged in the dark arts and lacked spiritual ethics. Morgan had tried to look for the event that both Maggie's grandfather and aunt had mentioned regarding taking over the Coven decades before, but the WitchWideWeb seemed to be scrubbed clean of all mention of it. Morgan wasn't even sure what that might mean.

As he curved around to the other side of the mountainous trail, which created a roughly 2.5 mile loop back to the other side of The Hollow, he also wondered at something that had arisen in his mind while they were in the powerful spell casting with Esmerelda. Moments like that usually weren't very well contained by wards. Morgan knew that when casting, one took the chance that their wards might not be enough to keep other more powerful beings from completely noticing—if their enemy was also supernatural. For so long, the enemy had been mundanes, as for generations they had to keep their magicks hidden in order to even survive, so most wards were not designed anymore to keep witches and wizards out.

On Samhain, the veil between worlds was especially thin, which is what they needed next week in order to assist Althea in traveling from their world to the next to join her family. But such a spell and world travel may place them at risk of being noticed by Mulligan. Morgan could set all the wards he wanted to and even reinforce his uncle's wards on the estate that had kept the older man alive as long as they had—and it could all tumble down on Samhain along with their plans.

And it seemed that no matter how much he problem solved, everyone simply expected Mulligan to find Maggie anyways. Divination had never been Morgan's thing. He wasn't so much of a "my life is fated" person as an "I can change my fate by the choices I make" kind of person. But watching the pain Maggie's family had gone through to try to protect her from Mulligan, and now realizing she may have to face him anyways...was hard for him to accept.

He was damn sure she wouldn't be facing him alone anyways.

When he and Xander got back to The Hollow, he fed the hungry pup and jumped in the shower. Maggie was already hard at her own work, and he decided to push some of his frustration into writing. He wrote for a couple of hours, coming up for air only once to go to the bathroom and refill his coffee. Maggie came in to check on him once, rubbing his shoulders for a moment but then went out to fix herself some lunch. He wrote for another hour still, the creativity flowing better than he could have hoped a month or so ago.

He finally broke away from his train of thought around 2:30 and decided to grab a late lunch. A quick ham sandwich and a sliced apple on a plate later, he went to check in on Maggie. He found her slowly rocking on the porch swing as she thumbed her way through a journal of her mother's.

"You know, it's really rather sad," she said contemplatively, "It seems like my dad had stumbled on some of Mulligan's early story and had felt compassionate towards him. I guess he had grown up really poor, his dad had been abusive to his mom until she left him, and then he had had to watch men take advantage of his mom throughout his childhood to even survive. My mom wrote that early on, she had felt that compassion from my father, and shared it for a while. But eventually, she had felt like Mulligan just didn't seem to remember being a victim anymore, that he no longer had the ability for compassion, but that he had become the victimizer in order to feel powerful."

"She even wrote that what seemed to finally break the bank, was that Mulligan had cornered her at one of their corporate business events in an elevator. He had forced himself on her for a moment before she got away, and when my dad heard about it, he was finally done with his compassion toward him. Ironically, she also wrote that she had struggled with feeling aroused by the force, especially since Mulligan was such a charismatic man. Despite, I guess, my parents being an open couple, she never did tell him that. She felt bad that he lost out on what was a big financial opportunity in working for Mulligan and that he had done it for her. I guess she had felt strongly that they shouldn't go on this last trip, but since it was to avenge his father after he had already lost so much to Mulligan, she went anyways and didn't speak up."He had sat across from her in the chair, pulling it to face her. At this point, he put a bare foot up on the swing alongside her leg and stopped the unconscious swinging.

"How ya doing with all that?" he asked seriously.

She met his eyes. "I don't know. I guess I am feeling a bit uncertain, but I also feel like I know my mother more now. She was very open sexually as well, more so than my father, it seemed, not that he was mundane-rigid or anything. But I get the draw to the sexually violent."

She shrugged. "But it can be hard to talk about sometimes. Not that he had a right to do that to her, Mulligan. They didn't have any kind of trust or agreement or anything between them. I mean, from some of the things you shared, he very well might have killed her eventually through stealing her power—before he finally killed them both in the automobile accident."

He heard what she was struggling to say and could feel her struggle even without words. "You and your mother aren't the only ones who feel alone in being turned on by violence. It can be hard to vocalize. Some sense and are drawn to those animalistic urges more than others. We all have our own inclinations. There is room for our consenting partners to meet our needs with safe agreements and plans when we are ready," he said softly, sending reassurance her way.

"Her not talking about her feelings to my father may be what killed them in the end," she hesitantly said, and he could sense her guilt at admitting it, at thinking such a thought of her mother.

"Mulligan is what killed them in the end," he offered softly but firmly.

She crawled over to him and onto his lap. He wrapped his arms around her as she curled into him, rubbing his scruffy chin gently against her forehead and kissing her there. They sat that way for a while on the sun-warmed porch. He could be content with a life like this...post-Mulligan, of course.

He hoped they had an opportunity to consider one.

"I was thinking about a seance, maybe tonight, to call Althea into the room to make some plans for next weekend. What do you think?" he asked, telling her a bit about his worries that the event next weekend would open a door for Mulligan as well. He was already concerned that the spell casting with Esmerelda might have been sensed in some way. "Whatever we can do to plan ahead will only help us," he finished, thinking aloud.

So together, they made some fresh tea and moved to the library, continuing their exploration of the books in his uncle's study, as well as some of her mother's books. The spread on the conference table seemed incredibly messy, but they did have a system amongst the chaos.

Morgan gathered items from the shelves that they would need tonight, the tablecloth, the candles he selected carefully, and the herbs. He set aside the items needed to cleanse the space at the beginning of the ritual, as well as items carefully selected for gratitude at the end. He poured a small bowl each of both new moon water as well as waxing moon from their tall glass canisters. He needed to make sure and gather more purified water at the next full moon, the storage was nearly empty on that.

Morgan prepared a list of intentions and plans possible for the night of Samhain. He wished he had his uncle's guidance in all of this. He would have turned to him in the past in such situations. He had briefly thought of summoning him, but he did have to figure some things out on his own. Although it was worth a thought regarding what to do with Mulligan. But tonight was about Althea.

They ate a simple Italian pasta salad for dinner that Maggie had thrown together that morning to chill. Morgan cracked open a bottle of Pinot Noir to share with the meal and built a fire in the fireplace to warm them as they ate in front of the fire together, a Spotify channel on the tv casting low tones of simplicity.

Morgan always preferred to have a quiet night to center himself before a ritual. Being able to set aside his own bias and needs was important—to be a conduit of the universal energies needed. Sometimes he would meditate a bit, but tonight the quiet together, the wine, and the waning moon helped him release the energy from the day, setting aside his worries and stress.

When they were ready and the moon was high in the sky, they moved to the study. Morgan led the cleansing rituals with selenite, new moon water, and burning common sage, walking the path around the table slowly three times and instructing Maggie to join and assist. He knew that eventually, she would lead spells on her own just fine, but for now, she continued to feel a bit uncertain, which was normal. Her heart was open and her energies powerful when she focused her intent. It had been a while since he led a ritual with someone else, but it was really much like riding a bike. Enhanced by Esmerelda's spell casting the day before, he felt far more ready and prepared than he likely would have been otherwise.

The pure white tablecloth laid out, he set out the candles, three white and three purple in the circle, adding two black candles for protection, one on each side of the circle. He hoped adding this portion might protect their circle from being intuited by scrying, were Mulligan watching. He spoke the words that opened the circle, putting his focused intentions into the lighting of each candle, first the black for protection of the circle, then purple to enhance supernatural intuition, and then white for clarity and insight.

From east to south, and north to west

We call gods and spirits, to attend and bless

May our work be just, right and true

This circle we cast, may it honor you

He had set 5 flat stones in the angles of the pentagram he knew was below the tablecloth in the center, carved into the wood, calling to the four corners of the earth, spirits, and gods and goddesses to honor them with safety and power.

He then placed the small, shallow tabletop cauldron on top of the stones. He placed dried clove and sandalwood pieces in the pan, along with a few drops of frankincense, lighting it with a match. Bowing his head in honor of the space, he took both of Maggie's small hands in his, across the table from him, and spoke reverently.

Beloved Althea, draw close to us

We open our hearts, we whom you trust

We offer an alter to your presence

As we usher in your essence.

Join us now as the power of three

As we will, so mote it be.

The offering in the center of the table suddenly billowed a small amount as they felt the energy change in the air. Both looked up as they felt Althea draw near. She joined them at the table, taking a seat.

"Hello, my loves," she said, beaming at them. "Am I here for another orgy, or do you have some news for me, I suspect? We can always do both," she added and laughed liltingly.

Maggie giggled. "Oh wow! That was so easy!" she exclaimed, her eyes wide.

Morgan chuckled. "Althea, while that would be lovely, we really called you here to prepare for Samhain. It's just a week away. We think that night will be the best time to reunite you with your family." He looked at Maggie. "However, we think there are some complications."

"No, no," insisted Maggie at Althea's worried face. "Nothing we really want you to worry about. You just need to be with your family!" she rushed in to assure the young ghost.

But Althea looked between them both. "Be genuine," she said softly. "What are you holding back? I can sense it."

"So, there is an old and powerful wizard who seeks to harm Maggie. He killed my uncle, I believe," replied Morgan. "We are not aware of him having any specific plans to find us on Samhain, but I know witches and wizards, and it's a powerful night. He could take advantage of the situation. We just want to be extra careful." He tensed, trying to hide the stress it raised for him, knowing he likely wasn't very successful with these two women, as intuitive as they both were.

"Your uncle is just as fun dead as he was alive, I must say," Althea giggled.

"What the hell, girl, you giving away all my secrets?" Morgan heard his uncle's gruff laughter as a chill ran down his spine. In the chair next to Morgan, he suddenly appeared as though requested.

"Get your chin off the table boy," his uncle chortled. "Yes, it's me. Yes, I've been around. That's what happens when a stupid ass wizard wants you dead. Gotta avenge my death before I can move on with things. Although I am clearly not having as much fun with it as my girl Althea here." His pale, ghostlike hand reached across the table and caressed her cherub-pale cheek.

"Now," he said more seriously. "What are we going to do about all this? I hear Mulligan is after your girl next?"

Morgan was trying to sort through all the unexpected changes. He hadn't planned for this, but he had thought about the benefits of requesting his uncle's presence, so he needed to get it together.

"Well," Morgan said, laying his hand on Maggie's small one again. "First of all, I miss you uncle."

"I hear ya, my boy," Uncle Castian said, voice softer. "I see it too, in all you are doing for me." His uncle's rasp from many years of cigar smoking still lingered even post-death. Morgan even caught the sweet scent of the old Maduros he had favored. Wait, he had wondered why he couldn't get the wafting smell out of the house, thinking it was the old curtains. Maybe it had been his uncle's presence all along.

"Second," Morgan said, always seeming to think in lists. "Yes, this is Maggie. I'm going to guess you are fairly aware of how we met. I do hope you weren't being a dirty old man."

His uncle pulled a cigar out of his pocket, running it beneath his nose for a sniff. Winking at Maggie, he chortled again. "You bet I'm still a dirty old man. But I do like my women to be agreeing, so don't you fret, little girl. I'm not doing anything you haven't approved of. You can always ask Xander."

Maggie laughed out loud. "You do have a penchant for amazing bathrooms, don't you?" she asked him, still giggling.

"Yes, ma'am," Castian smirked, winking again. "I don't stay around too long, though. That old cat of yours usually threatens to tell on me to the mutt. Xander would happily run me off if I took advantage."

Morgan wasn't even fully sure what that was all about. But they needed to focus, or they would lose their intent.

"Okay," he said. "Well, since you are here, let's start with why you never helped Althea rejoin her family." He looked pointedly at his uncle, fairly certain he knew the reason.

His uncle's face grew sad and repentant. "Well, that was all on me, and maybe why I am still here as well. When I met this sweet young thing," he said, gesturing to Althea, "I had just taken over the place from my own great uncle. I was young and just out of The Academy. I had taken work with a Coven in New York, business work. I had an apartment in the city, just like you—but I wanted to be able to get away, and Uncle Quinn had left me the estate. I thought I was a strong wizard then, at the rise of my prime. But how little I knew even then," he grimaced.

"When I began to visit the estate and get it back into working order, I eventually stumbled on this breath of fresh air," he smiled wistfully at Althea and took a long sniff of his cigar again. "I was lonely. I had just left England, heartbroken from ending a college affair. My friends had all gone their separate ways. I have always been more attuned to ghosts. I met them everywhere, really, London is full of them. So, when I stumbled on a young pretty thing like her—remember I was much closer to her age back then—and she offered to help me finish something I had started by myself—ahem," he cleared his throat, "I sure as hell let her."

He smiled widely at Althea, who giggled, "And that was the beginning of an almost half century-long, wide as hell open, torrid love affair." He looked at his cigar again but changed his mind and put it back in his pocket. "I was young and lonely in a new country. But that wasn't an excuse not to do my homework. It was a good year before I took the time to learn more about her, about her family. But by then, I couldn't imagine losing her. When she grew sad, I would cheer her up. Over time, my guilt should have grown. I wasn't a weak wizard even then, I just didn't know how to mess with different dimensions and worlds. Then, by the time I actually started to consider freeing her to her family, I was worried the rituals would open the door for Mulligan to find me." He winced. "So, for a second time, it became about me again. And he found me anyways." He ran his hand through his thick, pale white hair.

"But we will get you released to your family. Of that, I am sure," Castian stated firmly, his eyes focused on Althea, who blew him a forgiving kiss.

"So, uncle," Morgan began, "what else can you tell us that might help? I was just explaining that your old friend Mulligan may be targeting Maggie next. And I would like to avoid her being noticed on Samhain as well, if possible."

Castian turned to Maggie again. "You are Wil's granddaughter, am I correct?" he asked her directly. When Maggie nodded in the affirmative, he continued, staring off into space. "I didn't quite realize that moving to the States after we all separated might've saved my life."

"Mulligan had been growing in power while we were all still at The Academy together, and somehow Wil and I just didn't seem to recognize it." He took another long sniff of his cigar. "Mulligan had always been a bit of a trickster of sorts back then, wanting to win at all costs. It wasn't as bad as it has become now when we all first met. But every taste of power that he received seemed to go straight to his noggin. I didn't learn until almost twenty years later that he was the one who killed William. It was such a terrible tragedy when we all learned of his death, leaving young Talon and his mother as a widow. I had never dreamed Mulligan would harm anyone other than when he would do anything to win. But I didn't know that Wil had stumbled on news that I still think very few Coven Council even know. I myself only stumbled on it in an old journal of Wil's that was sent to me after Selene's death."

He looked at Maggie sadly. "Your maternal grandmum loved you. Enough that she participated in that plot with your grandmother to protect you. Yes, I know about that. It was in Selene's letter to me with the journal, to be delivered to me on her death." He looked at Morgan. "You should find those in my lower left desk drawer. I know it's been difficult to face my death, face my things. But find that, it's useful."

He sniffed his cigar again. "Anyhow, the journals outline William's awareness that Mulligan had been selected by old Kragon to fulfill an alignment with Atë, the goddess of mischief and folly. She had somehow promised them power of some kind after she attained control of the Coven Council. When Wil confronted old Kragon and Mulligan, it did not seem to go well, but the journal ends there. It was shortly after that that his car was found at the bottom of a ravine. Much like my old roadster." He grimaced. "She was such a beauty, my baby girl," he said sadly with another long sniff of the cigar.

"I began to research quietly. I had known over the years that Mulligan had changed. Grown in power and took advantage of others for it. No matter what those of us under the Crown did to investigate him, we couldn't seem to get close enough to catch him where someone didn't die, or he couldn't get his lawyers to get him out of it. Damn scoundrel," he harrumphed. "I knew if I wasn't careful, I might end up in a ravine as well, especially once my search led me to the deaths of Talon and

Allegra. I actually wasn't aware of you, until old Selene's letter. Mangus did a good job there, he did."

"I never was quite sure why they were choosing the path they took with you, your grandparents. But I kept their secrets, they weren't mine to share. And I continued my own quiet investigations into Mulligan. But he remained ever the trickster. I knew that with Wil's death being so like your parents, they had to both be by Mulligan. But finding proof was nearly impossible. I was just investigating a new lead when I heard from Mulligan, and then next thing you know," Castian motioned, his throat cut. "The information on that lead is with the journal and letter in the drawer, boy. I suspect there is something to be found there, or I wouldn't have become a threat."

"You know," he said, "old Mulligan called me right before the accident. He tried to ply me with money and power and sex. Can you believe that? Like that would work on me at this age when I already had everything I wanted."

Castian leaned toward Morgan, "Now show me your plan."

Morgan pulled out his notes, going over the ideas he and Maggie had come up with together the last few days. But he hadn't been able to think of anything additional for protection other than the usual wards, candles, and talisman. He pointed out Maggie's pendant, but his uncle agreed that it wouldn't be enough. Not even Mangus was as good as Mulligan would be on Samhain.

Old Castian got up and began to pace in front of the library shelves. He would stop every now and then to leaf through an old book of history or spells.

"Your releasing ceremony looks intact," he approved. "Esmerelda's additions were perfect. She always was a bright young witch. Talented mouth as well," he said, smiling to himself. But then he glanced briefly at Maggie. "I should apologize, but I do believe you understand your aunt fairly well."

Maggie nodded and then chuckled.

Castian stopped for a moment and pulled out a rather large, leather-bound book from the corner of his desk. "I'm surprised I haven't thought of this," he mumbled, leafing through the book quickly. He settled on a page about three-fourths of the way to the end. "Yes..." he mumbled, sticking the unlit cigar in the corner of his mouth, "Yes, that's it."

He brought the book to the table and laid it open. Morgan saw that it was his uncle's old grimoire. Why hadn't he thought to look there? Oh yeah, he was avoiding it. He glanced over the spell his uncle had opened it to. Morgan raised his eyebrows.

"Well, if anything would work, that would," Morgan said slowly. "If we all don't go to hell for it."

Chapter Eighteen

Maggie

If Morgan were anything like his uncle, he would be one happy, quirky man to grow old with.

Maggie couldn't believe she had thought that thought. She had known him for only a few weeks, and already she was considering spending the rest of her life with him? She tucked that in her back pocket for now as she poured her first cup of coffee the next morning. Too much other stuff to freak out over.

Like dying. They all might die.

If Mulligan didn't kill her, this spell they were talking about doing damn near might. But it also could be the absolute best moment she might ever be alive. But she wasn't going to get ahead of herself. *She had a lot of living she wanted to do in the next five days if she might die.*

Maggie thought Morgan might be feeling the same way. While her first thought had been "*try all the toys he brought home from New York*" last night, she was content with the slow and sensual, and simple lovemaking they enjoyed. Like they might not have another tomorrow. Like maybe he was coming to care about her as much as she was about him. And really, that had been better anyways.

Morgan definitely had the better shower, though, of their rooms. Better bath too, but she still liked the clawfoot one in her own bathroom. But for a quick shower, she was using his. She walked back into the bedroom with her coffee, but noticed he must have gotten up, as the bed was empty. Having similar thoughts, she noticed, as she saw he had hopped in the shower. The window was cracked, making the bathroom a bit chilly, so she stripped down and got in quickly—where it was warm and steamy.

"Happy to see me, are you?" he quipped as he noticed the chill to her nipples. He wrapped her in a warm and wet, soapy embrace and kissed her good morning. He had already washed his hair and his hands were all soapy from being mid-wash on his body. She had also noticed when she stepped into the bathroom that he had had his cock in hand.

"I mean, don't let me stop you from what you had going on," she said teasingly, stepping back to sit on the edge of the black-tiled seat, letting the steam envelope her and warm her after getting somewhat wet by his embrace.

He looked at her, his eyes darkening to a smokey gray, as he took his cock back into his hand. He slowly stroked it a few times, his thumb lazily stroking over the head as he let the water cascade down his body from over his shoulder, washing the soapy suds down the drain.

Maggie leaned back on the tiled shower seat, taking her nipples in hand, as she watched him look at her, stroking his thick cock, knowing he was imagining her mouth on him. She brought her feet up on the edge of the seat, spreading her legs, and began to play with her clit with one hand, her other still at her breast.

Morgan reached over to a small switch in the shower, and she saw the second shower head over her head come on and then watched as he took the shower head off its handle and began to fiddle with it. *Fuck*, it was a handheld, *and* it had different pulsations. Maggie watched as he smiled to himself and knew she was in for it. *Goody*, she smiled.

He stroked himself again, walking closer to her. "Let's try this, kitten," he said quietly. Using the handheld nozzle, he brought the pulsing water to her breast where she had been pinching. Its medium pressure wasn't too soft but didn't do too much. As he adjusted the settings on the shower head, she reached for his cock head. Bending to reach him in her seated position, she took him in her mouth.

Around wet lips sliding on his cock, he played with her and the different pulsations of the shower head, eventually turning the shower head on a high strong stream, which made her forget everything about his cock for a moment as she came with the pulse of the water against her clit.

As she moaned the last of her orgasm, he picked her up, and he sat on the tiled seat, positioning her facing away from him, legs on each side of his seated position, as he sat her right on the length of him. She moaned again as he filled her. He turned the pulsating shower head back onto a steady flow. She felt the water pulsating against her sensitive clit, and she suspected it also hit his hard cock and balls just right as he began to move his hips more intensely. She leaned forward on his wet knees as she rode him, allowing the pulsating water to take her up again rather quickly as he filled her this way.

"Fuuuuckkkkk," Morgan groaned out as he came, guiding her hips and pressing into her one final time, even deeper than before. Maggie caught the vision of their wet nakedness out of the corner of her eye as the steamless mirror beside them reflected the final arch of her back as she came again.

The water from the remaining shower head on the wall cascaded over the bottom half of their legs as the one in Morgan's hand continued to flow against their connected bodies, only he had turned it on the soft rain setting now, soothing them. Maggie was panting as she came back down to earth, watching their purple and gray swirling and washing down the drain with the water. Maggie giggled. *Who knew one could orgasm pretty purple sparkles?*

She felt Morgan start to shift, and he moved the shower head he held in his hand to begin to get her hair wet. She tilted back her head, enjoying the sensual care, still connected to him, even though he was receding out of her slowly. He took the shampoo bottle from the seat nearby without having to move and began to wash her hair for her.

She could definitely get used to this. She wasn't sure what was better, shower sex or having her hair washed for her.

"It's a good thing this huge place has an endless supply of hot water," Morgan chuckled in her ear.

"But that is so dangerous for the hot water bill..." Maggie groaned. She was not in a rush, though. Morgan applied conditioner to her hair like he was a pro, ends first. Then he lathered the soap sponge that she had added to the shower with her preferred lavender and amethyst soap from the other bathroom, using both his hands and the sponge to wash her body from behind her. Both hands ran all over her, washing every part, getting caught for a few extra moments on her breasts and then further down below as well.

"Can we stay in here alllll day???" asked Maggie, as he used the shower head to rinse her body and hair, staying on the soft rain setting to soothe, even when Maggie wondered if he might turn the pulsating on again. She knew they had to get going. They needed to get into town and get a few things for the week, along with picking up Margot. Plus, eventually get some work done, being Monday and all.

Morgan chuckled again. "While that would be lovely, that wouldn't be good for mother earth," he reminded her, kissing her shoulder as he stood her up in front of him, facing him, for a final rinse of the soap suds. He stood, backing her slightly into the spray of the shower head on the wall with a steamy kiss, and hung the additional shower head up.

Maggie sighed deeply, content after soapy orgasms. She dipped her head back into the spray and finished rinsing the conditioner from her hair while she watched him rinse himself off in the other stream of water. When she was finished, he gave her a final brief kiss while reaching around her to turn off the water.

Thankfully, there was a towel warmer because the chilly breeze in the room was especially cold after all that heat.

Maggie was startled for a second when Althea appeared, sitting on the edge of the bathtub and watching them as Morgan wrapped a towel around his waist and handed her another.

"I sure will miss watching the two of you," Althea said, appearing saddened at the thought. She stepped up behind Maggie in the mirror with another towel and towel-dried her hair, reaching for the amethyst brush to begin working it through her wet, dark waves gently for her.

"We will too…" Maggie agreed, tingling from all the care she was receiving. Morgan had stepped into the walk-in closet off the bath, dropping his towel as he traded it for underwear and his usual black jeans.

"But you will be with your family, where you belong," Morgan said softly. "That is what matters most," he said as he stepped up next to them in the mirror. He began to take out the items he used to shave. Maggie did enjoy his rough scruff, but watching him apply the lather in just his unsnapped jeans was rather sexy too. His pitch-black hair was getting a little longer, curling a bit at the ends.

She watched in the mirror as he slowly scraped a line of lather off his face as next to him, Althea combed Maggie's wet hair. She felt so much contentment in this domestic moment between the three of them, but she knew it wasn't meant to last. For sure not Althea, but she was also afraid of the same thing for her and Morgan.

But Maggie didn't like the way that thought was going, so she kissed Althea's cheek, and moved toward the closet. Since they had begun to sleep together, gradually, her clothing was ending up in his closet. Not that he didn't have plenty of room—more than half of the walk-in closet was still empty. She hung her towel on the door as she reached for a pair of purple panties from the metal basket she had taken over for her intimates.

Walking back into the bathroom in just her panties and glasses, she reached for her ponytail on the counter as Morgan finished the last of his shaving. Looking at her appreciatively as she stood there in the mirror, twisting her wet hair up into a top knot. He continued to watch them as Althea reached from behind her, cupping her breasts.

"This is what you wish you were doing, is it not?" Althea asked Morgan.

"It is," said Morgan, definitively. "But we will never get anything done today if you girls get things started again." He smirked, but his eyes had a smoky luster to them.

"Well, drat," said Althea, as she tweaked Maggie's taught nipple but then walked out of the bathroom haughtily.

Maggie felt Althea's presence leave, and she could tell that Morgan did as well, as he winked at her. Maggie couldn't believe what her life had become. Not the 'standing around naked and fucking all the time' thing. She had lived with pansexual and explorative roommates in college. It was more the 'poly with a ghost' kind of domesticity.

Maggie finished dressing, wearing one of her usual white tanks and jeans with a clean purple flannel, despite bringing a few more clothing options after stopping at her grandparents. Her pendant gleamed in the sunlight flooding the bathroom, reminding her they had a big week ahead of them.

Morgan grabbed a dark gray v-neck, pulling it on over his head. "Let's go get Margot."

Morgan

Traveling by classic car was fantastic. Traveling by classic motorcycle on an autumn day in the northeast was even better. Morgan had had Maggie wear his uncle's leather jacket, which practically engulfed her. But he knew she would be cold otherwise. When he pulled the rumbling Harley Davidson around the corner of the house, she had gotten so excited that she had bounced right down the porch and onto the bike. The ride together into town with her arms and thighs wrapped around him as they leaned into each curve had been even better. The mountainside was so beautiful in the autumn.

Morgan still wasn't sure when the intensity between them might dissipate to more normal levels. Even after sex in the shower, he had been just about ready to pounce her when Althea had tried to start things again. If Maggie had turned and started to make out with the younger girl, he might have caved quickly, he was pretty sure.

So, when Maggie ran her fingernails down his belly to find him partially sporting a hard-on on the ride, she shouldn't have been surprised. But she hadn't pushed it, and though he could feel her chuckle against his back, she returned to clasping her hands around his waist. Otherwise, he would have had to pull over and take her right there on that goddess-damned bike on the side of the road.

Edging into his awareness was the consideration that it might be because they potentially only had five days left of this whole thing. *Who was he kidding, he knew she felt the connection between them too.* He sensed that well enough.

He meandered the long way, enjoying the last of the colors on the trees as they wound around the mountain road in the chilly autumn wind, headed towards Rochester. He remembered taking this old bike out when he was 17. His uncle had trusted him with it, and he had thought he was the shit. The girls had been drawn to him, his darkness emanating from him on this badass motherfucker, a rumbling engine between his legs—in more ways than one in his youth. Most of the guys had just wanted to *be* him. Other than old Mike's grandson, Alec, who had been in his advanced English class. He had been impressed enough to actually ask for a ride—again, in more ways than one. Morgan still wasn't sure if Mike had ever known about him and Alec. He'd heard Alec had married a few years ago and seemed happy enough, according to his uncle. But for just a moment, he had a flash of bending Alec over the Harley, out on old route 91, by the old cabin.

They arrived at Mike's not too much later. Ironically, Alec was there with his wife, picking up her '86 Corvette, which had just had its convertible top repaired. Morgan listened as Mike proudly talked about his great-grand-baby on the way by the two, but Morgan also noticed Alec stutter the introduction of Morgan to his wife, whose eyes seemed to flick between the two men knowingly.

Morgan wasn't interested in helping people cheat on their spouses if they were monogamous. But it was definitely still there, that attraction between them. Alec had reportedly gone into finance and did fairly well for himself, looking fantastic in his tailored gray suit, his slicked-back blond hair freshly cut like the affluence he carried. Morgan allowed himself just a brief moment of imagining him on his knees in that expensive suit, feeling confident Alec would likely still happily take orders—before he cut off the imagery. He knew he was half hard again in his jeans and didn't mind when Alec's eyes strayed down just a little longer than they should have. He wasn't surprised at that point.

But he didn't look again as Alec and his wife left, his wife gushing about Maggie's car while Maggie looked at him, smirking with knowing eyes and a wide smile.

"You have totally fucked him before!" she exclaimed teasingly the moment they got far enough away from the shop that Mike couldn't hear. Laughing and nodding, he opened the door for her as she got in Margot. She ran her hands lovingly over the leather steering wheel cover. "Oh, my baby girl..." she cooed, sighing as she took in having her beloved car back. Starting her up, Margot purred to life in response.

Turning her attention back to him, she raised an eyebrow and said, "Don't think you are getting out of this story. I need to have it, eventually. It sounds *hot*. But where are we going from here?"

They made plans to run by a few stores, getting a few final items for Samhain, as well as the grocery store for everyday mundane living. Maggie also mentioned needing to stop for gas before heading back home. Hearing her call The Hollow home, did something pleasurable to his gut. Something sweet, which of course was followed with the worry it might not last. But he wasn't going to think about that.

By the time they got home, it was well into the afternoon. They grabbed sandwiches and split to different parts of the house to work. The temperature had dropped outside some today, so Maggie was setting up in the formal dining room that never got used. The long, dark-walnut table sat 12 people, with a matching buffet against one wall. The other wall had empty built-in shelves with running lights to display expensive china or special items. The room hadn't been used in decades, as he and his uncle had always eaten in the sitting room while watching TV. He mentioned it would be easy to set up an office in her suite across the hall from their bedroom or even just add a printer on the buffet here. The second idea was thrown in when he realized how much the first sounded like something long-term.

They really just needed to see if they survived this week first.

Morgan settled at the desk in the office on the second floor, almost immediately reaching for the lower left drawer. He hadn't had a chance to follow up on what his uncle had mentioned since last night. He pulled out the journal, the letter tucked inside and a file beneath it. Setting aside the journal and letter for later reading, he perused the file briefly. Interesting. There were some photographs taken of a younger man with a much older man, as well as what he might guess was a female ghostly deity. The same goddess and the younger man were in a handful of others, in a place that seemed otherworldly. He noted a few jotted notes in his uncle's handwriting, catching the names of Mulligan, Kragon, and Atë. There were a few printed-off emails as well, between Mulligan and Kragon. And there was a death investigation report for what looked like the elder Kragon Night.

He set it all aside and, for now, turned back to his computer. The frustrations and fears for the upcoming week, the mystery before him, and even some of the memories of Alec became fuel for his work.

He surfaced much later, not noticing the time fly by until it was almost 8. As he checked the time, he noticed a notification come through of an email that looked like it might be from Alec.

```
7:54pm


From: AMeister@gmail.com


To: MSmithe@gmail.com


Subject: Still here?


So, not sure if you still use this old email address. But thought I'd reach
out. Care to meet for a drink, for old times sake? It was nice seeing you
today. If you are up to it, I'll be at the old bar on 91 around 10pm.


-A
```

Morgan sat with that for a moment, his cock still somewhat stiff from the sensual scene he had just been working on between his protagonist and the assistant, which he had fueled with some of his memories from Alec. It had been a while since he had his cock in a man's mouth. And while it might be presumptive, he knew where this was likely to go. He wasn't a fan of secretive liaisons, however—from either side.

He set aside his work for the night. They needed dinner anyhow.

Walking into the kitchen, Maggie was just wrapping up preparing some chicken and freshly steamed vegetables. She was working at the stove in her short cut-offs and one of his t-shirts, and braless as usual. She saw him and smiled, turning to the sink to wash her hands as she said, "It's just about ready, I was getting hungry."

Walking up behind her, he pressed his hard-on into her ass as he roughly pushed into her from behind, grabbing a nipple as he sunk his teeth in gently to her neck.

"Well damn," she said, immediately panting as she tipped her head to the side, giving him better access to her neck, her wet hands coming up and back into his hair.

He spun her around and ground his pulsating cock into her pussy there against the sink, growling as he captured her mouth.

"Well, I mean, *fuck*," she said breathlessly as she pulled back and looked him in the eyes. "Not that I won't take it, but dinner is ready, and I'm not even so sure all of that is about me?" she insinuated, a twinkle in her eye. He pulled back a little, realizing she was right. Her nipples were still tight against his shirt. She moved around him to take the vegetables off the burner and uncovered the chicken.

Turning back to him, she put her hands on her hips and cocked her head at him. "Sooooo writing or Alec?" she asked cheekily.

"Both?" he both asked and answered. Taking plates down, they began to spoon their food onto them.

"I was working on a sex scene in my newest book before coming down to find some dinner," he mentioned.

"Oh, interesting!" she responded. "I didn't notice any intimacy at all in the first of the series. I just finished that earlier. It was fantastic, I can't wait to start the next one."

Honored that she was reading his book, he expanded for a bit about how this was the first book he was going to incorporate any kind of detail regarding sex while also being the first book where a relationship occurred between two men.

They moved into the sitting room.

"You seem uncertain about that?" she asked.

He explained a bit more, "I'm hesitant to incorporate many of the more openly sexual aspects about supernatural folks when mundanes can be *so goddamned rigid*. I have a decent chunk of both as reading fans. While I'm hesitant about losing a potential large following of mundanes," he sighed deeply, "I'm also tired of limiting my writing to please everyone. Especially in areas that really are very healthy and normal and had been for centuries in many cultures."

Maggie agreed with him, sharing that she had struggled a bit in college with how much more open and free she felt than many of her friends.

"My undergrad roommate and I were involved with each other for a while, and we seemed to help some of our friends open up more too. Jenny was always really open." She paused and considered. "I wonder if she might have somehow been supernatural of some kind?" Maggie wondered thoughtfully before shaking her head briefly, her eyes focusing on him again.

"But you also mentioned Alec. Tell me more about him," she encouraged acceptingly.

While they finished eating, he gave her a brief background of Alec and how he had been interested in the bike his senior year in high school, likely because of his grandfather's love of old vehicles. How that had turned into much more after the long bike ride, and how they had hooked up a handful of other times throughout the rest of his senior year, gradually shifting into some Dominant/submissive play when they would meet. But they had never acknowledged anything other than basic friendship everywhere else, especially at school.

Morgan knew some people just struggled with accepting all sides of themselves. The feminine and the masculine existed within them all, and Morgan hypothesized that many more people than not would appreciate pleasure in many forms. Sadly, current mundane culture far too often ostracized what felt different. Witches had embraced what was different from the start, often being far more open to the intuition of all creation around them, including but not limited to sexuality.

Maggie nodded her head. He picked up on the fact that she found his story erotic and would willingly accept his frustrations were he to take them out on her. But he also sensed her greater acceptance. So, he mentioned the email.

"Well, I mean, do you want to go and see what happens?" Maggie asked, smiling at him. "I actually have to be on a guest lecture tonight that's in a weird time zone, so it's at 11. I really am okay if you were interested in meeting him tonight."

He gauged her response, both in word and energy, assessing it to be honest and true.

"If you are okay with that," he tentatively nodded. He'd been with other polyamorous witches or wizards. They had just never *mattered* to him this much.

"Just, you know—protection or tell me if not," she said, winking at him and reminding him of his original words. He knew he wasn't interested in sharing medical concerns with his various partners either, so if he played openly, it was always with protection.

"Always," he assured.

He noticed the time, and after he put his plate in the dishwasher, he took a quick shower. He traded one pair of dark jeans for another, pulling a black v-neck over his head. Running his hands through his wet hair, he grabbed his leather jacket and took the Harley, as he had left it in the front from earlier. It seemed appropriate anyway, given the history.

He arrived at the old bar on 91 just after 10:15. He wasn't sure how long a straight-laced financier would wait for an old friend, but he saw him sitting alone in a booth in the back corner, nursing a beer.

"Hello," he said as he slid in across from him. Letting the bar girl know he'd take one of whatever his friend was having.

Alec looked a bit nervous, his eyes quickly scanned the mostly empty bar on a late Monday night.

Morgan smiled patiently. Yep, he knew why he had messaged.

They talked for about an hour or so about how life had been the last decade, school and business for both of them as they developed their careers. Morgan was a gentleman and didn't bring up any uncomfortable subjects, allowing Alec to lead the way for now. If anything were to happen here, he wanted everyone to be on the same page and ready for it.

Things eventually grew quiet and a bit more awkward. Morgan began to figure that he likely might go home with his cock still half hard. Which was fine. He'd enjoy Maggie and maybe Althea, who had seemed disappointed this morning.

"My wife knows," Alec suddenly blurted out. Awkwardly meeting his eyes, the intensity suddenly growing between them.

"She knows...?" Morgan raised his eyebrow, asking for more.

"About us...before..." Alec stuttered out. Rubbing his mouth and chin, he sat up straighter. "She's actually way cooler about it than me, I think. I wasn't the only person she openly dated in college. But she's my best friend, and sex is fine between us. But she knows sometimes I...I crave something else..." he hesitated.

"You haven't been the only one," Alec said quieter, looking around again to make sure no one could hear him. "But no one else has ever been quite like you..." he swallowed, their eyes meeting again.

Morgan noticed the grey smoke at the tips of his fingers and tamped down his response. It had been a while since he had fucked a mundane. He had to keep that part of himself turned off.

"Up for a ride?" he asked, offering the privacy that he knew would make Alec feel better.

Alec's eyes lit up, and he agreed, quickly setting a 50 dollar bill down on the table to more than cover their two drinks and a hefty tip for the young girl working the bar. Morgan had barely nursed half of his, knowing he might drive.

Alec had left his suit coat in his car, but he loosened his tie and undid the top button of his shirt as Morgan handed him the extra helmet from the compartment beneath the seat. Tightening his own, he felt Alec swing his leg over and climb on behind him, taut abs and cock ridge flush against Morgan's back.

He remembered that cock.

Morgan started the Harley, not sure he didn't growl himself along with the old hog. Alec's hands came to rest on his lower abs, just a hands-width away from his throbbing cock. Morgan peeled out of the old bar drive and headed down the old, dark road of their past. Periodic streetlights flickered as they rode the empty old highway through the mountains late at night. After a while, he felt Alec's hands begin to tentatively investigate, slowly moving and exploring underneath Morgan's shirt and jacket. Running his soft fingertips and short nail edges over Morgan's clenched abdomen and even lower, slowly moving toward where Morgan had been wanting all along.

Alec's fingers began to explore the ridge of Morgan's cock through his jeans, eventually becoming impatient and unsnapping and unzipping him to circle the wet, uncovered tip. Morgan approached their old spot, the abandoned cabin along the highway by the river. He wasn't quite sure how someone hadn't torn the old thing down yet, but it offered shelter from the road and from prying eyes for a much more private Alec.

As Morgan slowly pulled the old Harley around back, parking, Alec pulled him fully out of his unzipped pants, stroking him slowly and firmly. Morgan got off the bike, pulling Alec off with him, barely getting their helmets off before he had Alec against the outside wall of the cabin, mouths fused intensely. His hips fucked into Alec's hand as he continued to hold him tightly, pumping him until Morgan came with spurts, Alec dropping to his knees to capture the spurts with his mouth, sucking him until he began to recede.

That one had been coming on all afternoon.

The streetlight on the other side of the cabin flickered, although they were in the dark shadows anyways. Morgan took Alec by the hair, pulling his head back and off his softening cock.

"Such a good little cock sucker," he added, knowing what turned Alec on. Or at least he had. But he wasn't disappointed, as Alec's eyes lit up, panting on his knees in front of Morgan. Morgan had known he would enjoy the sight of him with his pretty suit knees dirty. He pushed him back and walked away from him, leaving him to get himself together and follow him into the old cabin.

They had done this before, it wasn't new. Alec liked a little degradation. His pretty little rich boy ass liked to be taken down a peg or two. It only made him hornier. And the darkness of the cabin often allowed Morgan to infuse a little magick to enhance Alec's orgasms. He figured that was what Alec had meant by no one else ever being quite like him, the blond kid had never found another witch to be fucked by.

He cautiously opened the old cabin door, hearing Alec following him not far behind like a nervous puppy. Alec had always been afraid of the dark unless he was blinded by lust. Once they were inside the old cabin, Morgan took pity on the mundane and pushed him against the wall with the nearby window. The moonlight cast its glow, lighting the space nearby enough that the two men could just see each other well enough.

Morgan grasped Alec's tie at first, twisting it in his hands until the blond's bright blue eyes went wide, Morgan's fists tightening the tie against his Adam's apple. The lack of oxygen for a moment, heightened the puppy dog eyes. "Please..." Alec barely got out, shifting right back to their pattern of 10-plus years ago.

Morgan let go of the tie, pulling it loose and letting it hang down both sides of the financier. He gripped the shirt where it came together at the top button, pulling hard as the buttons popped off down the front of the shirt.

If his wife didn't know, she would wonder, at least.

"YES!" Alec exclaimed excitedly at the increased aggression. So, Morgan took the loose tie and wrapped it once around the blonde's mouth, tying it tight behind him. Morgan figured Alec could still talk around the tie, as this wasn't a first for him. But he also remembered how much Alec had enjoyed the feeling of being gagged.

Morgan ran his hands roughly up and down the man's chest. Mostly still fit. A little bit of soft tummy at the waist didn't surprise him, as finance didn't require much activity. Alec's nipples were hard as a rock as Morgan twisted one, slapping it gently at first. Alec's eyes rolled back into his head as he lulled his head back and groaned. He was nearly coming out of his suit pants, a wet spot just forming near the tip of his penis under the material.

Morgan took the man's belt off. Snapped it, but set it aside for now. Alec had always appreciated the threat but hadn't responded well to the actual pain of the belt when they had tried that before. But it did come in handy for additional bondage if needed. He undid the front of the trousers, letting them slide down to the man's ankles. White traditional underwear, some things never changed.

Morgan gave them a yank on one side, ripping the cotton, and it hung precariously off one hip. Alec's mouth dripped drool around the now wet tie, his eyes on fire, begging for more. Morgan took the pleading man's smaller but throbbing cock in hand, the tip pulsating and wet with pre-cum under his thumb, infusing just enough magick to enhance and not release much smoke in the shadows. He gripped the cock a little harder than some might, milking the straight-laced financier as he begged to be fucked.

Morgan turned him around, the blonde's face to the wall, still gripping him from behind. His own cock had begun to harden again.

"You want to be fucked in your tight little ass, don't you cock slut?" he ground out into Alec's ear, pressing his cock against the man's ass through the hanging dress shirt as they leaned into the wall. Morgan's hand continued to pump the panting and slobbering blond, no longer all put together and pretty. He enhanced his magick just a bit more with a final tug, and the man burst with orgasm, releasing a stream of cum that Morgan was counting on. His hand wet, he pulled up the back of Alec's hanging shirt, rimming his asshole with his hard bare cock. He slipped the condom from his pocket out, ripping it open with his teeth and sheathed himself. He used the remainder of the semen to wet his protected cock.

"You thought about this all day too, didn't you?" he whispered roughly into Alec's ear, pressing in a little at a time at first. "About how it feels to have a hard cock in your ass in a dirty, dark old cabin where anyone could find us at any time." He pushed to heighten Alec's excitement—the fear, the intensity, the awareness. He felt himself sink in fully. "Your wife's pussy feels good, but it's nothing like a good ass fucking, is it?" he asked, knowing he was talking to Alec but also to himself.

Alec nodded eagerly, his answer muffled by the slobbered-on tie. His hands free, he was playing with his own cock again, and Morgan let him. He gripped the back of the blonde's hair tightly, jerking as he began to pound into him. Alec began to jerk off furiously again, and Morgan knew he would come soon.

"Take my cock, you little cock fucker. Little cum slut," he grunted darkly as he exploded into the man's ass, groaning in release. The tightness of the financier's ass had sucked his cock right in, and dear gods, it had been a while since he'd had this. He leaned against him, against the wall that barely held them up. It took something out of him to be degrading, but it had its own edge as well. He gathered his strength and pulled out, removing the condom and tying it off.

Alec turned around, pulling the tie down off his mouth as he slumped against the wall in his torn underwear and hanging open shirt. "Damn," he breathed, "I missed that." He smiled. Almost like old times.

Morgan winked at him. "Anytime, stud," he said. He hadn't really thought about Alec living here in town since he moved back to his uncle's place. Well, his place now. He zipped and snapped his jeans, having never really taken anything off. But Alec looked down at himself with a wry grin, unsure of what to do with his torn clothes. It wasn't the first time, though. He balled up his torn underwear, tucking them in his pocket. Tucking his torn shirt into his pants, trying to keep it more closed, he hung the tie around his neck.

"Well," Alec said, looking awkwardly up at Morgan. "Thanks?" he added and chuckled.

On the ride back, he could feel Alec's semi-hardening cock against his back. But he didn't initiate anything more when he pulled the Harley alongside the car he indicated. He did notice, though, when Alec grazed his stomach and cock one last appreciative time as he got off the bike. He took off his own helmet, while he accepted the other one, watching the man get into his small four-door BMW sedan. Alec gave him one final look and a nod through the window and pulled out of the parking lot.

Morgan put his helmet back on. Revving the engine, he took off down the dark and quiet highway in the other direction. Damn, that had been good to get out of his system, for tonight at least.

Chapter Nineteen

Maggie

Morgan had come home late the night before, showering and crawling into bed and curling up against her in her sleep. Her lecture had only been about an hour, so she had already crawled in around midnight, reading for about an hour before falling asleep. She had just started his next book, and it already had her on the edge of her seat. She could see why his books did so well. She wondered, though, why he held back his sexuality in his writing, noticing that the characters in the book she had just finished had very vanilla and basic relationships, not really writing about their sex life, focusing more on the mystery to solve.

But the lead character was supernatural, and from all she was gathering, most supernatural folks tended to be very passionate people. Honestly, it helped her understand herself more to learn that. She had started at what she had thought was a pretty young age in exploring her own body in the bath. Auntie had even bought her a vibrator for her 12th birthday, saying she would know what to do with it when she was ready. But she had already been ready, already bringing herself to orgasm while humping her pillow after watching that old movie her friend had dared her to watch, Cruel Intentions. That led her to Buffy, and well, she had her first girl and boy crush at the same time. Looking back, so many signs of inclinations and being drawn to supernatural things. And then there were the Winchester Brothers. She would have taken them both on if she could have.

She had slipped out of bed, giving him time to sleep in, but she needed coffee. As she started the pot, she thought about how her first little girlfriend at 12 had thought her vibrator was cool too. Just friends at the time, but secretly crushing on her, Maggie had innocently offered to show her how it worked—really just intending to show her how to turn on the button. But when her friend had immediately pulled up her skirt and pushed down her panties, Maggie had just gone with it. Her grandparent's none the wiser. The door had been allowed to be closed because they were both girls and "just friends." Maggie had shown her friend how to use it on her clit, her friend not even knowing what a clit was, so Maggie, of course, showed her the book she had that explained it all to teenagers and assisted with both the vibrator and her fingers when her friend had been interested.

Looking back, she and Ashley had been so innocent really in their early explorations. When Ashley excitedly told a friend that Maggie was good with her own body and knew how to orgasm well, the friend asked Maggie for help. For a year or two there, the sleepovers were more fun than Maggie would often admit until one religious girl told her mom in a fit of shame, and the sleepovers ended. But no one had ever blamed Maggie for anything or mentioned her to their parents. Friends who were loyal to the end.

Before long, parties started in high school, and by then, Maggie was exploring with both sexes. She played around a little with alcohol but tended to avoid hard drugs. They just tended to make her feel more agitated and scattered, more than she already was, and she didn't like that. But jello shots were her jam, whether on her own body or someone else's.

By the time she had reached college, she was primed for the scenes she found. Her roommate introduced her to some of the Cruel Intentions style crowd, although Maggie veered towards the geekier ones like she was. Each year, they had a few new people in their apartment hall, but eventually, most fit in. By the time she graduated and prepared for graduate school, Maggie had burned out a little bit on her intensity. The last year had been much quieter. It had been nice to have quiet nights at home alone sometimes. Last night was no different. Not that she didn't like Morgan, on the contrary, she felt like she had never met someone who fit her more.

And giving him space to go fuck Alec had actually felt more comfortable than not. At least she figured he fucked Alec, since he was out fairly late. Did she high-five him when he got up? She had really only done the poly-partnered relationship thing with Jenny before. They had often talked about their other hookups or side relationships, but this time it felt more emotional, more intense. She didn't want things to be awkward.

Morgan yawned as he came into the kitchen, pouring himself a cup of coffee. He saw her quietly sipping her cup by the door as she waited to let Xander back in. After he took his first drink, he set down his cup and came up behind her, wrapping her in his arms.

"Sleep well?" he asked, kissing her cheek sweetly. His scruff was comforting as it scraped against her, first her cheek, then her neck as he kissed her there as well. She let her head fall back on his chest and sighed deeply.

"Yes," she said, yawning. "I started your next book last night. I had no idea how fantastic you were."

She felt him smile broadly against her cheek. "Oh really? Then I must not be doing something right..." he teased as his hands came up beneath his t-shirt that she wore, holding her breasts and letting his thumbs circle her nipples.

She groaned and clenched her thighs together. "You know what I meeeeaaannn...as a writer..." she said breathlessly. His hand slid into her panties, his middle finger finding her clit. She was already wet, she supposed due to her earlier reminiscing about her sexual development.

"I'm so glad you are enjoying my books," he said appreciatively as he began to suck on her neck, the scruff of his facial hair rubbing just the right way to add to the sensation, making her squeeze her legs together on his hand.

"Did you have fun last night?" she asked softly.

"I did," he said, his finger entering her as he swirled his thumb at her clit. "Alec was always a little fuckboy. He likes it hard and dirty, a little mean. Sometimes I enjoy dipping my toes into my shadow side." It did not miss her fuzzy awareness that they were standing in front of the screen door and were anyone to be outside or pull up, she was half naked with his t-shirt pulled up to expose her naked pussy and a breast. She could just glimpse a reflection of them as he stood behind her with his low-slung sweatpants, barefoot, his arms wrapped around her at her chest and hip.

"I hope he showed your shadow side some appreciation," she said as she rubbed her backside against him, noting his hardening cock. Some might be less turned on hearing about their lovers metamours, but not her. She only burned a little hotter.

"That he did, kitten," he said, growling a bit. "I find such good cum sluts," he remarked. Turning her, he removed the t-shirt and pinched her nipples just tight enough to make her jump a little. He gently pressed at her shoulders, and she immediately went on her knees in front of him, in front of the screen door. She imagined others seeing them there like that as she knelt naked, and he took his cock out of his pants and entered her mouth. He held her there for a moment, his cock deep as he ran his fingers through her loose hair, grasping ahold of handfuls of it.

"I fucked his mouth, just like I fuck your sweet little mouth kitten. They are such pleasing mouths," he said, holding her head there until she gagged briefly. He let her pull back. *Oh god, this was so fucking hot.* Her clit was throbbing. She could totally see them in her mind's eye, and it was such a turn-on, almost like she was watching. Almost like she had been there and knelt next to the blonde, both of their mouths used for fucking.

He took his cock out of her mouth, pulled her up with him, and finally picked her up and placed her on the center island.

"And—and—what else did you do?" she gasped out, super turned on as he pressed her back on the counter and began to kiss his way down her stomach to the heat between her thighs.

"Well, he doesn't have one of these, now, does he?" he asked as he slapped her pussy. *Oh fuuuuck.*

"Noooooo..." she got out between pants, his thumb circling her clit again.

"No, he doesn't," Morgan said quietly. "But he does have one of these..." he said as his middle finger gently circled her asshole.

She writhed in response. Ass play was take it or leave it for her sometimes, but when he had put that vibrating dildo just inside her in New York, she had just about gone insane with the orgasm. And right now, he had her wild with images of him fucking Alec.

He circled her clit with his thumb again, then he spit on his middle finger. As he began to edge the tip of his finger into her ass, he added, "The tip of my cock began to penetrate him, just like that kitten. He liked it just like that, but do you like it like that...?"

His thumb circled her clit again, stroking her flames with his own intense desire.

She couldn't think of hardly anything else at this point. She was so wild with wanting him, with or without Alec, although she definitely had visions of his hard penis fucking the blonde guy's ass.

"Please, Daddy..." she begged, so close...

"Please, what kitten?" he asked quietly. His thumb had stilled on her clit, his middle index finger about halfway inside her asshole, which only drove her more insane.

"Please let me come, Daddy, I am so close," she whimpered.

"You like hearing about all this, do you? As I make you come?" he asked, his middle finger working its way in further as he flicked across her clit once again.

"Yes!" she barely got out when he smacked her pussy again with his other hand. This time she came against his hand, clenching and whimpering as her tightest hole clenched around his finger spasmodically, noticing he had enhanced her orgasm with his magick, as his gray smoke flowed from her sex, mingling with her purple once again. Her head fell back as she rode the orgasmic wave and his hand, her muscles clenching his finger as his thumb continued to circle her clitoris, first fast with the orgasm and then slowing as she slowly came down.

"Yesssss...." she moaned again as he drew up back up and forward, setting her on his cock as she wrapped her legs around his waist. He held her there, their eyes meeting intensely and holding as he turned her against the wall and pressed her hands above her against the wall. Fucking her into the wall, he twisted her breast with his fingers, then captured it with his mouth, first suckling, then biting. He pushed into her again, and she knew he was getting close.

"You are so fucking beautiful, I have never met anyone like you..." he grated out as he began to come, his hand grasping the back of her hair and pulling as he bit down again, and she went over the edge all over again.

"Fuuuuuck..." she cried, the orgasm spewing forth purple fireworks from her as he rammed into her one last time, overflowing with his own gray smoke, their passion intermingling before slowly dissipating.

He leaned there against the wall with her for a moment, wiping a sweaty strand of her hair back behind her ear and glasses. Eventually, she slipped her legs down from around his backside. Catching her breath, not even sure where her forgotten coffee was...again.

"We're going to have to stop meeting like this over coffee..." she giggled.

"I think it's a rather lovely way to start the day, kitten," Morgan replied, pulling his sweatpants back up over his softening cock. She went to clean herself up quickly in the nearby small bath but eventually came back to join him with her coffee. He had let Xander back in and shut the inside heavier door.

"Phew," she breathed, following him into the sitting room with her coffee. She sat on his lap on the couch, while he turned on the morning news for a few moments.

"So," he said cautiously as she snuggled into him. "Do you always like to hear about your partner's hookups? I don't mind. That was rather hot, but not everyone wants to know," he added seriously.

She shrugged. "I don't know. I've really only ever been in a poly relationship long-term with Jenny, I guess. All the other times, I was just consensually non-monogamous with different people. I've just always been pretty open. It's kinda rare for me to get jealous, I think I get turned on by knowing. And if anything hurts me, it's secrets or dishonesty. I guess deep down, it's more like I know something big is being kept from me," she said softly, thinking about her family.

"You deserve to know things that affect you," he said simply, understanding her deeper meaning, both relationships and her family. "Lies and secrets only hurt people and separate them."

"So true," she said. "On that note, what is your plan for today?"

They worked through the things that needed to be done, knowing it was Tuesday and Saturday was Samhain. They would get the things together for the releasing spell on Thursday now that they should have everything. They would actually set it up Friday, just to be safe. Fall break started for her after some work tomorrow, so that would help. She had more to do today to wrap up her current project goal.

They eventually separated, Morgan heading to work in the office, and Maggie took a quick shower. She settled in the dining room eventually, with a brief virtual call with her lab partner for one class, as well as tracking outcomes for her project, which was just long, tedious work.

They finished the day fairly productive, and Wednesday was really just more of the same. Both were nervous about Saturday, so they dove into their work to distract themselves. Wednesday evening, Morgan drew a bath for the two of them, adding lavender and amethyst soap to the water, to help soothe and calm their nerves.

Maggie leaned back against him in the warm, soothing water, the bubbles rising nearly to the top of her breasts. Every now and then, Morgan would cup them, sliding his wet thumbs over her nipples absentmindedly. Her hair was up in a messy topknot to keep it mostly out of the water. Morgan had turned on his chill Spotify list, and he had already added hot water once to warm things back up. Maggie practiced bringing her magic in her palm in front of her as Morgan slid his hands along her form, infusing soothing magick with his touch, the gray magick floating to the surface at times to blend with the bubbles.

"Oh!" Maggie exclaimed. "What did you ever figure out from the file your uncle left about Mulligan?"

"Well," Morgan began, "not as much as I'd hoped, really. I mean, there are items in the file that show proof of his connection to both Kragon and Atë, and your grandfather's journal is there, and your grandmother's letter—you should have those, of course, but there is minimal to lead to anything that I can tell. I can't figure out what my uncle had been recently tracking, not something that was enough to push Mulligan to end his life anyways." He leaned his head back against the edge of the large tub and sighed. She knew he was checking the wards on The Hollow again for the hundredth time today. Three days away from Samhain, and while they had a tentative plan for assisting Althea to the other side and a suspected outcome that just might assist in protecting them from Mulligan, there was no guarantee that he wasn't already nearby. And their backup plan had possible negative outcomes if things didn't go right.

Maggie had been practicing various things that she could the past week. Spells from her mother's book, things her Auntie would send to her, and small steps she could add to her intuition from Morgan. But she really feared she would not be enough. She felt like such a baby witch. She should have had nearly 20 years of experience under her belt by now. She let her breath out slowly, focusing on her center like Morgan had been teaching her with meditation. She felt him notice, and his hand came over her heart, and then hers over his, and he joined her. He had taught her a trick when she struggled to focus her attention. He had her imagine a soft space within her mind. She imagined a purple forest with purple trees and purple clouds, and purple grass. She knew it was silly, but he said that was okay. And he joined her there. At first, he had to be touching her, and then she would see him there. She could hear his voice in her mind, and he could hear her, enhanced, she knew, by both of their intense intuition as well as their intimate connection.

Even now, as she centered herself, she saw him join her there, and she heard his voice, low and patient, "Shhhhh... I've got you."

She had often struggled to quiet her mind. Usually, it was like she heard way too much—too many things, feelings, and thoughts from her own mind and those around her. But practicing this with him had helped quiet some of the uncertainty at times and some of the overwhelm. Feeling her heart quiet down, she opened her eyes and snuggled back into him. Their fingers and toes were squishy like raisins at this point from being in here so long, but she didn't care. Next week wasn't promised. She'd stay for just a few more minutes.

Chapter Twenty

Morgan

Friday dawned cloudy and rainy, which worked just fine for Morgan. He got up early and collected the full moon water from the night before that he had purified and set out in the old, blessed glass pitcher. He poured it into the tall glass container in which it was normally stored and placed it back on the shelf, ready to be used as needed. And they would need it.

With the full moon last night and Samhain tomorrow, he went ahead and began some of the deep cleaning that he preferred to do around full moons, which he also did around Samhain. The cleaning company had come and gone the day before, doing the general cleansing of the home. He knew Christine, the lead witch in the cleaning group, had taken extra care with the moon and Wiccan holiday, or Sabbat in mind.

Morgan felt it was time to sort through more of his uncle's things and sat down at his desk with the intention of clearing what should be. He took a moment to focus his energy and then opened himself to what he would be drawn to. A few hours, drawers, and books later, he had piles of items to donate, items to throw away, and items for offering tomorrow.

Stopping for a break, he headed downstairs to grab a late lunch. Maggie was working in the kitchen, and it smelled like oranges and cinnamon. She was just taking a batch of what looked like cookies out of the oven. He snuck a bite of a warm piece from an edge that was falling off, but she smacked at his hand, laughing and saying the cookies were offerings for ancestors. She had found a recipe for "soul cakes" but did her own take on them, and they were pretty good, with a hint of apple cider, clove, and orange peel.

He also noticed she had the windows cracked, with a white candle steadily burning for cleansing alongside an obsidian point, despite the light breeze keeping the room a bit chill. She had a small cast iron crock on the back of the stove, simmering orange peels and cloves, adding to the scent.

"You've done some of your own research on preparations for this week," he commented, smiling approvingly.

"My mother wrote a great deal about her favorite traditions around different Sabbats," she said, gingerly moving cookies one at a time onto a beautiful autumn tray he remembered seeing in the dining room. "I'm just trying a few I saw that looked like they might be lovely."

They definitely smelled lovely, and homey. He'd never been happier to be in this kitchen. He made a quick sandwich, adding sliced veggies on the side for snacking. He sat at one of the stools at the center island, quietly watching her work as she finished her cookies and began to clean up. She set the last cookie on his plate and kissed his cheek sweetly.

"For me?" he asked, pleased. They were damn good cookies.

That afternoon, they went on a walk through the woods. She was already fairly educated on herbs and their uses for mundane tasks and had picked up some others in her reading already, but he talked a bit about the celestial year and offerings of nature and honoring the end of the season and year with Samhain being the new year for many in the supernatural community, while simply being Halloween celebrations for the mundane crowd. He gathered some pinecones, apples, and mushrooms he recognized and found some mint and rosemary still holding out with the end of the seasonal rains.

Morgan eventually found the old orchard, where a memorial plot had been created centuries ago. His uncle had explained that a familiar pet cemetery had been started there with a few burials and small monuments by previous supernatural beings, and then over the century, their family had added headstones or memorials of various kinds to represent their family members, despite their bodies being either cremated or buried in the family plot in England. Morgan had created a transitional headstone for his uncle on the first night that he had returned here and ordered a more ornate version that had yet to arrive.

He laid various autumn remembrance gifts before the makeshift reminder, including a shot of his uncle's favorite whiskey he had brought in a small stoppered vial, which he opened and poured. Maggie was quiet and respectful as he took a few moments, head bowed, thinking about his years with his uncle and how influential he had been for Morgan.

With this Samhain, may your heart find rest

Be at peace, you brought the earth your best

May you find your way to the light

On this blessed, revered night

My uncle, my friend

May you find your way to the end

By all powers that be

As I will it, so mote it be

Morgan then visited his uncle's familiar, a cat by the name of Onyx, who had died a few years prior. His uncle had refused to take on another familiar in honor of the powerful relationship the two had shared. Morgan knew his uncle would have wanted him to be remembered as well. Then Morgan finished his time cleaning up the space a bit, gathering a few squash and a medium size pumpkin he found, offered by the old orchard as a gift in return. That was how his uncle had taught him years ago, bringing gifts to the earth and past generations, and they would offer them gifts from nature in return. Maggie had joined him, finding a small stash of fresh garlic, as well as some mandrake roots that would be beneficial for his storage in the study.

Walking together back to The Hollow, hand in hand, he observed their trail of purple and gray smoke dissipating behind them, noting the energies within and between them, as well as what he could feel rising in the earth strengthened as Samhain drew near. Maggie fairly radiated with her energy, primed from her intense focus recently on practicing her magicks, as well as their profound, intimate connection enhanced not only her developing skill but but also by the generations of energies who had lived and died The Hollow. It seemed clear to him that past generations were approving of her growth at this blessed time.

Morgan had been quietly considering something that might even intensify the power at the site of the ritual they planned tomorrow. When they returned, he mentioned their needing to move some of the items down to the old cellar, where his uncle had mentioned knowing the strength of the connection to the underworld was strongest, especially as the stars and moon aligned around Samhain. Maggie moved to put things away that they had returned with, so Morgan told her he needed a few more items from the old attic that he hadn't found yet, but would meet her in the study to gather the rest.

It took him a bit, but he found the items he remembered seeing during past hunting trips into the secrets of the family when he had been younger. The dark attic hadn't scared his friends as much as the cellar dungeon, but had added just the right amount of tension to plausible fear. It had been the place Morgan had been much more willing to go when friends would ask for spooky ghost hunts in The Hollow. A little bit of fear added well to arousal, whereas too much often emptied it out as they ran for their life. There had been Alec against that wall the one time he had visited, and Clarice had sucked him off by that rather large box his first year here. He figured he likely had Althea to thank for the second one. While he hadn't seen her, Clarice had sworn she saw a female ghost and had clung to him in fright, starting the whole thing.

He pulled himself back from a trip down memory lane and gathered the items he was looking for in a box, heading to meet Maggie in the study. Together they took a few trips, bringing the altar and ritual items they would need the next day down to the cellar's kitchen. The electric lamps cast an eerie glow across the dark, stony space. The energy was already enhancing here with the shifting season. Morgan saw Maggie shiver in delight as she looked around the space and hoped her sensing the power would only enhance what was to come even more.

He talked through the plans for tomorrow and what they hoped would occur. Then he began to fill her in on his most recent thoughts, how their intimacy seemed to enhance their powers, and he wondered if it might down here as well. As he suspected, her eyes lit up with possibilities as she asked if they could have sex in the dungeon. He had hoped she'd feel that way.

The cellar dungeon was one space in The Hollow where he had never been intimate with anyone. Not for lack of fantasizing or desire, but for lack of partners who were interested, as the place truly was scary. While it had clearly held people in true bondage or slavery at one time, Morgan sensed he wasn't the only one who had used it to fulfill a fetish through the centuries.

Morgan filled Maggie in on his thoughts regarding the items he had brought from the attic. When she excitedly agreed, he helped her strip her clothing, chuckling when he noticed her lack of underclothing, both braless and pantiless today. He trailed a finger over her berry lips, trailing down her body until his finger came to rest on the line of her vaginal lips, already noting the dampness.

He kissed her gently on her forehead as he lit a bound clump of sage, passing it over and around her naked body, coming just close enough for the small but steady stream of smoke to almost touch her at various places. Using a selenite point, he traced her body gently, cleansing her for the sensual ritual they would complete together.

May this body be a portal, this heart be a light

An offering to please the gods and goddesses tonight

Enhancing what is, what will be, and what can

Keeping her safe, by the power of your mighty hand

All evil be bound, what is pure be set free

As the Universe wills it, so mote it be

He brought out the old, yellowing chemise he had noticed in the attic years ago, and assisted Maggie in putting it on, as she put her arms through it, and he brought it down over her head. The thin shift was transparent in places, Maggie's beautiful tight nipples visible through its sheer fabric. It laced up the front, much like Althea's, but Morgan left the laces hanging loosely. He brought out the dried woven branches that someone at some point had crafted into a wildflower crown. He let down Maggie's hair that she had wound on top of her head in a topknot, the waves cascading over her shoulders and down her back as he laid the garland of dried twigs gently on her head.

Walking around her as she bowed her head dutifully, he asked, "Are you ready, my love?"

Her eyes flicked up to him at his words, their connection intensifying as she read his emotions there. And she simply answered, "Yes."

He led her to the next room where two single lanterns lit the space, casting shadows that seemed to shift and move with the powers that be in the room. He led her to the wall that held the open shackles. For a moment, he kissed her there against the wall, softly.

"Stay," he said firmly, taking off his shirt. He walked to the opposite wall, taking the old rusting metal ring with the old skeleton key off the nail on the wall, exchanging it for his shirt. He took off his shoes and socks as well, walking barefoot on the sacred ground of this ritual. Walking back to her, he tested the locks briefly, to assure everything worked as it should, he didn't want her getting stuck in rusted metal locks. Taking one arm, he encased her wrist in the first cuff. Trailing the key slowly from her wrist and up her arm, he intentionally gave her additional time to back out if she wished, reminding her she held the power. But he saw her eyes deepen with purple fire, as he circled a nipple beneath the sheer dress with the key and his finger.

"Try to make me leave," she whispered breathlessly. He might just take her up on her taunt, he responded, kissing her other loose hand, biting her forefinger gently.

Adding the other wrist shackle, he clicked the lock. His cock hardened a bit with each added restraint. He checked back in with her again silently, taking her chin, kissing her as his other hand roamed lower, cupping her heated sex through the thin shift roughly. He brought her on her toes as she yearned towards him. But she wasn't even close to being allowed to orgasm.

Hunching down, he pulled one leg roughly to the side, causing her to stumble a bit as he attached the first heavy foot cuff. He ran his fingertips softly up her leg beneath the knee-length thin shift as he stood, slapping her naked pussy beneath as he gripped her there tightly against the wall, and she fucked her hips towards him. But rather than giving her what she craved, he kicked a foot out at her other ankle to spread her thighs wider, holding her up with his grip on her wet sex. But he avoided entering her with his fingers as he leaned down again to lock her other ankle in the spreader bar locks.

Stepping back, he assessed the sight she made, unsnapping his jeans to ease the pressure on his cock. The lower bar and locks were far too wide for anyone to have designed these for anything other than pleasure. Or rape, he winced. His eyes met hers again.

"Red, yellow, green," he reminded her, checking in.

"Green," she said, smirking fearlessly. Daring him to push her further. He saw her short panting breaths, however, as she strained at the locks towards him. She was already fairly aroused.

"You won't break me, Daddy," she said, smiling widely. "I promise."

We shall see, he heard the dark voice within, causing him to step back.

He redirected, heading back to the cellar kitchen, gathering a few items that he wanted as he took a few steadying breaths. He lit the bound sage again, and as he cleansed the dungeon around her, he sensed his frayed edges just beyond his control. His fears for her the next 24–48 hours pushed him beyond his usual balanced groundedness. He didn't mind losing control a bit more with men, full-bodied and able to take his shadow side on better than small waifs like the beauty in front of him.

The sage offered some stability, he sensed as he set the still smoking bunch further away from them on the floor, but within the circle he had cast as he cleansed the space.

He walked back to the box in the kitchen, bringing the other items. He set the rather large clear quartz flame as well as the medium red tiger's eye pyramid at the other points in the circle. And he took out the purple and black flogger.

"Margaret," he said her formal name firmly. "What gifts shall we offer the gods and goddesses tonight?" He walked closer to her, running his finger gently down the deep V of her loosened dress. Her nipples were already tight buds, he could practically hear them begging him to touch them.

"I don't know, Daddy," she said cheekily. "Do they like watching you fuck me?" She raised an eyebrow at him.

He slapped her begging tit. "And what if *they* want to fuck you, my sweet slut?" he asked, his voice a step deeper. He could sense that deeper, darker self, clawing at him from within.

"Mmmmmm..." She closed her eyes in pleasure as he slapped the other, begging breast more roughly. "I'm game," she said eagerly, eyes widening, wondering what that could lead to. She'd fucked quite a few people, but how would it feel to be fucked by a god or goddess? And were any of them even paying attention to them? They weren't really anyone to be known by gods or goddesses.

He paced for a moment, intently watching her. He flicked the flogger across her thinly clothed body, watching her respond as she jerked her body lightly, yearning towards him against the chains. The wreath of dried branches had fallen a bit to the side but still held a rather quaint innocence.

"Are you offering your body, little girl, to the gods and goddess tonight?" He challenged her, "To do with as they please?" He paced away a few steps, then turned and flicked again.

She mewled, then, "Yes. *Please*, I do."

"The gods like when they are begged," he heard as the shadows began to move a bit more around them. "Make her beg all the more." Multiple voices rose in murmur around them in unison, Maggie's eyes going wide and flying to his.

He waited a moment for her to register the direction this was likely moving and watched the moment she gave herself over to the night, nodding slowly at him. "Green..." she whispered softly.

Morgan slowly began to walk forward, flicking the flogger intently. Watching the soft red lines rise at her chest, where the strings had loosened a bit more with her movements. "You're going to be fucked by the gods, princess. You want that tonight, do you? Will you beg for them to allow you to come?" he grated darkly into her ear as he clenched her jaw, holding her firmly to the wall.

She breathed heavily, staring his shadow self straight in the eyes. "Yes," she said simply.

He jerked her chin up, and his teeth sunk into the skin of her neck as he ripped the dress down the center. The dress hung on both sides as a drip of her blood slipped down her neck, his teeth having bit harder than he had intended. His darker half had responded to her, and his control of the situation had slipped. He stepped back to gather himself, trying to push parts of himself that he despised back into the locked corridors of his soul.

She looked at him again. "Yes," she simply said, panting as her chest heaved in the torn dress, seeming to have followed his thoughts.

Morgan felt his darkest side rearing and lashing at him in response, stalking back to the other items he had brought to the room and picking up the whip.

The voices in the room, the shadows, increased their stirring and murmuring, encouraging the next step. The braided black leather of the whip twitched in his hands as he infused it with magicks so painful pleasure, but not further blood would be engaged tonight.

"Spill the witch's blood," he heard chanted but ignored for now. They had already received a taste of it without his intent.

She looked at him hungrily. "Mark me, Daddy," she taunted.

And he did. As he counted to ten, watching the red lines rise on her breasts and her thighs, ever higher than the flogger or crop had. He also noted her purple intensity deepen and darken within her. It began to spill from her fingertips and toes, even drip out of her sex. It was the only thing that continued to tell him that her body followed pleasure, and her words remained true, that she was fully in this moment with him.

The voices around them became more and more clear, willingly trading spilled blood for her magicks that spilled into the room, their voices blending with Morgan's as he paced within the rising powers of the shadows.

"How wet is she, how wet is she?" insisted a slightly louder voice from the shadows, and Morgan tested her cunt, first with the edge of the whip handle, then with his hands, as he again brought her to her toes against the wall with his grip. His other hand went to her mouth, where he gripped her chin roughly, his two fingers in her mouth as he held her firmly against the wall.

"She is pleasingly wet, my Lords," he stated, "on both ends."

Suddenly and overwhelmingly, he felt himself be consumed by another as he threw back his head and his darker self spoke—

May the gods of the underworld join us here

Taking their pleasure, the maiden offers without fear

May she writhe with passion and pain

As you take what you gain

She will know fear and contempt

by he who will tempt

But may fear empower

As she faces this darkest hour

And from around him, the shadows stirred into clearing as the spirits of gods and goddesses became visible, each emboldened by his words, as they paced the room, their eyes lustfully gazing on Maggie in her torn dress and restrained limbs.

Morgan, remaining controlled by his shadow self, looked deep into Maggie's soul. He had held back while his righteous other half had led the way through this relationship. He wasn't sure though, why she wasn't afraid of him. She should be. But instead, she looked right back, tilting her head up defiantly, and she simply said, "Green," very distinctly and clearly, despite her panting.

Ghostly gods and goddesses paced behind him, each wanting their turn at her, as he traced a finger down her delectable body. *Oh, what he could do to her.*

But for now, he stepped back a few paces and decided to watch as the first bold goddess stepped closer to her, the dark-haired celestial running her fingertips over Maggie's straining chest, her nipples hard as cranberries in their puckered areolas. Maggie broke eye contact with him and looked at the voluptuous naked goddess before her, and whispered, "Please..." her hips undulating in her need.

The goddess cackled and smirked. "Why, little girl, don't you know how much we love to play?" She threw her head back and laughed. "We just got here." She picked up the crop that Morgan had brought as well but had not yet used tonight. Another goddess stepped up and kneeled down before Maggie.

"Oh, don't think she is bowing for you, lovey," said the first goddess. "She just knows where this is going." And the second goddess began to play at Maggie's vaginal lips teasingly.

Morgan watched as other gods had their ghostly cocks out and were stroking their own, or some even each other's cocks. The room had turned into a literal god and goddess orgy. Each one looking at and discussing Maggie and what they might do to her, but some were too eager to wait and had started to show one another.

One such god stood separate from the rest. From the horns, Morgan guessed it must be the Norse god Loki. Loki watched Morgan instead, a sardonic smile on his face. When Morgan couldn't look away from him, Loki sauntered closer. Another god had stepped forward to the crop owning goddess and the young one playing with Maggie's clit. Maggie's eyes were on the new god joining them, as his heavy, thick cock bulged in front of him.

"You're turned on by her experience, but also my cock, are you not?" asked Loki, stroking himself slowly. Morgan's eyes shifted back to the intriguing deity. He hadn't expected to engage any of the gods, but he recognized the invitation for what it was. As his darker half began to wrap his lips around the handsome trickster's thick cock, Maggie as well serviced the elder god's penis.

For a time, the room was filled with heavy breathing and unexpected moments of laughter or chants as the various naked gods and goddesses played out their desires on both young witches. But eventually, they were led back together, where Morgan's much darker side happily fucked Maggie against the wall. While some of the goddesses had taken pity on her and allowed her to come previously, as he entered her, she looked deep into his eyes and demanded, *"FUCK ME."*

Clearly, she had not had enough, so he did. Fucking her harder than that righteous other within him ever could, he slapped her cock fucking mouth. "Cunt, don't tell me what to do. *I* will tell *you* what to do." To which he got a mouthful of irritable goddesses but laughing and cheering gods as he felt that righteous inner bitch trying to climb its way back out.

He fucked her harder against the wall as he sought to slam that ethical hardlined prick of himself back into the dark places he himself was usually resigned to. *'How the fuck does it feel to not be allowed out of your sniveling corner?'* he asked himself. He noted the shift in Maggie's eyes as she registered what he'd said. Damn him for letting her in so closely.

'What if I want both of you?' she intuited back to him, which startled the fuck out of him—enough to allow his other half to slip back into the driver's seat.

Morgan breathed a sigh of relief, thankful she hadn't seemed to have been hurt beyond what she wanted. But he hadn't planned on her seeing that side of him. He brushed his hand down the side of her face and smoothed her hair, the wreath long ago knocked off.

"I'm so sorry," he whispered quietly, his eyes soft and apologetic, as he gentled his thrusts, to the disappointment of the spirits around him.

"For what?" Maggie panted. "I agreed to this—all of it. And have rather enjoyed it." She smirked, although tiredly he sensed.

'See!?' exclaimed his inner darker half, locked back where he kept him, in the darkest and furthest corners of his being.

He reached between them and circled her clit, knowing what helped pleasure her the most. He nipped at her breast as she began to roll over into another orgasm, her eyes rolling back into her head a bit as she groaned deeply.

A few meager cheers from the gods around them, but he also noticed pleased smiles by the goddesses, as they shone their light upon them. Maggie's body began to rise somewhat off the wall as her power rose in their approving light, her deep purple mist rising like a cloud around her as the goddesses began to chant softly, their voices steadily rising with Maggie's power, enhancing her orgasm as they enhanced her spirit. Morgan felt a remnant of the powerful surge run through him as he remained connected to her, rising beneath him.

As the orgasm faded, he noticed the spirits were gone, the shadows fell still on the walls, and it had become quiet in the dungeon.

"Are you okay, my love?" he asked quietly as she slumped against the chains.

Her eyes blinked open sleepily as she whimpered, "Yes, Daddy. I'm tired now." So he retrieved the key from his pocket and began to unlock the locks. She sank to the ground on her knees, and curled up at his feet, almost immediately falling asleep. Red lines crisscrossed her chest, and the thin dress hung off her shoulders, the wetness on the soft material from various gods' semen already fading as the spirits had.

He picked her up, carrying her carefully back up and into the house. Xander followed worriedly from the kitchen, asking if Maggie was all right and letting him know how rudely inappropriate it had been of Morgan to leave him locked in the kitchen with such a miserable cat, and neither of them had been able to get to them when they felt the spiritual world tilt on its axis.

He lay Maggie for a moment on their bed, selecting an ointment from the dresser and applying it to her marked chest, and as his magick enhanced the healing serum, he watched as the red marks slowly faded from view. He applied a small amount to her neck as well where he had bitten too hard when he broke, but the healing treatment only worked so much, leaving a small red mark where his tooth had pierced her flesh. His guilt was heavy for that. He had always worked hard to contain his darkest side. He had never broken his control like that, generally allowing his darkest self to play only within certain limits and agreements.

"It's okay," she whispered, her eyes fluttering open to look at him.

"It's not," he said firmly. "I usually control myself better than that," he added, his face grim.

"I imagine you have never been so influenced by multiple gods and goddesses' intent on an orgy," she offered, a weak smile escaping. "You were face fucked by a Norse god," her eyes filled with mirth.

He smiled back, teasing, "Well, Odin did you as well, soooo... We both seemed to have been blessed by the Norse moon tonight." He had removed the torn dress before applying the ointment so the only remaining sign of the night was the minuscule red mark on her neck that would take longer to heal.

"Are you feeling up to a bath?" he offered.

"Only if you are in there with me," she whispered sleepily.

He drew the bath, lighting a few healing candles and adding additional ointment to the water. He added a few dried chamomile leaves for additional anti-inflammatory purposes. He undressed and returned to pick her up from the bed, carefully stepping into the tub and settling her in his arms. She curled to her side against him, falling back into a healing sleep.

Morgan let her rest there for a few minutes before he eventually soaped the sponge and began to wash her gently, trying not to disturb her. She had been through a great deal already, and they still had so much more to come tomorrow.

He wouldn't let himself lose control of his other half like that again.

Chapter Twenty-One

Maggie

Saturday dawned bright, with very few clouds in the sky. Maggie had hoped it might, as that would potentially mean a cloudless sky tonight, to access as much energy from the moon as she could. She stretched out, noticing that the bed was empty and Morgan was already up. He'd likely gone on a run with Xander.

She knew he had taken last night heavily in the end. She had sensed something deeper in him before and a core of guilt that seemed to run early in his life, having a childlike sense to the guilt. She wasn't certain she fully understood it all yet, but he had clearly split at one point, probably when young, and felt deep shame for it.

He shouldn't on her account. She wasn't afraid of him. She noted the small remaining red mark on her neck as she bound her hair on top of her head. The red mark barely stood out against her pale skin, as she stood naked in the bathroom mirror. He had left the ointment he used last night on the counter, and she went ahead and applied a fingertip size amount. She felt the space on her neck tingle as the red mark faded a bit more.

The bite had surely been an accident. He had bitten her many times before, giving her hickeys even. She noted he hadn't offered the ointment for those, and smiled. He generally had a wealth of self-control when it came to his mouth, she could definitely attest to that.

But she had never felt afraid of his darker side last night either. She wanted to ask it some questions before she was sure, but she still fully sensed it as being *HIM*. And he not only cared about her, but he protected her—even from himself last night.

Not that she'd needed it. She actually wondered what the culminating orgasm might have been like if he hadn't switched back. The intensity of that side of him was fire—and she wasn't afraid to get a little burned.

She dressed in the long flowing goddess dress her aunt had sent with her for this special day. Her aunt had mentioned that it was her own creation, and she had worn it to some special event when she was younger. The deep purple and scarlet shifting between glistening black shone as it hung from the gathering below her breasts in soft muslin. The dark boho style was edged in old black lace along the three-quarter length sleeves and floor-length style. Her protective pendant rested at her neck, but her chest was mostly bare with the deep square cut of the neckline.

While somewhat dressy for a day at home, the soft sundress feel of the material was perfect for Samhain and boosted her spirits. *If she were to die tonight, at least she would be dressed for her funeral.*

As she took out her makeup bag, Althea appeared behind her quietly. Maggie jumped slightly, muttering, "I'll never get fully used to that." But Althea stepped up quietly, kissing Maggie's cheek and taking her blush brush from her.

"I shall miss the two of you," Althea said quietly, sadly even, as she added the blush to Maggie's cheeks. Maggie's eyes filled with tears, and Althea shushed her. "Stop that, or this will all wash right off. You know we found our own ways to add color to our cheeks and eyes in my day, but I have been watching, and your way is so much easier."

She opened Maggie's eyeshadow pack, tilting her head in amazement. "So many options..." she said, going with a light sparkly violet. She looked up at Maggie. "Just as you had so many options last night."

Maggie smiled, trying not to move too much, "You saw that, did you?"

"Absolutely, I watched," Althea exclaimed. "Although Castian did not, once Loki engaged his nephew." She began to apply eyeliner, and then handed the mascara to Maggie. "You'd best do this one. We didn't have these fanciful little magic wands in our day. I don't want to get the paint on you."

Maggie leaned into the mirror and began to apply it.

"All is well for you, right?" asked Althea quietly. "I sensed the shifting in Morgan. But you never seemed uncertain." She watched Maggie apply the mascara in the mirror.

Maggie capped the wand and put it back in her bag. "I mean, I can't say I have ever experienced that before. But I was never afraid of him. He didn't do anything I would have said red to." She shrugged. "And I think even his other 'darker side' as he calls it, would have respected red if I had said it. I think..." She turned toward the ghost girl. "He was still Morgan to me, either way. I trust him."

Althea nodded her pale head. "Truth," she said, agreeing. She wrapped Maggie in a deep hug. "You are truly my sister, as if you were from my own coven," Althea said, kissing her cheek again.

"Sweeter words have never been spoken," Maggie expressed, smiling at her.

Althea faded and Maggie went out to get her first cup of coffee. She noticed it was already almost 11am, and Morgan and Xander were nowhere around. Morpheus, however paced the floor.

'Darling girl, it's about time you were about yourself,' the cat started in on her. *'After leaving us out of the loop last night, you sleep forever this morning when danger approaches.'* The cat paused his pacing to look at her as menacingly as a cat could. *'I sense trouble on the horizon. The boy and his dog are walking the property and reinforcing their wards as we speak. They sense it as well. But why don't you?'* He looked at her inquisitively.

"I don't know, Morpheus," she said aloud, still not fully used to this 'talk to animals as familiars' thing. "All I can say is that I have a sense of peace around me. I feel no ill will from any direction, I promise you I would tell you otherwise." She took a sip of her coffee as Morgan and Xander came in, a worried frown on his face.

"Hmmmmm..." Morgan mumbled. Looking at her after closing the door and removing his shoes, his eyes softened. He took in her dress and makeup as he wrapped his arms around her softly. "You seem to be feeling better this morning, love."

For a moment, she laid her cheek on his dark gray t-shirt, snuggling into him. "I do," she said contentedly. But she leaned back and looked him square in the eye and asked, "But what's this I hear about danger from Morpheus?"

His eyes darkened, but he tamped that down. She wasn't sure what it might take for her to help him see that all of him was trustworthy in her eyes. "It's just a sense I have, as does Xander. Morpheus does as well, huh? I do think a dark presence is close. Not here specifically, but I can sense it drawing closer. Clearly, it must be Mulligan," he added, frustration rising in his voice. "The wards are secure, though. Xander reports that my uncle's ghost is patrolling as well." She knew he hated not being able to stop what was happening.

"I don't know why I don't sense it as well," she admitted. "I mean, my intuition was fairly on target before having my powers turned on. But all I feel is a stillness inside of me."

He searched her gaze, laying his hand over her heart. For a moment she felt him searching within her, like quiet footsteps through a mossy field. He left traces of himself behind for a few moments after he separated. "I don't sense any harm or sorcery over you," he said quietly, but his brows were furrowed in concern.

"I know," she said quietly, meaning more than Mulligan. He saw that, but ducked his head as he turned to the sink to wash his hands from the outdoors.

She let him shift away from the moment. "I would like to set an Altar for tonight," she said. "My own gratitude to the gods, goddesses, and spirits who have and will protect us and who brought us to this place in time." She thought for a moment. "I was thinking in the greenhouse." She knew he would prefer her to stay in the home where the wards were most secure, and that would be a compromise.

"Okay," he said hesitantly, kissing her forehead after he dried his hands. "I am going to start some squash soup. It will need to simmer throughout the day on low, and I will be starting some fires beneath the various cauldrons in the house and opening windows and doors to usher in the new year and out with the old. Xander will help guard," he assured her.

"Morpheus said not without him," she smiled. They would be fine, she just knew it. Why else would she not sense otherwise?

An hour later, she had laid out her first altar on the workspace in the greenhouse. She felt proud of her work, and sensed the spirits had heard her gratitude. She had much to be thankful for this year as she had come into her own sense of self in a whole new way. The beautiful red, gold, and purple scarf she had laid out to place everything on had been purchased from Mangus's shop. It had called to her in the window when they first arrived. She laid out various flowers and herbs, some fresh and some dried to represent the old and the new. She placed a squash and an apple, and a few crystals from the small collection she had brought with her. If they survived the night, and she was finally feeling hopeful they might, she would need a trip to her small apartment in Boston for more of her things.

"Please let us survive," she whispered to the wind as she set down the leather-bound book that had become like a friend to her. *Wait, wind?* She was in an enclosed greenhouse. She looked around but sensed no disturbances. Uncertain, she continued. She would add a bowl of the squash soup when it was made, as Morgan mentioned he would add one to his. She bowed her head in reverence and thought of her parents, and her father's parents, all gone but not forgotten.

Mulligan

He watched the girl through the mossy glass enclosure as a tear slipped down her cheek. This multi-generational daughter with the borrowed power of the gods was more discerning than he had given her credit for before now. He must not have sensed that through his crystal, but here in person, he sensed her potency even greater.

But just as he entered her spaces like a breath of wind, he would capture her tonight, and nothing would stop him. He had already foreseen it. He would have to thank her for the sacrificial blessing she'd purchased from the gods with her body, as it would only empower him more when he siphoned the power from her.

And oh how he would consume it from her lithe young body, ripe for his plucking. She had her mother's enchanting figure, but her father's stimulating passion, and he hadn't had the opportunity to savor those as he had once planned.

He would eat tonight, and he was starving.

Talon

"That bastard better not lay a hand on my daughter or so fucking help me goddesses..." Allegra ranted as she paced. Or paced as only a ghost could do, flying from one tree to the next and back again. The heat of her anger came off her in waves.

"My love, will you please take a moment and breathe," Talon told her, speaking calmly despite his own fury that raged within. He was glad the bastard hadn't noticed their presence. *To think that he had once believed in this man...* made him want to break things, but he had long ago accepted that as a ghost, you couldn't always quite grasp real objects, let alone lift them, at least not that they had figured out how. It had greatly limited their travel and investigations. "We have been protecting her for almost 20 years now. Today isn't the day that we stop."

"*YES*, we will never stop protecting our baby," his wife raged, her eyes seeping purple as she plotted the older man's death for the one-millionth time in her mind. "Do you think what the children plan will work?" She took a deep breath, not for the first time today.

"The boy's uncle feels strongly that it will," he told her. The older ghost on the property had been friends with his father. He trusted him, as his father had.

"Then we wait," she said, her deep violet eyes locking in on his. "We wait for tonight."

Chapter Twenty-Two

Morgan

The home had been cleansed thoroughly without incident. Xander and Morpheus had been on the ready lookout while the doors and windows were open, ushering out the old energies and welcoming in the new year. Morgan had started fires in the hearths in the study, the sitting room, and the cellar kitchen—all the spaces that had been active this year that he was aware of. At each fire, he started a cauldron to simmer with various spices and fruit peels that he had been saving the past few weeks for this purpose. Over each pot as he added the ingredients, he spoke a variation of gratitude.

This Samhain, we reflect upon the past, looking forward to the new year

Bringing honor to those who have come before and all we hold dear

Letting go of the past, we release what no longer serves

We look to the future, thankful for filling our reserves

Be with us, kind spirits, protecting what you foresee

As the Universe wills it, so mote it be

He had set his own altar, choosing to do so in the greenhouse as well, to combine his power and gratitude with Maggie's. Proud of her first altar, he set his across the way from hers to the east. Praying that hers facing west, his east, the home's protection and recent cleansing to the south, and the cellar's to the north might lend even more strength from the four corners of the earth to the safety in tonight's events.

He set the bowls of soup for any guests at their altars. His gut told him tonight was not going to go well. But he prayed they had done everything they could. Now it all depended on the help they might receive from the others.

Morgan knew bringing multiple generations of ghosts to this dimension was not always safe for witches to conjure. Never mind last night, as gods and goddesses did as they pleased, and humans were often much more likely to survive keeping a god happy. But tonight, was playing not just once with the multi-dimensional, but potentially five times all at once. The power dynamic shift in the world could be too great. He took a breath and centered himself.

'Let me do it, you need my power.' He heard the dark one say.

"NO," he said aloud this time.

Xander rounded the corner. His pup licked his master's hand before cocking his head at him. *'He's not quieting?'* Xander knew him too well. He'd fought his internal darkness most of the night.

'No,' Morgan intuited to him. *'But he often doesn't, especially when we are in crisis.'*

'You know that's because he was borne of crisis.' Xander reminded him gently.

Xander didn't need to remind him. He had been just 6 years old when his father's friend had first touched him. It took him almost two years of the abuse before he felt bold enough to speak up to his mother. While she had done the right thing, believing him and reporting the man to the police, she had never spoken to Morgan again about the topic. And his father had actually resented Morgan for the loss of his friend.

It had been his uncle who had stepped in to help the great-nephew he had never met. Not even knowing what had been happening as his niece refused to discuss it, he had somehow intuited that her child had desperately needed a lifeline, and he had found him Xander. His mother had been sending him to a child therapist for three months at that point, but he had stopped talking to everyone—his teachers, his friends, even his family. His darker half had risen up and taken control and felt safe with no one, convincing him he needed to remain in charge if they were to survive not only what happened, but the pity offered by those who knew.

The therapist had been kind, also a witch, and thankfully trauma-informed about dissociation in children, he would later learn. They would play silent games for their hour, but Morgan had just never begun to build safety, even when the therapist never used her magicks to try to trick him into talking, the way his darkest side had said she would. So when he met Xander, he somehow knew he could bury his young face in his pup's thick black coat where no one could see him cry. Even as a puppy, Xander had felt safe in a way that humans just hadn't in years.

Morgan hadn't brought out this memory in a very long time. He guessed it was due to his darker half taking over unexpectedly last night. Morgan preferred to stay in charge, as his darker half didn't always stay connected to his empathy, or respect limits. Like when not to take charge. Morgan preferred to feel more balanced.

Learning how to accept love and support again through Xander had been a miraculous start. After a year of therapy, with Anne allowing him to always bring Xander, he had begun to take tentative steps back into friendships again. He stopped believing that side of himself, that no one in the world was trustworthy. While he would always remain cautious, he began to learn he could recognize who was trustworthy—and who wasn't. And that side of himself was not always trustworthy.

Anne had frequently tried to teach him to have compassion for that side of himself, but Morgan knew if he didn't keep him in check, one day, he might harm someone or even himself. Anne had tried to tell him that that thought as well likely came from his shadow side—the fear of harming others the way he was harmed. But Morgan had no doubts about his lack of interest in small children. It was his rage at the injustices of the world that often caught him slipping up.

And it wasn't right that Maggie had to face Mulligan any more than when she was forced to face his dark side the night before.

'That's why you should let me handle it,' the deeper, darker voice said from within.

'NO,' he responded. He didn't trust him. He had no limits. He didn't listen.

'That fucker doesn't need any limits to what I would do with him,' the darkness growled.

'I can do this just fine without you,' he responded one final time and then turned off the internal speaker. Sometimes you had to mute your inner voices when they wouldn't stop the ceaseless arguing.

Xander walked beside him quietly as they made their way to get Maggie, sensing his inner turmoil. But Morgan was not going to talk about it anymore, not with himself and not with his familiar.

Maggie was in the kitchen, staring out the window past the lit candle on the windowsill. The sun was setting, and Samhain was here. "The moon is bright," she said quietly. He knew she sensed its strength within her.

He moved to stand behind her, his hands wrapping around her. So many things he wanted to say to her, like "stay," or "I love you," or "if you only knew how safe you made me feel." Safe was a feeling he often offered but rarely fully felt with others.

But instead, he said, "Are you ready?"

He felt her take a slow deep breath, and then she said, "Yes."

The familiars refused to be left behind this time, so they followed them to the cellar through the greenhouse. Althea was already waiting for them in the cellar kitchen.

"Look," she said excitedly, holding out her ghostly quivering hand. "I'm shaking I'm so excited!"

Morgan began to set out the items they would need on the counter. Herbs—both fresh and dried, a bell, chewing tobacco, crystals, candles. The fire still burned in the hearth nearby, and he would light various things from there. Maggie began to walk the room, as they had planned, with the bound sage—smoking and cleansing the sanctity of their space with his uncle's three-foot narrow selenite wand. He watched her light steps, her hair and eyes radiant in the low light around them as she walked.

Morgan paused to give thanks for the Abenaki family from the north, who had introduced past generations to sage for cleansing, teaching them to replenish the earth each year to refill their own supply. His uncle had taught him this, and he intended to teach the next generation to honor the earth as well. *What we took from her, we always replace as best as we can, and she would bless it.*

Maggie set the metal tray from the hearth in the center of the cement circle. In the center of the tray, she set the large clear quartz, a large white candle, and she lit a small bundle of sweetgrass, gently blowing it out but letting the smoke rise from next to the candle, as he did the same with a small bundle of mugwort.

To the north, he called to the earth to join them in their journey tonight, as he placed smokey quartz and a small clump of red earth from their walk the day before. To the east, he called the air, presenting her with the black-as-night obsidian and a sky-blue feather they had picked up yesterday as well. To the south he called, welcoming fire with the smokey quartz again and a red candle lit from the hearth. To the west, he called to the waters of the earth and the moon who governs her—as he laid the additional black obsidian quartz and a small bowl of full moon water. Finally, at the top of the circle, he lit a deep purple candle, inviting the spirits of the governing worlds to join in their power.

"As above, so below," the three said in unison, opening the circle together, their familiars bowing their heads in reverence.

The three joined hands at the palms. Morgan pushed down the inner voice that nagged at him that things were about to get ugly and to let him through. His voice rang out:

Great spirits, gods, and goddesses draw near

Open our hearts, draw out any fear

On this night when the veil is so thin

We seek your great guidance, your power within

We invite all beings who are ready

To enter the light of your divine energy

Releasing the past, the pain, the shame

We draw on the power of those we call by name

Samuel, Shyanne, Ganon, Causette and Anna

Come be a doorway, a portal, a channel

Release Althea through the power of the light

Protecting those who remain here tonight

Go now spirits and take thy leave

Unto the place predestined for thee

As we will it, so mote it be

Maggie

With a great flash that came from the center of the circle, suddenly the sounds of joy filled the air as Althea greeted her loved ones, all five appearing, including the young children in addition. Maggie felt a tear slip down her cheek as she watched Althea rejoice with her family lost to her so long ago.

Looking around wildly, wondering if what she had hoped had come true, she saw Morgan embracing his uncle, who had also appeared once more, and she saw an older man that she did not know coming towards her from the other side of the room. He couldn't have been Mulligan, as his face radiated love and joy as he greeted someone who was—behind her?

Maggie felt a tingle on her shoulder as she turned and looked into the most beautiful burgundy eyes she couldn't remember.

"Mother," she said, weeping as the women gathered her close. She sensed Morgan's attention as he watched her protectively from across the room. The man at her mother's side gathered them both close, and she knew it had to be her father.

But over her head, she heard him address the man who had walked towards her. "*Father?*" he asked incredulously.

"*WILLIAM!*" Castian bellowed as he walked around the circle, clapping his friend on the back.

Maggie couldn't believe it, her mother was here, and she could feel her! No ghostly pastiness, but in full form. *AND THE WORLD HADN'T EXPLODED.*

Maggie turned excitedly towards Morgan when she saw Althea waving excitedly to her as she and her family began to fade into the distance in the brilliant portal still shimmering between the candle and the quartz. Through the glistening light, Maggie could see the sun was shining brightly in the other dimension with a gentle breeze flowing through the field of wildflowers that seemed endless on the other side.

Morgan came to her side. "We must close the portal before things come through that shouldn't," he insisted impatiently.

But Maggie just wanted to hold on to her parents for just a few more minutes. She clung to her mother's hand, tears streaming down her face. Castian and her grandfather were speaking animatedly about Mulligan and their deaths when two small bright flashes flew from the portal.

Each orb of light flew through the room. One flew out the open doorway immediately, while the other hovered for a moment in the door. The light formed into the figure of a man, enshrouded in a cloak. Tipping back his head, he let out a throaty, evil laugh, jeering at them all.

"Why thank you, my old friends, for saying my name," he smirked. "The two of you were always so easy to manipulate back then, and today I didn't have to hardly do a thing. My name on this side of the portal was the final thing I needed in my spell to access within these wards."

Using his deep dark red magick, he shot a band of binding rope around William and Castian's hands that were next to one another. His fire-like magic exploded out of him again, throwing Morgan back against the cement wall, and he fell, a streak of blood sliding down the wall with him.

"Morgan!" As Maggie cried out and ran to Morgan, she didn't even notice Mulligan send a ray of magick toward her parents, binding two of their hands together as well.

And everything went black.

Chapter Twenty-Three

Maggie

Maggie felt sandpaper on her foot. *Why was there sandpaper on her foot? And why did she have such a huge headache?*

'Wake up, girl, quickly, before he sees me.' She heard Morpheus as he licked her foot again.

Maggie slowly blinked open her eyes. It was fairly dark, and she didn't know where she was. Her hands were losing blood in them and achy as they were over her head. She was in some old cabin with dirty floors and walls, almost like no one had been here in years. Maggie had been bound by Mulligan's magick, and currently, her bound hands were tied with his brand of red magick to an exposed pipe through the old ceiling.

"Mmmmmmm..." Maggie groaned. She must have hit her head or something.

'Shhhh child. Yes, you hit your head when you were thrown forward against the wall by that great oaf's magic. Far too forceful, I say.' The cat grumbled something about magick being more delicate than that.

'How did you get here too?' Maggie asked, remembering to stay silent. She was still trying to clear her head. She felt so nauseous. She hoped Mulligan would come over to her before she threw up, so she could vomit in his face.

'I jumped in the man's cloak when he wrapped it around the two of you and teleported out of that old dank cellar. What I wouldn't give for that

old dank cellar right about now, though,' Morpheus stated, disgusted with the dirt on all four of his usually pristine paws.

'He saw me when we arrived but somehow thought I was already here. Oh, what pray tell, would I—such a clean cat as I am—be doing in this disgusting hell hole,' the cat said unpleasantly, shaking another cobweb off his tail.

'Where is he?' she asked, hoping the cat knew. Looking around, she seemed to be in a bedroom. Ironically, while the whole place was dank and dirty, the bed was made with immaculate and expensive sheets. Maggie knew the white sheets had to be at least a thousand thread count.

'That horrific man who brought us to this vulgar place left out that door after tearing out the ceiling and tying you to that pipe.' Morpheus licked his black paw and then spat, gagging on the dirt. *'All with magicks, of course. A disgraceful use of magicks for sure. This is why we get the bad reputation that we do—repugnant psychopaths like him.'*

The cat sat again, this time trying to touch the floor as little as possible. *'I'm not even certain where we are, I can't get a good read on this place.'* He looked at her intensely for a moment. *'I do, however, sense that the mutt's owner has been here before, although his energy is faint, and not in this room actually.'*

Morgan had been here before? Hell, this was when Maggie was reminded how short of a time she had known the man. A few weeks only meant that gave her no clue.

'Why don't you lay on the bed,' Maggie suggested to the cat, shaking her head again to clear the fog. She tested the pipes by pulling on them. *How the hell in an old, falling down place like this, were the pipes this secure?*

Morpheus looked at her like she had grown two heads. He gingerly walked over to the bed and jumped on it. His paws made dirty prints on the edge of the bed. *'My dear, that is why,'* he said absurdly. *'Now that monster will know I have been in here. However, now that I have dirtied it, I shall stay. Until he returns of course.'*

Maggie kicked out at the nearby wall, but she couldn't even reach it. And her weight still didn't budge the damn pipes.

She heard a vehicle rumble up outside. She looked frighteningly at Morpheus.

'Just comply for the moment,' said the cat quietly. *'We will figure out a plan. But I must hide or he and his hawk will sense my energy.'* And he jumped up on the nearby broken dresser and slipped out the broken window.

Shit. Shit. Shit. What the hell was she supposed to do with this old wizard?

She heard him come inside the building. It sounded fairly small, as she heard him walk from one side of the next room to the other. He seemed to be talking to his familiar, as no one else's voice spoke back. Did Morpheus say it was a hawk?

For a small place, it sure was insulated better than you'd expect. She only heard him mumbling. He opened the door and threw light into the room with an old oil lantern. Maggie squinted against the light. For being an old man, Mulligan had aged surprisingly well. Come to think of it, so had Castian. *Damn wizards and their glamour needs.*

The older man walked directly to her and gripped her chin tightly.

"Well," he said, sneering. "Look at you, finally awake." His lip curled up under his thick black and silver van dyke of a beard.

"Whatever shall I do with you, *kitten,*" he leered.

Fuck him. He had watched them somehow. "Fuck you, you asshole," she said through gritted teeth.

"Why yes," he said, raising an eyebrow. "You will. In time. How else do you expect me to drain your power, my dear? You have truly enhanced it beautifully with all this extra work you have been doing to strengthen them," he said, sniffing the air close to her. "Do I even smell a god's semen still on your breath?"

She spit in his face.

"I would never fucking sleep with the likes of you, you ugly ass old wizard," she said disgustedly. I mean, she really didn't have a thing against age. Older men could be distinguished, and he kind of was with his well-trimmed facial hair and long thick head of salt and pepper waves. And his English accent didn't hurt things. Plus, old guys still got it up.

But she sensed that it mattered to him.

"You bitch," he sneered, his face twisting into an ugly snarl as he back-handed her across the mouth. Maggie tasted blood as her lip busted against her teeth. "You will fucking *beg me* to let you come before I am done with you. And when I am done, you will be of no use to anyone else, let alone that candy-assed boy of yours." She winced. He narrowed his eyes. "Maybe I will bring him along, and you can see him tied up and fucked til his little uncle cries. How would you like that, bitch?" he sneered as he backhanded her once more.

Maggie had tears streaming down her face, but she was pissed. She had to play this smarter, not harder. She quieted her voice to sound more compliant. "No," she whispered. "Please don't hurt them. I'll do whatever you say."

If worst came to worst, she could fuck an old man just fine, as long as he took off this gods damned magick fucking rope and then she would be free. She'd tried to twist out of the magickal red rope, but it was steadfast. And the pipe wasn't going anywhere, he must have reinforced it somehow with magick, as a real pipe that small should have busted with her weight. She couldn't break his magick.

She might have to play him at his own game. And dear gods, if she did not win, she just might die. Either way, losing her magicks after having them for such a short amount of time would surely feel like death as well.

Morgan

'If you had just fucking let me handle things, we would have her right now.' Morgan heard from the darkness.

'You would have just made things worse,' he responded.

'I would have fucking closed the portal, not waited for permission!' the darkness shouted at him. Well, he couldn't argue that one. Mulligan wouldn't have gotten through.

'She had just needed another minute with them,' he responded hesitantly. Uncertain, but the darkness *was* probably right.

'Of course, I'm fucking right,' the darkness retorted. *'Closing the portal with those there who remained, and then finding a way to open it again would have worked in the meantime. It worked once, it would work again,'* his darker half said logically.

'Or, once he got through, you could have let me handle things. He'd be fucking dead right now,' his darkest side added sardonically.

There it is. *'Why do you have to always be so vengeful?'* Morgan asked himself.

'Maybe because some people don't deserve to live.' Was the simple answer given.

'You are not a god to decide who lives and dies,' Morgan responded quietly.

'Well, then the gods need to do their fucking jobs.' His darker half laughed.

Morgan began to see light at the end of the tunnel. He wasn't dying was he?

'No. Take a breath buddy, 'cause we still got more living to do,' came from an altogether different voice, one he had known and loved since he was a child. He heard a whoosh as he blinked open his eyes to a big fat tongue licking his face.

'Alright Xander, I'm all right,' he reassured his worried familiar.

Damn his head hurt. The low light of the cellar kitchen came into his blurry view. He leaned up on his elbow, peering through squinted eyes past the Shepherd. The portal had closed. How long had he been down? "Where the fuck is Maggie??" he shouted, suddenly realizing he already knew Mulligan had taken her.

"Calm down son," he heard Maggie's grandfather say.

"Why the fuck should he calm down?" he heard his uncle say to the younger man, one of each of their hands still bound together by Mulligan's red magick. Maggie's grandfather just grumbled back that Castian had always been so argumentative.

Morgan saw Maggie's mother pacing the floor, pulling her husband behind her, as they as well had a hand each bound together. Maggie's father was trying to calm her down, and she was saying, "Don't tell me to calm down, Talon. This was not supposed to fucking go this way. This was not what we talked about—" her voice rose into a shriek as he saw his uncle cover his ears.

"Dear mother and baby fucking Christ," his uncle said in his English accent. Morgan never did understand why he used that phrase, as he wasn't Catholic, but he always had. And somehow it was reassuring to hear him say it again.

His uncle lasered through his and William's red magick binding and stood up.

"What the hell, Castian?" yelled William at the older man. "You knew how to do that this whole time, and you didn't say anything?" It was ironic to see the roughly 25-year-old man yelling at the one in his early 80's. Like someone wanted to tell him to respect his elders. But they had been best friends all throughout boyhood and college.

"Well, y'all would have left my boy here, and I needed him to wake up first," said his uncle. "Plus, I got an additional almost 60 years on you to study magicks, and blood magick is different. You have to add some moon water, and I didn't have any until the pup spilled it on my pant leg, rushing to check on the boy as he woke up."

The older man hobbled over to the younger couple and released their bond as well. He rubbed his hip, and William laughed, calling him an old codger. Castian grumbled back at him that he hadn't gotten to grow old like an 80-year-old man.

"I wish I had," William said, looking sadly at his son. They embraced for the first time since seeing one another. "Does anyone know what happened to Selene?" he asked, looking around.

"Well," said Castian, grimacing. "She sent me a letter when she died, a little over a year after Talon. Only she died from breast cancer. She said she found out too late, old mate. I'm sorry." But then his face cheered some. "Maybe that means she's on the other side of the veil waiting for you?"

"I mean, she shouldn't be too old, maybe her early 40's? Some say women are in their prime right around then," Castian quipped. But William punched him in the shoulder, quickly apologizing at the older man's pain.

"I keep forgetting you aren't in your twenties anymore," said Wil. "Same old sarcasm. Always got you in trouble with the women. And the men." He laughed harder.

"Gentlemen!" interrupted Allegra, voice pitched higher than normal. "What are we going to do about Margaret? She's been gone for an hour already, and we don't even know where..." She wailed at the end into her husband's shoulder, still rubbing the remaining marks from the blood magick rope that had marked her wrists.

"Xander reports the cat jumped in Mulligan's cloak with her," Morgan spoke up, petting the dog in appreciation for his help.

"Morpheus is with her?" Allegra's eyes widened at the news. "Well, that is something. Two are better than one I suppose. Maybe he can offer her advice or fetch her something she might need to escape. Unfortunately, our line of communication closed with my death, though." She fretted her hands together anxiously.

"If only we could figure out where he might take her," Talon added.

Castian shook his head. "There could be so many different places where he teleported with her. For instance, he could have taken her back to his home fortress just outside of Blackpool."

"Well," Allegra said, "in your 60-plus years of additional experience, did you get any good at teleporting with others as Mulligan did?"

Castian puffed out his chest proudly. "Of course."

"Well, then, let's go, old fool," said William. "We might as well check some of those places."

Chapter Twenty-Four

Maggie

It was late. Mulligan had brought his dinner in to sit and watch Maggie fight against her binding. He had drawn a chair in from the old kitchen table in the other room. Using magick he had wiped the chair clean as he sat down in his pressed black slacks. Maggie couldn't believe he was dressed in a designer three-piece suit and tie in this old run-down cabin.

Mulligan laid his black suit jacket on the clean linen on the bed. Noticing the paw marks on the corner of the bed, he began to remark when Maggie blurted, "Why the three-piece suit but the run-down hovel, huh?"

"Did you think you deserved a five-star hotel when I fucked your tight little ass?" he asked viciously, making eye contact. She looked away from him, but he gripped her chin as he forced her eyes back up to his. Loosening his tie with one hand, he trailed his fingertip down her chin and along the low neckline of her dress. Her hands being over her head and compressed together to hang from the pipe had pressed her chest closer together, creating cleavage she didn't often have. His short fingernail traced her cleavage, causing her to shiver.

He smirked. "You may enjoy this yet, my sweet."

"I'm not your sweet anything," she hissed back at him, forgetting for a moment that she was trying to play this out. He smiled and backhanded her again. Shit. How many times would she learn that lesson? Each time she talked back to him, it only seemed to give him a thrill. Antisocial sadist. Psychopath. He liked giving nonconsensual pain. He got a thrill out of it. She needed to stop giving him a reason to enjoy it.

He took off his belt.

"No, no, I promise, I'm sorry..." she began. But he backhanded her again. She spit the blood out of her mouth at his feet, but he just leered at her. Running his fingers along her neckline again, he jerked at the dress, tearing the neckline further down a few inches.

She knew he could see her breasts through her bra. She knew her nipples were hard. *Fuck him for that.*

"See, my pretty," he snickered. "I thought I read you right. You can pretend all day that I disgust you, but I bet if I tapped that pretty little cunt of yours, it would be wet right now, wouldn't it?"

Only 'cause bondage turned her on.

"No," came out of her mouth. *Shit. That would just egg him on.*

He laughed darkly, a thick eyebrow rising at her.

"Shall I check, then?" He trailed the rich Italian leather of his folded belt down her cleavage, stopping to smack a breast, the hard metal of a thick platinum ring adding to the reaction she gave, as she stumbled against the rope and clenched her thighs together.

"I don't really need to check, do I? You're a pretty little whore who loves to be fucked up, don't you?" he sneered. "I bet you even have fantasies of being raped, that you don't tell anyone," he laughed, reading her right as she blushed.

Pulling her dress up quickly, he grabbed her pussy hard. She knew her heartbeat was in her sex right now, the heat emanating from it. But she wasn't going to give him the glory of responding.

"Why so silent now, little cat?" he grated out into her ear, his fingers finding the wetness in her panties. He ripped them and shoved two fingers into her roughly, and she gasped, almost coming immediately, feeling the heat of his power on his fingertips.

"No," he said flatly. "You will beg first."

She spat at him. "I will never beg for your ugly cock."

That one was almost worth the backhand that made things go black.

Morgan

Morgan was getting more and more worried by the hour. It had been five long hours, and they still had no clue as to where Mulligan had taken her. They had been to his fortress, which was dark with no presence of anyone. They had checked his home offices in London and his offices in New York and Beijing. Morgan had scoured the darkwitchweb, looking for any sign of him in the last 24 hours. Nothing.

He placed his hand on his chest as he had with her so many times before. *'Maggie?'* he reached out.

All he got was Xander raising his head and whimpering at him, and a grunt from the darkest recesses of his soul.

'I told you, let me step up to the plate.' He heard. But he didn't respond. At this point, what could *anyone* do differently than they already were?

He had pulled out the items from his uncle's desk when they returned from the last trip. He had asked about them, uncertain as to what he was missing.

"Why, Mulligan killed old Kragon," Castian had exclaimed, with William sitting nearby.

"Ya don't say?" responded Wil.

"Yeah, but that's when Mulligan disappeared off the face of the earth for a while," said Castian. "I was trying to figure out what happened with the missing time in the timeline."

The conversation hadn't really led anywhere in Morgan's mind, as it didn't lead them to Maggie, and that's all that mattered right now. Maggie's mother had paced for the last 20 minutes since their return, wringing her hands and muttering about 20 years wasted if Maggie was dead, raped, or had lost all her magick.

He couldn't believe Maggie was dead. He'd know. *You knew when your soul mate died, didn't you?* He would not give up hope. But he knew every hour that passed by, her mother's worries were more and more likely.

Morpheus

It had begun to rain outside.

Morpheus did not like getting wet. First, he was dirty, and now wet. The two didn't go well together, as he had mud between his toes.

He hadn't been able to get back inside the ridiculously filthy cabin, with the old wizard in there. His hawk was in the front room, keeping an eye out the front window.

The weather was interfering with his familiar intuition. He had had moments of sensing the girl's arousal, which didn't worry him. She had been far more active than her mother and could handle herself where that was concerned. It was the fear that kicked in every now and then that he listened for. But now he heard nothing, and that terrified him.

A century old, and he just now fucked up the job?

He sensed her heartbeat rising and breathed a sigh of relief.

The lightning cracked right outside the door of the old shed he hid in.

Dear mother of gods, he longed for the comforts of home.

Maggie

Maggie's eyes began to blink open again. *Fucking head... hurts.*

'Maggie?' She sensed from a distance. She could hear him. But if he came, he would bring the rest and it would be all her fault. She pushed him out of her mind.

"Well," said the older wizard. "If the little hellcat hasn't woken again."

"You're not as fun when you're asleep, darling," he said, sharp eyes pierced on her. At this point she was bound, her dress gaping open, blood drying on the corner of her lip that she could taste, and the small gash at her temple from his ring still stung. He looked at the insignia ring on his middle finger, clearly this wasn't the first time it had come in handy. "Maybe you'll play nicely next time, little girl."

"You don't want me to play nicely," she said under her breath. But she knew that he heard, as he smiled.

"You really are a smart feline," he said, "it's too bad things must end the way they do. You could have learned well from me as your parents should have."

She didn't say anything. She was trying to keep her loved ones out of this.

When he didn't get the rise he wanted, he drew closer to her, running the tip of his folded belt along her bra line again. Gods help her but her nipples responded to the mild threat. She wasn't scared of a belt. She'd felt the welts before, they didn't do much for her. The threat, though, had always been the more successful part.

He smiled. Tearing her bra down the middle roughly, he exposed her breasts completely. She didn't expect him to show her nipples any positive attention, so she was surprised when he trailed a fingernail from one nipple across to the other. Her nipples reacted by tightening. He laughed.

"You think you have me all figured out, do you?" he asked, smirking. He had unbuttoned a few more of the buttons on his shirt while she had been knocked out. A swirl of dark salt and pepper hair scattered across his chest. He sat forward in his chair closer to her. He grasped both gaping sides of her dress, tearing it the rest of the way down. She saw his thick cock tenting his pants. Gods help her if her mouth wasn't watering.

"No, sir," she said meekly, trying not to react like a brat since that only seemed to make him meaner.

He leaned back in his chair. "Look at the pretty little mess I've made. It's going to be rather lovely to strip you of your power, little girl."

Her arms were still over her head, tied by his red magick to the secured pipe overhead. Her hair had fallen half down, her makeup had been ruined as she cried and bled. Her dress hung wide open, with her bra laying pitifully wide, her small breasts heaving as she tried not to pant, but her nipples puckered and called her a liar.

He ran the edge of his belt along the slit between her thighs, nudging her panties that hung in a torn mess off her hips.

"How wet are you now, little slut?" he asked. But she refused to answer him.

He flipped open the belt and whipped the side of her ass with it twice. But his eyes tightened as he noticed her lack of response.

"Not scared of the belt, are you?" he smirked. He unzipped his pants and pulled out his hard cock. Sliding his fingers along it, he ran a finger around the tip and looked at her. Her nipples had hardened again, and she had unknowingly slightly opened her mouth as she panted deeper.

"You are a little cum slut, aren't you, my dear?" he asked, stroking himself again, long and slow. Her eyes slowly left his hardened cock and she looked into his eyes. He stroked the length of himself again, his gaze never wavering from hers. Tipping his chair back on all fours, he reached forward again, his right hand remaining on his long cock, as his left slid along the wet crease of her cunt.

"Ah yes...." he said, his voice taking on a hard flinty edge. He began to just tease her, with about a half inch of two of his fingers inside her vagina. His left thumb flicked over her clit as he flicked his right thumb over his swollen cock head.

She let out a groan, embarrassed that he seemed to be reading her so well. *FUCK.* She was so close. She was supposed to be playing him, but he was playing her all too well.

He leaned forward in the chair and took her nipple between his teeth, tugging hard with his teeth. His rough salt and pepper goatee played havoc with her skin, and he nudged the hair against her nipple before biting again.

"*Fuck,*" she let out between clenched teeth.

"Beg first, slut," he said simply in his gravelly voice, sitting back. Watching her writhe as he stroked himself again, not even in a hurry.

Fuckity fuck. Her pussy contracted with her heartbeat.

"I just—" she gulped.

"BEG, bitch," he said, face flat as he stroked himself again, a drop of precum on the tip of his cock. He ran a fingertip over the top, licking his finger, eyes never leaving hers.

'Maggie?' She felt Morgan reach out again. She went still so she wouldn't let on in any way. She watched the older wizard watch her, stroking his cock again.

'If you can hear me, moon water breaks the blood magick of the bonds with the releasing spell.' Morgan's voice was so distant. In response, she said nothing but flashed on an image of the inside of the old cabin, hoping he might understand.

"Not going to beg, little witch?" Mulligan asked, standing up, his cock still in hand.

Nope, she wouldn't beg. She was going to figure out how to find some moon water before her people arrived, and this pervy old fucker hurt them all.

She knew her nipples were still aching and pointing toward the older man. His cock still made her mouth water. Damn sex and the human body. He stepped behind her, much taller than she was. She couldn't see his eyes now, which made her nervous. She couldn't guess his next steps. He pressed against her back, his penis against her spine. His hand came around her as he gripped her by the pussy and lifted her small body onto his hardened cock.

OH. *Fuck.* She slid onto him, but he was so big that he hurt. Even as wet as she was. He didn't care.

"I'm tired of waiting, little bitch," he said roughly in her ear, heightening her senses. He gripped the front of her pussy, as he rammed up into her again from behind. *Fucking fuck, there she came.*

He laughed, pulling her off him smoothly and setting her asshole first on his hard cock, pushing inside her without any fluids but her own on his cock.

"FUUUUUUCKKKKK—" she screamed. "*You fucking fucker,*" she yelled as she writhed against him, trying to get off his hard cock, but her weight worked against her, and the movement only helped him to shift inside her more.

"Ahhhhhh..." he said, entering her further, forceful inch by inch with each thrust. His hands came around to pinch her nipples painfully. The pain of her nipples being pinched only enhanced the pain in her ass, and she trembled as she began to orgasm again. He laughed darkly as he raised her by the hips and lowered her faster and faster onto his thick cock, going further in each time. She would probably be bleeding before the night was over. He pulled out of her, finishing with her sitting on his left leg while he stroked himself to a finish all over his other bare leg and somehow getting his old man semen on her wet little pussy as she sat on his knee with her dress and underwear gaping wide.

I mean, the picture was hot. She couldn't have asked for a better non-consenting experience, especially since she was kind of consenting as she tried to play him.

Gah. There was something wrong with her that she would even think that, that all this turned her on in spite of the pain, in spite of her fear.

Chapter Twenty-Five

Morgan

Morgan racked his brain, something about that image she had sent him felt so familiar. He'd been in many cabins and old buildings through the years. But he couldn't think of where that was. He definitely didn't recognize that bed. Maybe it just felt familiar even. So many cabins felt the same. The paneling walls, the dark lack of electricity. The emptiness.

Those walls, though, something was familiar...

Morpheus

"Moon water?" Morpheus thought he heard her say. What the living and dead hell? How was he supposed to get the girl moon water? It's not like a cat had thumbs to carry things with.

The lightning flashed. The moon hadn't been out all night, either, not with the heavy storm.

He was not the witch here.

Maggie

She didn't know if Morpheus had heard her or not. She hadn't seen him since she first awoke. But she hadn't seen Mulligan since he left her bound again to the pipe a while ago. She figured it had been maybe an hour. And she knew he hadn't left.

The older man stepped back into the doorway, his hair wet and with clean pants on. How the hell did he have clean, *pressed* pants here, of all places?

"Magick or money can get you anything your heart desires, my dear," he said, shrugging when she looked at him angrily.

"No need to fucking mind read," she said. *She was going to have to be more careful.*

"That mouth is going to get you into all kinds of trouble in life," he responded nonchalantly. "One doesn't have to mind read, your eyes speak volumes." He laid his clean, freshly ironed shirt on the bed with his jacket neatly.

"Magick can do all sorts of things." He shot a ray of red at the bed, turning the sheets a deep burgundy. He looked at her. "Live as many years as I have, and you will learn how to use your magicks in all sorts of ways. If you have any left after I am done with you, of course."

"You should feel lucky I didn't start with that last little round," he winked. *Did he think this was fun?* Of course, he did.

He flicked magick towards the corner of the dirty little room. A glass shower appeared, modern and clean. "I imagine a shower would be lovely." He nodded his head towards her. *Yes, it fucking would, as his semen dried on her thigh, and her asshole was still gaping and raw, maybe bleeding.*

She flicked her eyes annoyingly at the binding attached to the pipe.

"Beg," he said simply.

She rolled her eyes. She didn't beg him to suck his damn cock. Why would she beg him for a shower? She noticed the ridge of his cock in his pants at her rising annoyance. Damn, she swore the old man must have a line of Viagra in his blood.

"I did allow you to come twice," he stated calmly. "I do believe I am being far nicer than I usually am." He raised his templed fingers to his mouth and studied her. Watching patiently as her nipples began to pucker once again.

He smiled. "You should just ask your mother how nice I can be."

"Fuck you," she spat out without thinking. "I read her journals."

His smile grew, and he raised a thick eyebrow. "She enjoyed it enough to write about me, did she?"

"No, asshole," she rolled her eyes again. "She didn't." She wasn't going to offer him the pleasure of knowing that, and that wasn't her information to tell.

He walked forward towards her, his hand coming to grip her chin again. "That is the second time you have rolled your eyes at me in the last few minutes." He reached for and pinched her nipples hard, pulling her up on her tiptoes with it. "Don't think me daft, girl. You're smarter than that."

Fuck. He had her there.

She couldn't help it that she had always had an intense sexual appetite.

Plus, if she could get Mulligan to let down the magick rope from the pipe, she might even be able to find a way out of there, even with the binding still on her wrists.

She looked pointedly at his cock, ridging his pants. "If you were smart, you'd have your cock in my mouth," she threw at him, unsure how well the taunt might work.

"I don't know how much I trust that mouth, girl. Those teeth are pretty sharp," he said, raising an eyebrow again. *Damn, she hadn't even thought about that.* Really, she had just thought about a good cock sucking and then slipping out somehow.

She shrugged. She couldn't promise she wouldn't have thought of it had she gotten mad enough. He did push all the right triggers.

"I have been thinking about a workaround, though," he said, reaching for his belt on the floor. He held it between his hands and snapped it. *What the hell was he going to do?*

"Maybe, if you are a good girl, you can shower afterward," he said, nodding his head towards the shower in the room. "But I will watch."

She shrugged. Watching never bothered her, as long as she knew.

He unzipped his pants, taking his already hardening cock out. Slipping his finger around the slightly wet tip, he held his finger to her lips this time. "Suck," he commanded.

She opened her lips, recognizing this as the test it was. She lapped out her tongue onto the tip of his finger, licking the salty liquid. Taking his finger into her mouth, she sucked until he stuck another finger in, coming closer to her and twisting her tit tightly in his other fingers. His cock was as hard as a rock now.

He took the belt, wrapping it around her neck. He looped the end through, tightening it a bit against her neck. "One bite and I pull, little bitch," he said threateningly.

She nodded. *Okay, she hadn't planned to bite his dick off anyway.* It really was a pretty cock, longer and thicker than any she had fucked. She couldn't believe it had been in her ass. She would enjoy this, and then she would go.

He sent a laser of red to the pipe, disconnecting the rope from the metal. As her arms came down, the blood rushed into them, and she winced, trying to wiggle her wrists and fingers to get the blood moving.

The belt still around her neck, he tugged and said, "Kneel."

She kneeled. His pants unzipped, he stepped closer to her, her dress pooling open around her. She had always loved sucking cock. She'd take one for the team.

His thick penis pressed against her lips. She lapped her tongue out at it like she had his finger a moment before. His eyes glazed shut for a moment, and she took his hard cock in her mouth, sucking first the tip and then the long thickness of it back into her throat. She tentatively began to use her bound hands in front of her, as she took ahold of the length of him, manipulating his balls as she held the base of his cock, raising up and down on him with her mouth. His hand came to her hair, and he gripped her head, holding her down for a few moments.

She wasn't afraid to gag. She'd either throw up, or he'd let her up eventually. She felt his cock convulse against the back of her throat. He let her up instead of coming. *I guess he wanted that Viagra to last, huh?* She shrugged and continued, returning to sucking the tip, its thick bulging mushroom head fitting just inside her lips as she flicked her tongue back and forth over the spot beneath that she knew was usually sensitive.

She slipped her hands down below, playing with her own clit as she continued. He noticed.

"I didn't tell you that you could pleasure yourself, little slut," he said, his eyes tightening with tension. He jerked her head back off of his cock by her hair. Pulling her up by her hair, he bent her over his knee.

"You've been asking for a good spanking from the beginning," he said, his hand coming down to slap her naked ass as her dress spilled over his knee and onto the floor. He rubbed her pussy from behind, sliding two fingers in deep.

"You are a wet little thing, aren't you? You like to suck cocks?" he asked, making her wetter. He slapped her ass again. This time, three fingers, and one of them went in her asshole, and not slowly. She came rearing up off of his lap, but he jerked her down by her hair.

"A good little cum slut listens and doesn't have to be disciplined," he grated out as he fucked her holes. He jerked her head back towards him and said between his teeth, "But you like the discipline, don't you, little slut?" She was so close to coming again.

He jerked her up on top of his lap, facing her towards him, setting her directly on his thick cock. He raised and lowered her hips, as he filled her quickly. This time she had been a little more ready for him, a bit more stretched. Hands still bound, she bounced with his help. Slipping over the top, she came, riding him as he came as well. He seemed to forget his insistence once again that she beg, this time seeming to enjoy orgasming with her for the moment, his head falling back as he closed his eyes for a moment. She considered wrapping her hands around his throat, but with the blood magick still binding her wrists, she continued to not have access to her magicks and she knew he would still overpower her. *She had to figure out how to get access to moon water.*

In the end, he offered no support or connection afterward, she didn't know why she thought he might. *Aftercare was clearly too much to ask of a psychopath.* But she would get her shower. She almost got him to consider undoing the binding to take the dress off of her, but instead, he ripped the sleeves off, and the once beautiful dress fell to pieces on the floor.

She took her shower, telling him she had earned all the damn hot water. But the water that ran down her cheeks in the stream was her own. She had never heard a peep from Morpheus, and while she had gotten released from the pipe, she would never get home with her current binding, or naked.

Uncertain if it was to use the bathroom or because he didn't know what to do with her tears, Mulligan stepped out with a gruff, "I'll be back."

And in scampered her cat.

'I thought he would never leave. God damn, does the man have a line of Viagra in his system?' Morpheus chattered low outside the shower door.

'I know, right?' she thought. She was so tired. *'Did you hear me on the moon water?'*

'Yes,' groaned the disgruntled cat, *'Now open the damn door, child. Don't ever say I didn't do anything for you.'*

Maggie inched open the door, and the cat slipped in, mud and all. *'Ewwwww!'* Maggie thought, *'What the hell did you get into?'* And then Morpheus proceeded to shake his fur, and droplets of water cascaded across her, the cat saying the words to the release spell. Maggie saw the red binding suddenly release at her wrists. *Moon water! There was moon water in his fur from the rain and the mud under the moonlit sky.*

Maggie moved quickly, *'Hurry, get back outside, I'll be right there.'* She inched the shower door back open again, leaving the water running. Slipping out without a towel, maybe he had gone to get her a towel, she grabbed his suit jacket from the bed. Thankful for the backdoor being off the bedroom.

She slowly clicked open the lock, hoping he hadn't heard, when suddenly she heard him roar from the other room, "Oh no, you don't, you little lying slut!" And she spun around, magick flying from her fingers faster than she could even think. Two purple ropes slammed into his arms and backed him into the chair, wrapping around the arms of the chair and binding him there.

He sneered at her as he leaned forward, expecting to break the binding. But he couldn't. Maggie had slid a little something into her binding spell as well, and it kept him from being able to access his.

"You think you're so clever," he mocked. "I won't be bound here long, and I have already proven that I can find you. Next time, I won't wait so long before I consume your energy. I left you with far too much," he said, his eyes narrowing. "I thought we were having a grand ole time.

What will your little boyfriend think about your inclinations, my dear? I guarantee he won't like them."

Like he knew something about Morgan. But she just shrugged her shoulders. "I trust him. He trusts me." *And she was not her mother.*

"But what I don't trust *is you*," a dark voice said from the doorway. Her head jerked to the door, but Morgan was looking at Mulligan and not her.

"Oh, my gods," she said, finally fully breathing again. "You found me!"

"I will always find you," he said, his voice steely. But as Morgan stalked into the room, his eyes remained on Mulligan, spinning the older wizard's chair towards himself. His eyes zipped shards of pitch-black magick binding around Mulligan's upper arms and down his legs, reinforcing the hold. He stood back, arms crossed at his chest, and towered over the old man.

"*What* do you know about me?" Morgan said, clearly having heard the same thing she did in Mulligan's last statement.

Mulligan's eyes narrowed at the young man. "I know everything," the older man stated. "I always do when I have a plan."

Morgan's eyes were pitch dark, like when he had switched in the dungeon. Maggie tentatively spoke up, "Morgan, you okay?"

"With you?" Morgan asked dismissively, glancing at her face. "I'm fine. This fucker won't be, though." And he swung, his fist connecting with the older man's cheek. Mulligan's head swung back, his cheek split and bleeding.

"That all you got, kid?" Mulligan taunted. And suddenly, Maggie realized Mulligan would enjoy the pain as well. She stepped up. Morgan smashed his fist into the old man's nose. Maggie wasn't sure how Mulligan hadn't been seriously harmed yet. The man was in his mid-seventies.

"Morgan, something's not right here," Maggie hesitantly spoke up again.

"That's right, people who leave marks on other innocent people get hurt," Morgan said through clenched teeth as his fist connected again with the older man's face, but Mulligan only laughed, not even wincing at the pain.

"You think you are hitting that whiney little sniveler, Johnson," Mulligan said, his eyes narrowing again but not even wincing in pain as he stared down Morgan. "Margaret is a full-grown adult, capable of making her own decisions. You were a mere child. There is a world of difference."

Maggie wasn't quite sure what was being said here, even if she thought she could guess. But surely Mulligan wasn't deluded enough to think kidnapping her and keeping her against her will was consent? I mean, yes, her orgasms had been consenting to her, but overall, the whole thing was a big fat no from her.

But Morgan spoke next. "Mac Johnson's name doesn't get said around me, and it hasn't for a long time. It's scrubbed from any legal record connected to me on the darkwitchweb and mundane spaces. How did you get access to that?" The shock of hearing the man's name again had caused him to take an unexpected step back.

His uncle walked into the room. Her parents and grandfather were right behind him. Her mother ran to her, wrapping her in her arms. No one mentioned her nakedness under the suit coat wrapped around her.

Castian had heard Morgan's last statement and, looking around, took charge. "That's enough," he said to Morgan firmly. "Mulligan has his devious ways that seem to go far beyond reasoning. There is little to make sense of with him." He looked back at Mulligan. "And you will face the Witches Council, my old friend. Only this time, with mounting evidence, now including kidnapping charges.

Mulligan looked like he saw a ghost...or four. "But—but—I had you killed, your brake lines cut—*all four of you*! How are you in human form again?!"

"Well, at least for now, we are back, just like the portal you took advantage of yesterday," Castian said firmly. "And maybe a testimony of four attempted murders that are now admitted to, thanks to my recorded audio you just fantastically created.

"But, but! Atë!" the older man screamed shrilly "*Atë*!" he cried even louder, desperately.

"What, what?" said an annoyed voice, as the dark-haired goddess appeared, clad in long Greek robes. "Dear goddess, I have given you more beauty treatments than any man should have the right to ask for," she complained, super irritated as she picked at her nails.

She glanced around at the group and back at Mulligan, assessing the situation quickly.

"Do I have to save your old ass *again*?" she asked the older man as he sniveled and whined about not being old and about not asking for too many beauty treatments.

In the next moment, however, another god appeared. One who had sat back and watched the ritual in the dungeon on Friday night, quietly admiring without interaction. Neither Morgan nor Maggie had considered who he was.

"Dammit, Zeus," said the beautiful dark-haired goddess, throwing her hands in the air.

"I knew our paths were likely to cross again, my obstinate daughter," said the powerful booming voice of the god. "But this one is off limits," he said, gesturing to Maggie, nodding his head at her supremely.

With a snap of his fingers, he and the goddess were gone, leaving the older wizard gasping about a promise owed him by the young goddess. Zeus snapped back into the room. "My daughter does *NOT* owe you or yours another thing, young man, and will not be seeing you again." His powerful voice echoed in the room after he snapped back out of their dimension. I guess one was young when nearly 80 years old in comparison to Zeus.

"Well," said her grandfather. "I guess there went your only remaining out."

Epilogue

Maggie

Well.

She had finished exams that year while traveling to and from The Hollow. She really only had her thesis work to finish up and present, but that would take time.

Morgan hadn't really wanted to talk very much about his childhood but had filled her in on the basics. He definitely hadn't wanted to talk about his dark side. Maggie was hoping that with time, maybe they could build trust there, as she really longed to connect to that part of him as well.

But he did say he would see if his old therapist was still working in the field, and that he would reach out to her if so.

He'd asked her to move in with him permanently, and of course, she did. She couldn't imagine being anywhere else. And helping him turn The Hollow into a fantastic haunted old Bed and Breakfast? That was the best part. She could only imagine what kind of events the place could host once it was fully renovated.

Mulligan had been taken to London and was being held by the Witches Council to address and discipline with a hearing scheduled in the spring. Morgan had hinted that he wasn't so sure how well that would go, as Mulligan's connections ran deep in London. But her parents, grandfather, and Morgan's uncle were all remaining in this dimension, at least, until the Council addressed him, as to testify. Which also meant that they had unexpected time with the family members once so lost to them.

Only time would tell how things would resolve.

Enjoy the beginning of the shenanigans at The Hollow? Keep an eye out next year for more, as Esme learns a few lessons about life, love, and the ultimate surrender.